HIVE MIND

TAMAR SLOAN

HEIDI CATHERINE

SEQUEL HOUSE

CHAPTER
ONE
ECHO

E cho slips in and out of consciousness, floating in an endless sea of confusion.

Her body disconnects from her mind.

Her mind breaks away from her soul.

Time is stolen, like it never existed in the first place.

Then it all comes back in a rush, and she's cocooned in a web of bewilderment, the golden light that's bathing her doing nothing to ease the terror that's rising to the surface.

Snippets of awareness hover before her and she snatches at them, remembering the giant mechanical bee that captured her. She hears River's screams as he fought to hold onto her, feels the pain of being torn from his grasp, recoils at the sticky slime that coated her. When it gets too much, she shuts down, her memories morphing into shadows that she buries in the recesses of her mind.

Minutes turn into weeks that turn into days that turn into seconds. Echo imagines a clock, the hands turning forward then backward, before blurring into a haze, leaving her with no idea how long she's been trapped in the Hive.

She thinks of her father. She thinks of Chase. Of Flora. Of Jupiter. Of Nola. And Vernon. But most of all, she thinks of River. Is he in here, too? Or did Oren spare him the same fate she's being forced to endure? Although, if Oren was prepared to send his own daughter to the Dead Zone, then why wouldn't he trap his son in this sticky, golden tomb? The man has no heart. What she and River had witnessed after breaking into the Restricted Area had proven that. Images of Vernon being tortured by the Sovereign as she'd fed on him with her sharp antennae haunt Echo, no matter how many times she tries to banish them.

Slipping into waves of oblivion becomes a relief.

There's a violent jolt, waking Echo from her nightmare. And now she's moving. Light splinters. Fear flares. Sound reverberates. With some difficulty, she sits up, realizing the sound she hears is a scream pouring from her open mouth.

As she fights against her bindings woven from slime, warm fingers press to her lips, and a face appears before her. She recognizes it, but her brain is coated in fog, and she struggles to connect what she's seeing to the part of her that can remember what it means.

"Quiet," the face hisses. "You must be quiet."

But her screams continue, providing a strange comfort as they release some of the confusion that's exploding in her chest.

"Quiet!" the face says.

With a rush, she realizes the face belongs to Tuff. He presses his fingers against her mouth harder, trying to hold back her screams.

"You have to stop," he says.

So, she does. The screaming vanishes almost as mysteriously as it began, and she blinks up at Tuff. Is he here to save her? Or is he going to finish her off?

Slowly, he removes his hand from her mouth, and she swallows down the sickly-sweet taste of the slime that coats her skin.

"I'm not going to hurt you," Tuff says, sending relief deep into her marrow.

She goes to reach for him, but her hands are bound at her sides by sticky threads, and she only manages to raise them by a few inches.

"Is River okay?" she asks, needing an answer to the question that's plagued her the most.

Tuff tilts his head toward the Hive. "He's in there."

"You have to get us out." She fights tears to learn that River is experiencing this, too. "Please."

"Listen," he says. "We haven't got long."

She nods, prepared to hear anything this strange man has to say. Just as long as he releases her so that she and River can figure out what to do next. They can't spend the rest of their days locked in this prison of slime.

"I can't let you go," Tuff says, glancing around. "You're too important to Oren."

Echo moans, the thought of being put back into the Hive for even just another moment too terrifying to accept.

Tuff slams his hand back over her mouth to silence her. "I knew checking on you was a bad idea," he grumbles. "If it were up to me, I'd have left you in there. But Chase insisted."

These words give Echo the strength she needs to break her arms free of slime and she pulls Tuff's hand from her mouth.

"Chase?" she asks. "What does he have to do with any of this?"

"Doesn't matter." Tuff tries to push her back down onto the bench and she resists, only just managing to remain seated.

"Don't put me back in there," she pleads. "Let me go. And River."

He pushes down harder while the slime wraps around Echo, binding her to the bench. "You need to be harvested."

Harvested? A scream winds its way back up Echo's throat but the slime cuts it off and she's moving again, being pushed back into the Hive, golden light wrapping around her like a blanket she can't shake off.

The nightmare resumes and she blocks it out, her mind turning gold into black, as she floats into the endless abyss, surfacing for snatches of time before being dragged under again.

She imagines the clock, the hands spinning so fast she can't make out the individual parts. Backward. Forward. Backward. Time bending and twisting in malleable circles that join and separate before merging again. She should have asked Tuff how long she'd been here.

After what could be a minute, or possibly a week, she's jolted once more, and a familiar movement starts. She's being removed from the Hive. Only this time it's not for a chat... Her only hope is that River's found a way to set her free, although that seems unlikely.

She's ready to pounce, and the moment her bench has been pulled from the Hive, she strikes out.

But Tuff's not there to warn her. His hand is no longer pressing on her mouth to hold back her agonized screams. Her fist connects with hard metal.

It's the mechanical beast that River had called the Sovereign. She's larger and more menacing than when she'd trapped them in the Hive. Because this time, Echo knows there's no escape.

The giant bee studies her with all five of her hideous eyes and pure horror races down Echo's spine. This is exactly what Oren wants. To extract her fear. She wishes more than anything she could deny him that gift. To push down her terror and fill her veins with calm.

But that's impossible. Not with the Sovereign standing before her.

"No!" Echo cries as the beast's middle set of legs shoot out and flip her over onto her stomach while more legs expertly pin her down. There's nothing she can do. No way she can fight against this queen of misery and steel.

A fire detonates in the base of Echo's spine, and she knows the Sovereign is using her long antennae to feed on her. *Harvest her.* Have her fill. She drains all of Echo's determination to fight, replacing it with a suffering that tortures every one of her cells.

The antennae disconnect, the mechanical bee whirring as if she's excited. It feels like the Sovereign's taken Echo's will to fight with her. She's depleted. A shell. It takes focus just to breathe.

The Sovereign turns Echo onto her back and the slime comes for her again. This time she welcomes it, desperate to slide beneath its golden blanket. Anything, just as long as it takes her away from this nightmare that's far worse than anything she could ever dream up.

River's face enters Echo's mind, and she holds it close, looking into his green eyes. She can't give up. Not on herself. Not on River. Not on everything they have.

They'll be together again one day. They'll put an end to this evil. They'll make the world a better place.

Now she's moving again, her awareness that she's being pushed back into the Hive her last thought before her world dissolves into ragged threads of ungraspable moments of time.

TWO

RIVER

River waits, knowing what's coming. The golden glow around him thrums softly, keeping every body trapped in the Hive alive.

So they can be harvested.

He heard the screams. His heart splintered when he thought one of them could be Echo.

Yet, he tried not to let them touch him. Worked hard to stop them from shredding him to the core, knowing the screams are all a part of this.

One word is on a loop in his head.

Adrenacure.

He'd thought the adrenaline was needed to reverse the effects of the venom when someone was stung. But just like everything else in the Green Zone, the truth is far more sinister.

Adrenaline is part of the formula for the life-saving injection. Whatever the monstrous metal bee is harvesting from a person's spine, it needs adrenaline in the mix. The Sovereign herself is designed to terrify.

His time comes far too soon.

He's pulled out of the Hive like some corpse in a morgue, yet he focuses on his breathing. He thinks of the times Echo helped him through his breathing glitches, her calm gaze and warm hands becoming his center.

In. Out.

In. Out.

And he does it, even with the slime coating his face, somehow suffocating him yet providing his body with oxygen. He works to keep his pulse as steady as his breathing. Even when the steel bed he's lying on jerks to halt. Even when he can hear the clattering of the metal bee's six legs drawing closer and closer.

Even when she appears above him.

He knows the only way he can save himself and Echo is to stay alive.

And get out of the Hive.

He swallows, his heart involuntarily lurching in his chest.

In. Out.

In. Out.

The Sovereign pins him roughly, antennae twitching and mandibles clacking. Then pauses.

Lights flicker behind her glass eyes, processing what she's seeing. A calm body. One without adrenaline coursing through his veins.

River stares back at her defiantly. He refuses to be cowed by her. Refuses to give her what she seeks to take against his will.

He's hoping his father is watching.

Above them, there's a flash of light from the large circle on the bee's back. It blazes bright enough to make River squint. It's like a surge of energy just powered through the thing. Rearing up, the Sovereign releases a piercing screech, front legs flailing and black wings flapping. Just as quickly, she bears down on River. He throws his arms up instinctively as her obsidian legs hit the metal gurney with so much force, the crash pounds his eardrums. She screeches in his face, her mechanical jaws snapping so close they scrape his skin.

An antenna jams into his shoulder, feeling like a molten blade. Then his neck. Then his shoulder again. The second antenna follows its mate, piercing the opposite side in quick succession. He blocks one aiming for his chest, the pointed weapon scraping down the metal beside his head.

Pain, fear, and fury climb up his throat and explode as a scream. The potent concoction becomes a primal drive for survival, pounding through his veins whether he likes it or not.

A strange whirring sound comes from the Sovereign and she flips him over. She's gotten what she wanted.

Then the real pain begins.

River tries to arch, but he's pinned to the metal shelf that's now his bed. He tries to kick, but he's mummified in slime.

All he can do is endure the agony that's a firestorm exploding up his spine. It somehow saps him of any strength he has and shoots an endless inferno through to every nerve ending. He can't move, even though all he wants to do is escape before the pain defines him forever.

Even when the giant, mechanical bee disconnects, the pain seems to skip over skeleton and sinew, as if it's memorizing him, seeing where it can make a nest.

Then he's rolled back over and the slime engulfs him once more. He's simultaneously numb and on fire as he's pushed back into the golden womb of the Green Zone.

Now, the focus on his breathing is purely to hold himself together. Each breath is a fragile shudder in, a whispered shiver out. A single tear squeezes from the corner of his eye. Echo must have gone through this. So did Vern.

And every other poor soul trapped in this wall of torture.

River's entire world is founded on it.

He closes his eyes, the glow that would be beautiful if it wasn't so menacing still seeping through his eyelids. Maybe it's because every inch of his skin feels as thick as a spider's web.

Except there's a jolt. The light brightens.

And then he's moving again.

His eyes fly open, a denial screaming through his mind. He's not sure how long ago the harvest happened, but even if time is ceasing to have meaning, it can't be happening again! Not so soon!

River braces himself, this time allowing the adrenaline to flow through his veins. In fact, he encourages it. Uses the memory of the pain still alive in his marrow to fuel it.

This time, he'll fight.

The moment he's pulled out of the Hive, River struggles against the hold of the slime. The opaque mucus responds by tightening around his limbs, but he just thrashes harder.

"River! Stop!"

The words are hissed in an urgent whisper, meaning they take long seconds to filter through his fight to survive.

"If you don't, I'll put you back in!"

The warning is enough to make him still. River slowly turns his head, blinking through the film over his face. "Tuff?" he mouths.

The older man watches him for a few more moments, then nods. "You need to stay quiet."

River nods in return. A quick glance around reveals there's no Sovereign.

Yet.

Tuff has spent years helping that machine harvest innocent people.

Tuff presses something on the side of River's bed-drawer, and the slime retracts. River draws in a sharp breath, even though he's been breathing this whole time. Air floods his lungs, making his head spin.

He's alive. Weak. But alive.

Which now means he needs to make sure Echo is, too.

"What do you want from me?" He squints at Tuff, tensing himself for the answer.

Tuff draws his chin back, as if he's offended. "I'm getting you out of here."

There's no way River's going to trust that. Cautiously, he brings himself to a sitting position, finding his bones feel fragile and sapped of substance, but he can hold himself upright. Tuff steps back, giving him space, but River's still vigilant.

"What about Echo?" he asks.

Tuff opens the hexagonal cell adjacent to River's. The metal drawer slides out, Echo's slight form in the center encased in slime. Another press of a button and the opaque coating retracts.

In the space of heartbeat, she's a seething mass of fury, arms and legs flailing wildly. River leaps to her side, glad his legs don't give out. "Echo, it's me!"

She stills instantly. "River?"

His chest constricts. "Yeah, it's me."

Her arms clamp tightly around him as she buries her face in his neck. Seems they can both find the necessary strength when it comes to the other. "I thought..." she chokes.

His own hold around her is just as desperately tight. "Me, too."

That their future was an endless cycle of agonizing harvests. Or death.

They pull away, simultaneously turning toward Tuff, no doubt thinking the same thing. Is he friend or foe?

He raises his hands. "I'm here to help."

Echo frowns. "You pulled me out, told me to be quiet, then pushed me back in!" She gasps. "You let us be harvested!"

"I had no choice," Tuff says tightly. "It had to happen."

River steps away from Echo, unobtrusively testing his weight. He's going to need every ounce of strength if they're going to fight Tuff. "Is that what you tell every poor soul in here?" he growls.

Tuff's eyes flash. "You had to be harvested first or Oren would know you were gone."

Echo slides off her shelf, coming to stand beside River. "What do you mean, gone?"

"He won't check the Hive again until the next Harvest Day in one week."

River blinks. "You're saying you let him harvest us, so that you could free us afterward without raising suspicion?"

Tuff's eyes roam over the golden, slime-covered hexagonal cells that make up the wall. "I thought it would get easier," he says, his voice rough with emotion. "That it would be worth it."

Echo's eyes narrow. "But you don't think that anymore?"

He shakes his head, glancing at her, then River. "You were right. Oren isn't doing this to gift Immunity to all. He'll choose." Tuff's face hardens. "And let the rest die."

River wishes he could deny that, but it was his own father who trapped him in here. To punish him. River glances at the strong, courageous girl beside him. Oren also wanted Echo in here...for a completely different reason.

Just like the rest of the captives in this prison of pain.

River's hands tighten into fists. "We need to release the others. We can't leave them in here."

Tuff takes a step forward, his own fists by his sides. "You do that, and everyone in the Green Zone learns they're a Vulnerable."

River freezes, thinking of Clover and Daphne and every other soul he grew up with. Their immunity is a myth. It's gifted through the drinking water.

Echo's hand settles on his arm. "River," she says softly. "Tuff's right. We have to get out of here without raising the alarm. Too many lives depend on it."

He looks down at her, hearing the truth in her words. Seeing the same agony the knowledge causes him reflected in her eyes.

To have a chance of ending this, they have to leave the others behind.

River turns back to Tuff. "What do you think we can achieve in one week?"

Tuff shrugs. "More than anyone else." His gaze zeroes in on them. "No one else has entered the Restricted Area without Oren's knowledge. No one else has thought to question him and his beautiful Green Zone."

River's stomach clenches. Oren is his father. The man he blindly followed all his life.

The man who lied to him, just like he lied to every soul in the Green Zone as he turned his back on the suffering of the Dead Zone.

And the pain of the harvest will no doubt pale in comparison to the pain of betraying him.

But River will. He has to.

"It's almost midnight. You need to get to the Dead Zone." Tuff glances over his shoulder, as if expecting Oren to be there. "I've taken care of the cameras, but not for long. I'm giving you an hour."

River has to hope that's enough. They can pick some fruit along the way to get their energy back. He's about to thank Tuff when the old man turns back to them.

His face hardens. "You'll need to be back before the week is up. If you fail, Oren will need to find your bodies back in the Hive. If he discovers you're missing, you put everything at risk."

Tuff's granite face says he plans on bringing them back himself if they don't turn up. It's a promise carved in stone.

Echo takes River's hand. "And what exactly do we need to do?"

Tuff takes a step back, clearing the way to the exit. "You need to find the true Sovereign before Oren does." His gaze darkens. "Or we're all dead."

CHAPTER
THREE
ECHO

Echo runs through the Green Zone feeling like her legs belong to someone else. Blood pumps. Muscles stretch. Bones ache. Fresh air rushes at her and she blinks, savoring the luxury of drawing it into her lungs.

Tuff said they'd been in the Hive for a month. It felt like a year. Or maybe a day. But now she's free. *They're* free. Because River is running beside her, his hand clasping hers as the Beta-dome looms before them.

"Are you hungry?" River slows to a jog.

Echo licks her lips, the sweet taste of the slime detectable. "I could eat."

"I'm starving," he says.

"Your body isn't used to going without food." She squeezes his hand, hating that if they're going to be hiding out in the Dead Zone, his body will quickly acclimatize to the discomfort of an empty stomach.

River opens the green door and holds it for Echo. Tuff said they have an hour to get through before the cameras start working again. They still have at least half that left. He also said the Hive will have given them Immunity that should last at least a few days without drinking the Green Zone's water. The bees can't harm them for now.

They step into the dark hexagonal garden and Echo notices a wheeze in River's chest.

"Are you okay?" she asks.

He nods. "It's just that breathing thing again."

"Yeah, the one-off breathing thing that keeps happening." She rolls her eyes. "Got it."

He pokes out his tongue in the moonlight. "It'll pass when we get into the Dead Zone. Just like it did last time."

"You're the opposite of a bee." She walks to the nearest tree and plucks two red apples, handing one to River. "The pollen attracts them. And it tries to kill you."

He smiles, taking a bite of the apple and closing his eyes in bliss. "I'm the anti-Sovereign."

"True. She brings pain and misery. You bring..." Echo's front teeth pierce the sweet flesh of the fruit, and she loses her ability to speak.

"What do I bring?" he asks, taking another bite.

"Happiness," she says with her mouth full.

He raises a brow. "Not sure how happy you've been since you met me."

She finishes her apple, thinking about this. It's true. She's been miserable since she met him. But that's not *because* of him. "If it weren't for you, I'd be curled up in a ball in that tower of death." She points at the Sting. "Instead, I'm out here eating the best thing I've ever tasted in my life."

River picks several more apples, stuffing them down the front of his shirt. "About that...how exactly are we going to find the Sovereign? What even is the Sovereign?"

Echo shrugs, realizing Tuff didn't mean the giant bee that harvested them. She picks some apples of her own to take

15

with her, trying to find creative ways to carry them. Tuff had given them old clothes. Little more than dirty rags really. But it will help them blend in. Now isn't the time to attract attention.

"Tuff seems to have faith in us," she says. "And it's either that or be put back in the Hive for the next Harvest Day."

"I don't want you to go through that again." River pulls her to him, and an apple rolls out of his shirt.

"Me neither." She pushes up on her toes and kisses him, doing what she'd dreamed of when floating in time in the Hive.

He kisses her back, the passion in his lips not quite able to spark given his ragged breathing and the hard lumps of apples pressed between their bodies. But there's love in his kiss. Tenderness. A promise of something more.

"We need to get you out of here so you can breathe." She pulls back.

"In a moment," he says. "First, I need to tell you something."

"What is it?" she asks.

He bites down on his lip. "I'm glad it was you."

"What do you mean?" She tilts her head. "In the Hive?"

"Of course, not." He touches her on the arm. "At the Confirmation. I'm glad it was you who was an Immune. Not Flora."

Echo's eyes flare. What he just said is huge. Bigger than huge. He'd been gutted when Flora hadn't made it through her Confirmation. He'd resented Echo and everything about her, making it very clear he thought she'd stolen Flora's place.

"I needed you." He draws in a steadying breath before he continues. "I just didn't know it at the time. Flora made her own choices. If you hadn't passed your Confirmation, I'd have been on my own to figure all this out. And...I don't think I would have."

"You would have," she says without hesitation. "It just

would have taken you longer. You don't give yourself enough credit."

"It's more than that, though," he continues. "You changed me."

Love swells in Echo's chest and she leans her head on his shoulder. "You changed me, too."

"Should we go change the world, then?" he asks. "Figure out what this Sovereign thing is all about?"

She nods. "No pressure, hey?"

"No pressure." He stoops to pick up the apple that rolled away and they make their way through the smoke at the black door and out into the silence of the Dead Zone.

It's eerie on the other side of the door in a way it shouldn't be given this is the place Echo grew up. Perhaps it's because Echo really has changed since she met River. She's wiser. Braver. And more determined. A fire lit in her belly that's refusing to extinguish. The new Echo needs to make all this right.

As they walk on, questions rattle at her brain, demanding answers.

If nobody in the Green Zone is a true Immune, how is it possible that Echo is? If Oren had been spiking the water, then why hadn't all the Green Borns passed their Confirmation? Why was River the only one? And why wouldn't Oren ensure his daughter also passed?

"I can breathe," says River, interrupting her thoughts.

A flash of guilt strikes Echo as she hadn't noticed his wheezing had ceased.

"Good." She smiles, the moonlight seeming dimmer now the sky is masked behind a giant net. "I'm glad the Dead Zone is useful for something."

They reach the outskirts of the village and River pulls on her arm, urging her to follow the creek.

"We need to see Chase," she says, holding firm.

He shakes his head. "We need to go to Ruff's to see Flora. She's the one with the answers."

Echo stops, doing her best not to drop the apples she's smuggling in. Thankfully, the darkness is saving them from being mobbed by the starving masses. "Tuff said something to me. In the Hive."

"When he pulled you out to talk to you?" he asks.

"Yes." Echo tries to remember Tuff's exact words. "He said he knew bringing me out was a bad idea. But Chase had insisted."

"But..." River seems just as perplexed about this as Echo.

"Chase must be in contact with Tuff," says Echo. "And I really don't know if we can trust Ruff."

"And you think you can trust Chase?" he asks.

Echo goes to throw out her hands, stopping herself so she doesn't lose her stash of food. "He was my only friend growing up."

"And Flora's my only sister." His voice drips with sadness, almost making her change her mind. "Okay. We'll see Chase first, but then we go straight to Flora."

"Deal." Echo's also keen to talk to Flora, even though she's not entirely sure they can trust her either. Not that she's going to tell River that. Flora may have been a wonderful sister for him to grow up with, but she's held so much back. How could Flora not have realized she could trust River with her secrets? It only took Echo a few days to figure that out.

They make their way through the quiet streets. Nobody has the means to produce electricity in the Dead Zone, which means movement is mostly contained within the rise and setting of the sun. After being in the constant glow and hum of the Sting, and then the Hive, the darkness is haunting. But it's also a relief. They don't want to have to explain themselves to anyone.

Echo leads River to her old house, assuming Chase will be there, rather than the home he'd shared with his family. He'd looked very settled there the last time she'd seen him with the new Green Born Vulnerables. Cascade, in particular, had been enjoying his company. Strangely, the thought of Cascade annoys her more now as she reminds Echo of her sister, Clover, and the way she'd thrown herself at River. This is just another thing about Echo that's changed.

She knocks lightly on the door, then opens it a crack.

There's a scramble inside then Echo is thrown against the wall. The apples hidden in her clothes tumble to the floor of the hut.

"It's me!" she gasps. "Echo!"

"Echo?" The tight grip is instantly released and a person who can be nobody except Chase pulls her to his chest. "It's you."

"Are you okay?" River asks in the darkness.

"Of course, you brought him with you," sneers Chase, letting go of her. "Come in. Both of you, I suppose."

The soft glow of a candle lights the inside of her home, illuminating a familiar face.

"Flora!" River dashes forward at the sight of his twin, his stash of apples sent falling as he moves.

Chase bends down to pick up the fruit and Echo helps him, while River scoops Flora into his arms. Echo's pleased to see Flora hugs him back.

"You brought a whole orchard with you," says Chase, biting into an apple. "Oh, this is good. Here, Flora."

He throws an apple in her direction, and she lets go of River to catch it. Echo's mouth waters at the thought of having another apple, but she resists. She only just had one and there are plenty of others here who are starving. Perhaps she can cut one up into tiny pieces and bring it to Nola in the morning. If she's still alive.

"What are you doing here?" River asks Flora.

"Shouldn't I be the one asking you that?" she asks. "I thought you were in the Hive."

"We were harvested," he says, taking a step back toward Echo. "It was hell."

"You poor things," says Flora. "We've been so worried about you. I've barely slept a wink."

"We need to talk." Chase sets down the apples on a table and perches on the edge of Echo's old sleeping mat. Echo can't help but notice her father's mat has been packed away, leaving only one bed. Flora sits beside Chase, positioning herself close enough to him to confirm Echo's suspicions.

Averting her eyes, Echo pulls up an old crate that's used as a stool and sits down on one half, motioning for River to join her.

"Maybe we should blow out the candle," says Echo, aware of how precious a resource it is. "We can talk in the dark."

"No," says Chase. "This is too important. We can keep it on for now."

"Who even are you?" Echo asks, cutting straight to the point.

Chase looks stunned as he presses his palm to his chest. "Me?"

She nods. "I thought I knew you. But now I'm realizing I don't have the first clue who you really are."

"I know that feeling," River mutters, looking straight at his twin.

I'm so sorry, Flora mouths back at him.

Chase lets out a long sigh as he runs a hand through his

blond curls. "Echo, you do know me. I'm still me. It's just that there are parts of me I've protected you from."

She crosses her arms, feeling more betrayed than protected. "Tuff said you made him check on me in the Hive. How did you know where I was?"

"Let me start from the beginning." Chase speaks slowly, choosing his words carefully. "I've been sneaking into the Green Zone for years now to raid their crops. You know that part of me, right?"

Echo nods.

"That's how it started. Innocently enough. But you've seen the Green Zone for yourself now. You know what I saw over there. Complete and utter greed and abundance. It's not fair. I knew I had to do something about it. So, I formed the Razers."

"The what?" asks Echo. "Razers?"

Chase nods. "A group of likeminded people working to raze the Green Zone to the ground, along with everyone in it."

"But that's evil!" River leaps to his feet. "Most of those people are innocent!"

"Relax, Green Boy," says Chase. "Flora taught me that already. I'm just telling you how we got our name."

"Who's in this group?" Echo asks, pulling River back down to his seat. "And why didn't you ask me to join?"

Chase shrugs. "I guess I got that bit wrong, too. I thought you were too kind. Too sweet to be part of any rebellion like that. The way you cared for those with the scurge didn't exactly make you seem like the type of person ready to bring down a colony."

Anger flares in Echo's chest. "Maybe the way I cared for them would be reason enough for me to want to make a difference."

"I think what you did for those people was amazing," says Flora, wide-eyed.

Chase holds up his hands. "Like I said. I was wrong. I know that now. But while I was in the Green Zone, watching from the orchard, I met Flora."

"Flora didn't leave the Sting until her Confirmation," snaps River. "That's impossible."

Flora shakes her head. "I often left the Sting at night. I learned where Oren's cameras are. How to avoid them. I wanted to see what was out there. Then I met Chase..."

Chase puts an arm around Flora. Not in the petty way he'd done with Cascade when he'd been trying to make Echo jealous. This time, his eyes are shining with genuine affection. Never once has she seen that look when Chase has glanced her way. It's clear now that while he may have held affection for Echo, he's always thought of her more like a sister than anything else. And while that knowledge would have once broken her heart, she finds herself feeling numb. The warm leg that's pressing against hers has more than a little bit to do with that. In fact, the way Chase is looking at Flora reminds her of the way River looks at her.

"Flora and I began to meet up regularly," says Chase. "Next to the tree with the hollow in its trunk. She told me about her colony, and I told her about ours."

"I knew there was more to it," says River, clearly unimpressed as he scowls at Flora. "That there had to be more to the reason you left than justice alone. You've been seduced by this...Dead Born."

"River," says Echo, reminding him of exactly who she is.

"I'm sorry." He hangs his head. "It's just...You know I don't trust him."

"River!" says Flora. "You trust me, don't you?"

River nods without hesitation.

"Then you can trust Chase." Flora nods firmly, her short dark hair falling into her eyes.

"For the record, I don't trust you, either," says Chase, not ready to make River a friend just yet.

"You convinced her to fail her Confirmation, didn't you?" River asks.

"That was all my idea." Flora leans forward. "I did it all myself."

"You wanted to be a Vulnerable?" River is still trying to process what his twin did.

"I wanted to be with Chase." She puts a hand on Chase's leg. "Surely, you understand how that feels now?"

"And Chase wanted to get rid of me," says Echo, sadly. "That's why he gave me nothing but dirt when it was pollen I asked for."

"I didn't want to get rid of you," says Chase. "But I thought after what Flora told me that it was a certainty you were a Vulnerable. I didn't want more bees to sting you than was necessary. You know the medics favor Green Borns with their adrenacure. I was protecting you. And then you surprised everyone."

"No more than myself," she says, remembering the shock she'd felt to pass. "And how did you know we were in the Hive? Is Ruff one of your Razers?"

Chase nudges Flora. "I told you she's smart."

Flora nods. "You did."

"Ruff keeps Tuff informed," Chase continues. "I asked him to find out what happened to you. I was leaving notes for you in the tree, and you weren't answering."

"Tuff told us something," says River. "He said we have one week to find the Sovereign. Otherwise, we have to go back to the Hive. He sounded very serious about it."

Chase nods. "We knew about this. Oren will notice you missing if you're not there the next Harvest Day. Tuff wanted to keep you there permanently. We had to work hard to convince him to let you out. We didn't think he would."

"I still can't believe he did," Flora adds. "I was beginning to fear you were dead."

"What is the Sovereign?" Echo asks, wanting to get to the point. "We're not even sure what it is we're chasing."

Flora ignores her question, shifting her gaze from Echo to Chase. "Should we show them?"

Chase nods. "At first light."

"Show us what?" asks River. "You have the Sovereign?"

"No." Flora shakes her head. "But we know why Oren's searching so hard."

Echo's heart beats hard. Maybe finding the Sovereign will be easier than they thought? Although, if there's one thing the new Echo has learned since her Confirmation, it's that nothing is ever as easy as she thinks.

CHAPTER

FOUR

RIVER

The light is different in the Dead Zone. It's somehow harsher, more severe, yet muted as it filters through the net that encases the colony. River watches the sun crawl over the horizon as he sits outside the hut trying to process the difference, even as he knows he won't be able to. The Green Zone was saturated with color. Energy. Vitality. Yet everything has been bleached out of the Dead Zone. Even the rays of sunshine are lacking in life.

"How did you get used to it?" he asks Echo, looking down at her where she's sitting beside him. "Nothing's the same."

He wonders if he's even making any sense. They slept fitfully after Flora and Chase promised to show them everything at daybreak. River couldn't bring himself to sleep inside the hut, knowing his sister shares a mat with the one guy he really doesn't like. He'd just set himself up on the hard ground and was staring up at the night sky with the stars obscured thanks to the net, when Echo appeared.

Silently, she'd tucked herself beside him and for a few precious hours, River experienced the oblivion of sleep.

"You mean living in the Green Zone, compared to growing up in the death of the Dead Zone?" Echo asks, angling her head.

River nods, glad she understands. In fact, a little impressed that she practically read his mind.

Echo looks to the fractured rays that pierce the net, unveiling the drab world of dirt and desolation.

The world that, for now, is River's home.

"It wasn't easy, at first." Her dark eyes settle on him. "But if I hadn't experienced both, I never would've known there's far more separating the Green and Dead Zones than I could have imagined."

River watches Echo as the filtered sunlight climbs up her neck, her jaw, the almost-smile softening her lips, then lights her eyes. He finds himself captivated by the understanding sitting alongside the bitter truth in their dark depths.

The divide between the Zones is too great.

The difference too...wrong.

Life shouldn't come at the expense of this much death.

Echo leans closer, resting her hand lightly on his chest. "If I never experienced both, I wouldn't have had the chance to meet you."

River's breath evaporates, the knowledge that things have changed between them growing with every thud of his heart. His gaze drops to her lips as he remembers the times they kissed. That this girl can sear his very soul with one touch.

That she's right. Something strong and beautiful and special has already done what feels impossible—breached the chasm. No, blurred the lines.

In moments such as these, words like Green Born, Dead Born, Immune and Vulnerable cease to exist.

They lean in closer, breaths mingling, eyes drifting shut.

The sounds of shuffling footsteps have them drawing away

with a start. Flora and Chase exit the hut, eyebrows simultaneously hiking as they register the non-existent distance between River and Echo. Chase looks away, his lips twisting. Flora's "I knew it" expression is climbing up her face.

Ignoring it, River pushes to his feet, then holds his hand out to Echo. She takes it, even though there's no strain on his arm as she also stands. The warmth that was interrupted flickers back to life as he realizes she's openly touching him in front of Chase. Except then Echo releases his hand to dust herself off. River lets it fall to his side, ignoring the twinge in his chest. Maybe he's taking this too fast, especially considering these feelings between them sparked under such intense circumstances.

And as much as he doesn't like it, Echo and Chase have a history. He needs to respect that.

Even if it leaves a bitter taste in his mouth far more unsavory than the dust.

Echo slips her hand back into his, interlacing her fingers, making him still. She smiles up at River, and he realizes she was doing nothing more than dusting herself off. She *wants* to hold his hand.

And Chase has noticed.

River's fingers tighten around Echo's, conscious he's acting like a jealous boyfriend, and not really caring. He levels his gaze at Chase. "You said you'd show us what you can about the Sovereign."

Chase narrows his eyes, steps closer to Flora, and slips an arm around her shoulder. "We did. It's a bit of a walk. You think you're up to it, seeing as you haven't had breakfast?"

Or dinner. And River can't imagine lunch is going to happen. His stomach feels like acid is its only contents, which is probably the truth, but he's not going to let Chase know that. The hot churning sensation is more likely due to the fact the guy's holding River's twin sister so possessively. "We've been waiting."

"Great," Chase says, unsmiling. "Let's go."

The sound of shuffling in a nearby hut has them all clamping their mouths shut. Flora lifts her finger to her lips as she tugs Chase away from the hut. River glances at Echo, noting the tightness at the edges of her mouth as she watches. Is she jealous? Did she imagine herself with Chase in the same way Flora is?

What would it look like if Chase had chosen her...

River turns his mind away from the disturbing thought. He'll take it slow with Echo, give her time to decide what it is she really wants.

Which has him realizing what *he* wants.

River almost frowns. It's too soon to know that with such certainty, isn't it...?

A groan filters from the hut they're walking past, followed by a strangled wheeze, then nothing. Chase and Flora don't seem to notice, but Echo stiffens. River glances at her.

Surely not...

But Echo nods, her face drawn with deep lines of sadness. River points to her, then the hut, asking silently if she knew the person in the hut. The one who possibly just took their last breath. Echo shakes her head, the lines only deepening.

She feels the pain of loss, anyway. The price that was just paid for the existence of the Green Zone.

River squeezes her hand, wishing he could say something during this enforced silence as they creep through the colony, but also not knowing what. All he can do is nod at her.

Tell her without words that it will change.

It has to.

Echo nods too, the sadness hardening to determination. She squeezes his hand back, sealing the promise.

Ahead, Chase and Flora take a sharp right, and River realizes they're not only leaving the colony, they're actually moving closer to the Betadome.

They're not going back in there, are they?

The thought has reality hitting him all over again. He can't return to the Green Zone. His father believes he's trapped in the Hive. River was nothing but a means to an end for him.

He glances at his sister, realizing Flora must've known about the Restricted Area and the Hive, the lie that is Immunity, and their father's part in all of it. Exactly how much does she know?

How many lies has she kept from him?

The colony falls behind them, the sun now bathing its never-ending decay in a weak, dawn glow. Chase and Flora skirt the edge of the silver dome, the gentle hum of the bees seeping from the tiny holes, making him wonder how long the Immunity from the Hive will really last. For the first time in River's life, the sound of the bees trips his adrenaline as he remembers exactly how deadly the tiny insects on the other side are and he's unable to calm the response.

He's not an Immune. He never was.

He's a Vulnerable.

In fact, the Dead Zone is where he truly belongs.

Chase glances over his shoulder as he hooks a thumb in the direction of the Betadome. "Don't worry. We're not going in there. But if we ever need to, there's a way through without being spotted by the cameras."

Echo glances at the tight netting, the only one in this group who's guaranteed to be able to go in there without the threat of death hanging over her head. "Show me," she says, letting River's hand go so she can hurry over to Chase.

River's about to join her but Flora breaks away and moves around Echo, joining him.

His sister falls into step as he works to contain his frown, watching as Chase keeps walking, leaning in close to Echo as he points at various locations through the net of the Betadome.

"He's very clever, you know," Flora says softly.

One glance at his twin and River realizes she's looking at the scene ahead through a very different lens. One that's tinted in rose, a color that doesn't even exist in the Dead Zone. "Isn't clever another word for manipulative?"

Flora nudges him with her shoulder, a movement that's so familiar it tugs at something deep in his chest. "Chase doesn't like making the tough choices any more than you or I." She pauses, watching as he nods at something Echo said. "But he still makes them, and I respect that."

"You really care for him, don't you?" River asks, trying to keep the incredulity out of his voice.

Flora throws him a glare that tells him he failed spectacularly. "I really do, River. He's everything to me."

He nods, watching the dirt crumble beneath each footstep as he tries to think of a response. Even the soil is dead here.

"You really care for her, don't you?" Flora asks, watching him closely as she throws his question back at him.

River glances at Echo's back where she's walking beside Chase, her dark braid swinging down her back. His lips twist in a rueful grin. "I didn't want to." He thinks of how hard he tried to push Echo away in those early days. "I was hurting too badly after losing you."

"Our hearts don't let something like logic get in the way of who they beat for," Flora says softly. Almost tenderly.

"Seems so," River muses, still trying to accept Flora being so clearly in love with Chase.

He frowns. *Love.* Surely it's too soon to be thinking about a word like that when it comes to Echo.

"I'm sorry, River," Flora whispers.

He sighs. "I'm sure I'll get used to the idea eventually…" In fact, this way Chase is no longer interested in Echo. His twin has actually done him a favor.

Flora rolls her eyes, shoving him with her shoulder again. "No, I mean how I treated you back at Ruff's house. I thought…"

River's steps slow. "I know what you thought." His gaze drifts to the spire that is the Sting on the other side of the Betadome. "You thought I'd go back to the Green Zone and live a happy, oblivious life."

"In all fairness, I kind of wanted you to." Flora loops her arm through his like she has all their lives. "It was the easier choice. The safer one."

"I can't," River says fiercely. "I won't." And it hurts a little that the sister he shared a womb with would think he could.

"I didn't want you to choose this fight just because you love me, River." Flora tugs on his arm. "You love with everything you have," she adds, smiling up at him.

Yet, in some ways, he chose this fight because of Echo.

Which means that word just popped up again—

River focuses back on his sister. "We're going to do something about this, Flora. It's not right."

She nods. "That's why we need to find the Sovereign."

Echo turns as the last two words are said, making River wonder exactly how much she heard, rather than listening to Chase. "Which you still haven't told us anything about."

They stop, and River realizes they're now quite a distance around the Betadome. The colony is no longer visible as they've walked into the nothingness of the outskirts of the Dead Zone.

In fact, the netting that covers it is only a few yards away, dug into the ground so it can't come loose. There's more nothingness in the expanse beyond the net that's neither Dead Zone or Green.

"The Extinction Zone," breathes River, having never stood so close to it before.

Chase glances at Flora and she nods. He turns his back to the Betadome, and points at the ground. "The answers are down there."

CHAPTER
FIVE
ECHO

Echo studies the patch of dirt Chase is pointing at. The earth looks like it's been disturbed recently, but other than that, she can't see anything special about this location.

"You think the Sovereign's been buried somewhere?" she asks. "And Oren's been digging up the Dead Zone looking for it?"

River is still staring out at the vast expanse of the Extinction Zone as if in shock. She follows his gaze, seeing a tumbleweed blow across the horizon, making her wonder if there are plants growing out there somewhere. River's seen this wasteland from the Sting, but it must be different being this close. A reminder of all humanity has lost. Of all they could gain, if only they could unite the Zones and reclaim the earth.

She tugs on his hand to draw his attention back to Chase, and he looks down at the patch of dirt with his brow furrowed.

"Oren comes to this specific spot," says Flora. "We believe whatever's down there is the key to all of this."

"I'll show you." Chase drops to his knees and uses his hands to scrape away the dirt in long sweeping motions. Flora helps him and before long, a flat piece of metal appears. A little more work and it reveals itself to be a large disk with an electronic keypad in the center.

"What is that?" Echo's jaw falls open. She thought she knew every inch of the Dead Zone, but never in her life has she seen this. But then again, most of her days were spent weaving her way through the streets of the colony itself, not walking around the perimeter of the net.

"Oren comes here in the middle of the night," says Chase. "I first came across him on the way back from one of my food raids. I lay in wait and have seen him a number of times now."

"Has he seen you?" River asks.

Chase lifts an eyebrow. "I'd hardly be alive if that were the case. I hide behind that rock."

They turn to look where he's indicating and there's a small boulder that would be able to mask Chase's presence.

"What does he do here?" Echo asks.

Chase shrugs. "We're still figuring that out. He always comes with Tuff and one other Immune. When they arrive, he uncovers this disk. Then he punches some numbers into the keypad, and it opens for him."

"We haven't been able to crack the combination," says Flora. "I tried the numbers from the Restricted Area, but it didn't work."

River shakes his head like he can't believe what he's hearing.

Flora shoots him a sympathetic gaze. "There's so much more about our father than we can even begin to imagine."

"I've already figured that much out," says River, sadly.

"The three of them walk down some steps into the earth," Chase continues. "There must be a chamber dug out down there. And a while later, Oren and Tuff emerge. *Only* Oren and Tuff."

Echo's eyes fly wide open as the meaning of this sinks in. "What do you think's down there?"

Echo shrugs. "No idea. But what else could it be?"

"Chase has overheard a few interesting snippets," says Flora, looking at Chase like he's the smartest man alive. Echo is fairly certain this is exactly how she used to look at him. It's taking time to adjust to the new relationship she has with Chase, but a certain Green Born is making it easier. She wonders if she'd met River earlier whether she'd have fallen for Chase in the first place. Was it more a situation of him being the only guy around, rather than being the only guy for her? Because when River's nearby, Chase seems almost...invisible.

"What have you heard them say?" River asks Chase, leaning forward like he'll hear the answer sooner. It seems he's impatient, too.

"They call this place the Alphadome," says Chase. "Which is kind of a strange name, given it looks more like a dungeon than a dome."

"Tell them the important bit," Flora urges.

Chase draws in a breath. "I've heard Oren say they're testing for the Sovereign."

"That's the bit I don't understand," says Echo. I thought the Sovereign's in the Hive." Echo shudders to think of the giant metallic queen bee that held them captive.

"That's not the Sovereign," says Chase. "She's a Worker."

River frowns. "But the story we were told as kids—"

"Was wrong," Flora finishes. "Well, not the story. The Hive is real, as you saw. But that mechanical queen is what Oren refers to as a Worker. She cares for the Hive. Does all the work for it just like a worker bee in a real hive. But she's not the Queen."

"The Sovereign's something else," says Chase. "It's a person."

"I don't understand." River tilts his head.

"Flora can explain it better," says Chase. "She's the smart one here."

Flora beams at him, but then sobers as she turns back to Echo and River. "I learned things when I was helping in the LaB. It was all in my secret file."

"We didn't have time to read that," says River on a sigh.

"What else was in the file?" Echo holds her breath, sensing the answer is significant.

"The Code for Immunity is in a specific person's DNA," Flora says, her words heavy with the truth they carry. "Someone known as the Sovereign. A true Immune. Kind of like our very own human queen bee."

Echo draws in a sharp breath, reeling. A true Immune.

Someone who could save them all. No one would be Vulnerable.

"And Oren's trying to find them?" asks River, his green eyes wide. "And he's testing them down there?"

Chase and Flora nod in unison.

"But not *them*," says Flora. "*She*. I don't think Oren's worked that bit out yet as he's been testing males and females. Which means we're one step ahead of him already."

"I don't understand," says Echo, doing her best to keep up. "Why would the Sovereign need to be female?"

"Reed was doing some interesting research in the LaB." Flora points in the direction of the Green Zone. "He was exploring whether Immunity is contained within our mito-chondrial DNA. Which means a mother can pass it to either male or female offspring. But only her female offspring can continue to pass it on. It could explain why Immunity started out strong but has been waning."

"Told you she was smart," says Chase proudly.

"I've always known that," River reminds him. "Flora was born smart."

Echo sighs, accepting this foursome has some complicated dynamics. But for the sake of humanity, they really need to keep their heads level.

"Reed's the smart one." Flora waves a hand dismissively. "But I really think he was onto something. It makes sense. I mean, the Sovereign's a female in a bee colony. Why not for humans, too?"

Echo nods. Flora really is quite smart.

"So, let me get this straight," says River. "You're saying that somewhere out there is a female who carries the Immunity gene?"

Flora nods.

"And she's the Sovereign?" he asks.

"That's right," says Flora.

River nods slowly. "And if we find her, then we can make everyone Immune?"

Echo's chest fills with hope. When Tuff had tasked them with finding the Sovereign, she hadn't know where to start. But thanks to Flora, they're getting somewhere already.

"If we can achieve that, we'll have no more Zones," says Chase, his eyes burning with ambition. "We'd just have...the world. Like it used to be."

As idyllic as this sounds, Echo groans. This task just went to the next level of impossible. "How are we going to do that in one week?"

"Let's break it down," says River, putting a steadying arm around her. "First, we need to work out the combination to get into the Alphadome. Then we need to find out what's hidden in there. Then we need to find the Sovereign. Right?"

Everyone nods.

"See," says River. "We just take it one step at a time. We can do this."

Flora clears her throat and shuffles her feet.

"What is it?" River asks. "Say it. Whatever it is."

"It's just that..." Flora looks toward the vastness of the Extinction Zone, avoiding all eye contact.

"You can tell them," Chase encourages.

Flora looks back, her eyes filling with tears. "I can't say it, Chase. I can't. You tell them."

Chase nods and takes a step closer to Echo. "Flora thinks Echo's the Sovereign."

River lets out a gasp and hauls Echo closer. Her head spins as she remembers the way Oren had shown a special interest in her, wanting to keep her close as the first true Immune either Zone had seen for who knows how long.

"She can't be," says River, his voice full of denial.

"Reed was desperate to take a sample of my blood," says Echo, accepting Flora's words more easily as a few things start to make sense. "And he succeeded." She rubs her fingertips against the tiny red mark she'd found when she'd been gassed unconscious on the floor of River's room. "But if they found anything, surely Oren would have taken me here to test me."

Flora shakes her head. "You were the only Dead Born Immune for years. People would have noticed you missing. He was trying to find another way."

"The mentorship..." says River, nodding. "Oren wanted me to befriend Echo. To find out everything I could about her. To get her on our side."

"He was always so nice to me," Echo adds, remembering the kindly way Oren had treated her when she'd first been announced Immune. "Until he wasn't."

"He saw it was too late," says River. "That you were never going to be convinced to join him."

"Do you think that's why he made you his successor?" Echo asks, another piece of the puzzle falling into place.

"He did?" Flora seems shocked by this.

"He did." River nods. "He couldn't get Echo on side, but he thought he could win me over. And that maybe Echo would trust me. Then he found us in the Restricted Area and knew that wasn't going to work."

"So, he trapped you both in the Hive," says Flora, turning her gaze to Echo. "That makes sense. He found something in your blood that made him think you're the Sovereign, so he harvested you."

"But wouldn't people have noticed me missing then?" Echo asks.

"We forced his hand," says River. "We left him no choice."

"He'll have made up a story by now," Chase adds. "To explain your absence. And River's."

Echo glances at River as they both imagine what kind of story that might be.

"So, now that he harvested me, why wouldn't he want to take me straight to the Alphadome to test me?" Echo asks.

"Don't worry about that," says Chase a little too quickly. "Tuff's taken care of it."

"I don't like the sound of that." River scowls. "How?"

Chase shrugs. "All I know is that he said we don't have anything to worry about anything until the next Harvest Day. That Oren won't realize you're missing."

Echo swallows. "So, how do we find out if I'm the Sovereign?"

"We need to get into the Alphadome and test you ourselves," says Flora. "Before Oren gets the chance. We know he won't share the Immunity with everyone. We have to find it first."

"Hold on a minute." River tightens his grip on Echo, and

she finds herself sinking into his embrace. "That sounds dangerous. If we're so sure Echo's the Sovereign, why do we need to check? It doesn't sound like anyone survives."

Flora pulls back her shoulders. "That's only because the Sovereign hasn't been found. River, I wish there was another way, but there just isn't. We have to test Echo. She's the only true Immune we've seen for years. We don't have much time, either."

Echo feels ill to hear the fear that's been wrapping around her spine expressed out loud. Flora's right. As much as she doesn't want to admit it, she's the most likely candidate. It would be selfish of her not to agree.

They have to get into the Alphadome, so she can be tested.

And there are only two possible outcomes.

One. She's the Sovereign, and can save all of humanity.

Two. She never comes out.

CHAPTER
SIX
RIVER

The sun sets on River's first day in the Dead Zone and he already knows every day is going to be like this. A future defined by hunger. Inactivity.

And hopelessness.

He sat around the hut Echo grew up in, his future on display. There were others his age, gathered in groups, occasionally talking and joking, but mostly throwing rocks at nothing in particular. There was nowhere for them to be, nothing for them to do. If River were in the Green Zone, he'd have been preparing to spend the day in Eden, working hard to forge a tomorrow for the land they live on and the people depending on it.

Here, adults moved around with more purpose, children in tow or jugs of water on their hips. Yet their cheeks were sunken, their clothes hanging loosely on their frames. Hints of the scurge were starting to show in their bruised limbs, limp hair, and missing teeth. And the moment the sun climbed high enough, they all ushered back into their huts, the only shade that exists in the colony, no doubt to conserve what little energy they have.

As River had picked at the handful of dried corn Flora gave him, he'd registered there were very few people the age of his father. A few sat outside their huts, their frail bodies leaning against equally frail walls, toothless, gaunt and riddled with sores. Some stared into the distance with lifeless eyes, as if they were ready for death. *A longer life doesn't look like a blessing in the Dead Zone.*

Echo is the only one who seemed to have a purpose. When they returned from the location of the Alphadome after countless attempts to open the round portal to the unknown beneath the ground, she'd suggested they rest. Flora and Chase had disappeared into the hut, which meant River wasn't going in there. Echo had only just proposed that she and River sit in the meagre shade beside the hut when someone called out her name.

River barely saw her the rest of the day. There was always someone who wanted her. To talk. To ask a question. To bring her to their hut to show her something. She'd thrown him an apologetic look each time, but River encouraged her to go. *It's clear she's needed in the Dead Zone. That Echo found a purpose in a place with the sole role of holding the remains of humanity until it dies.*

Which gave him time to sit and watch. And think.

With each restless movement. Each painful cramp of his empty stomach. Each time he heard a soft, pitiful groan, two words had flared in his mind.

The Sovereign.

And she isn't a robotic bee painfully harvesting innocent people. *That's only a Worker. The Sovereign is a living, breathing beacon.*

The one who carries the genetic code to save them all.

And that person is probably Echo.

Which makes sense. She's the only one who was stung inside the Betadome on Confirmation whose Immunity was her own. He's just not sure how he feels about it.

Not when it's unclear how they confirm her Sovereign status.

Or whether she'll survive it.

River goes to pick up a small rock, wondering if rolling it around his mouth will make him forget about his hunger, then recoils when he registers it's a tooth. He throws it away, bile burning the back of his throat as he realizes losing teeth is normal here. He can just picture a hunched, sore-riddled man spitting it out and walking on without looking back.

Tucking his arms around himself, he gets up, then realizes there's nowhere for him to go. Nothing for him to do.

"Hey."

He turns, unwinding when he sees Echo approaching with a soft smile. "Hey," he responds, finding his voice raspy. He frowns when he sees her expression. "Is everything okay?" The moment he asks the question, River realizes how ridiculous it is. Nothing's okay.

Echo's shoulders droop. "I wanted to visit my friend, Nola. But Chase said she died a few days ago."

River remembers the screeching woman who was terrified at the prospect of him being in her hut. Echo was clearly the only person she trusted.

He engulfs her in a hug. "I'm so sorry. I know she was important to you." First her father, now Nola. "Just remember that the care you gave her made a difference."

Echo nods against his shoulder as she pulls in a halting breath. She looks up. "You're a good guy, River."

He's embarrassed to find a flush climb up his cheeks. "For a Green Born?" he jokes.

She steps back. "Especially considering you're a Green Born. I don't see any of the others here, risking it all in the Dead Zone." She smiles. "Nola would've liked you."

River's lips twitch. "That's not the impression I got."

Echo's own ghost of a smile tugs at her mouth. She opens the bag hooked over her shoulder and extends a canteen, sloshing it to show it's full. "Here. Have a drink."

River takes it, his mouth feeling like sandpaper, but then pauses. "Have you had some? Is there someone who needs it more?"

Echo shakes her head as she stops before him. "Water is something we can actually get in the Dead Zone. All we need to do is purify it. Drink up, River."

Still feeling like he hasn't earned it, River does as he's told, once more marveling at the clear taste. It's a stark reminder that even the water wasn't what he thought in the Green Zone. That his whole life was a lie.

Echo's hand lifts, hovering near his. "I, ah, wanted to talk."

River nods, knowing they need to discuss everything they discovered last night, but then he stills. Echo's voice was... softer than he'd expect. As if the topic isn't about the harsh reality that's weighing them down.

For some reason, his mouth is dry again. "Yeah?"

Echo opens her mouth, but before she can speak, Flora and Chase exit the hut. River frowns when he notices his sister's mussed hair.

Flora must see him looking because she flattens it with quick strokes. Then adjusts her slightly twisted trousers. Then flushes when she finds her top is caught up at the back.

Chase either hasn't noticed River's scowl, or he doesn't care. "We're going to collect some water."

"I have some," Echo offers, holding up the canteen River couldn't bring himself to finish.

"It's fine," Flora says, her gaze flicking to River, then quickly away. "We'll need more with four of us here."

Echo looks to Chase. "We could come and help?"

"No need," he responds as he grabs Flora's hand. "We've got it. We'll return before midnight to go back to the Alphadome."

Chase tugs her away before Echo or River can object. He flashes a smile at Echo, a cursory glance at River, then pulls Flora into his side as the two walk away...just a little too fast.

River crosses his arms. "My guess is it doesn't take that long to get water."

"No, it doesn't," Echo says thoughtfully.

A moment before they turn the corner around a hut with only three walls, Chase reaches around and gives Flora's butt a quick squeeze. She playfully swats at him, her delighted giggle sounding almost too bright for the Dead Zone.

River grimaces as he turns back to Echo. "Sorry. I know that must be harder for you to watch than me."

She turns to him, the dusk almost as dark as her hair. "It doesn't hurt like I thought it would," she says, looking just as thoughtful.

"Oh?" River knows he should say something more, but he's pretty sure he's not supposed to show he's happy to hear those words.

Echo steps closer, tilting her head to look up at him. "Chase can't break my heart," she says softly. "He's not the one who makes it whole."

"Oh."

This time, River breathes the word, at a loss for any more.

A slow smile tips up Echo's lips, bringing River's pulse with it. She moves in closer, grips him by the shirt and walks backward, taking him with her. She stops once they're beside the hut, her back against the flimsy wall, tugging him until their bodies are flush against each other's.

Echo pushes up onto her tiptoes so their lips are a breath apart. "And although I'm still not entirely sure what this is between you and me, I do know that you make my heart feel full in ways I didn't know were possible."

Although River realizes he's pretty darned sure, his only response is to banish the distance between their lips. To see exactly how full he can make her heart feel. He kisses Echo, fervently and passionately. Deeply and thoroughly.

With everything he has.

A shuddering breath ripples through Echo and her hands spear into his hair. She tugs, bringing his head down as she pushes further up. Then she's kissing him just as fervently and passionately and deeply and thoroughly. River's arms band around her, a groan rippling through him.

A groan of regret.

He pulls back an inch, panting. "Echo, I want to—"

"I know," she gasps. "I want it, too."

His knees almost give out. "No, I mean—"

She clasps his face, her hot gaze practically searing him as she smiles. "I want to check out the Alphadome as well." Her gaze drops to his lips, her own regret drawing a sigh out of her. "Before midnight."

River's breath whooshes out on a half-laugh. He drops his head until their foreheads are touching. "You're a mind reader," he chuckles.

She slips her hands from his hair and steps back, pulling down her top where it had climbed up. "And we now have the opportunity. It'll give us more time to try and figure out the combination to the door."

He nods. "If we're successful, we return before midnight with the good news. If not, we go back and keep trying."

Echo grins. "Unless you had a better idea of how to spend our time?"

River lets out another pained groan as he grabs Echo's hand. "Not a thing."

Echo's giggle has his own lips twitching up. Hands held, they make their way through the ramshackle huts, most of the streets and alleys empty. The knowledge why has River's shoulders dropping. If they were in the Green Zone, light would be everywhere, along with Green Borns. The children would be reading or building with hexagonal shaped blocks in the Sting, the adults would be chatting, all with full stomachs and minds free of worries. But what's there to stay awake for here? Darkness. Hunger. The knowledge tomorrow and every one after it is going to be the same.

The constant contrasts are why River's sneaking back to the Alphadome without Chase and Flora. Every minute counts. And as much as he hates to admit it, he doesn't know if Flora's told him everything she knows. There's a part to his twin that he never knew existed. One he's not sure she's ready to share.

As they pass the Betadome, River's stomach clenches painfully at the sweet scent of honey. If he breathes deeply enough, he can pick up the faint hint of citrus. His mind is suddenly tortured with images of fruit dangling from branches, of nuts sitting in husks, of breads made of millet, corn, wheat, and rye. Yet he can't get to any of it. Not without risk of a far quicker death than starvation.

It's the ultimate torture.

The Dead Borns are slowly wasting away. Yet they know a bounty of food is beyond a single stretch of wire netting. No wonder they hate the Green Borns so much.

47

Night has fallen by the time they reach the location of the Alphadome. It takes them a few minutes of scrabbling around on hands and knees, but Echo finally gasps. "Found it!"

River crawls over, blinking in the faint light of the stars and crescent moon when his fingers brush cool metal rather than gritty dirt. Shuffling until they're side by side, shoulders touching, he runs his fingers over the keypad. They tried dozens of words this morning, and were rewarded with harsh beep after harsh beep.

And a tightly closed door.

River grits his teeth. More secrets lie behind that door. Which also means more answers.

"We have to think like Oren," Echo murmurs.

River snorts. "Like a heartless, greedy leader?"

Echo sighs, leaning into him. "I'm sorry, River. I know you..."

He's glad she doesn't complete the sentence. She might've been about to point out that he looked up to his father, or that he craved the man's approval, or that he secretly hoped to be his successor. Any of those statements would've been true.

And each makes him as uncomfortable as the last.

"You loved him," Echo finishes.

River draws in a sharp breath. Of all the ways to finish, that truth cuts the deepest.

Echo gently nudges his shoulder. "Which makes you being here, doing this, all the more impressive. You've turned your back on everything you cared about, and that's not easy."

"Because the price for it is too high," he says roughly. "Oren's wrong."

Echo squeezes his hand, the sensation reverberating around his heart. "You're going to be our secret weapon, River. Right now, you probably know Oren better than anyone else. What are some words he liked to use?"

"Be in peace," he says bitterly. That was his father's favorite statement. River used to tell himself it was an endearment of sorts. A well wish for those he cared about.

But it was just another way to ensure compliance. A peaceful society doesn't ask questions. Doesn't look too closely beneath the veneer of serenity.

"Nice one," Echo says, a smile in her voice. "The code for the Restricted Area was the numbers for *fear*."

"I doubt the Alphadome is about peace." Still, River's brow furrows as he spells it out. "P. E. A. C. E."

Echo snorts. "Who comes up with these spellings?"

"That would make the code 165131."

She presses each number into the pad as he says them. There's the usual pause afterward and River sighs. "Seems I don't know my father—"

The door clicks open.

River and Echo jerk back in shock.

"It worked," she breathes.

River hauls open the round hatch the rest of the way and stares into the opening. An opening that holds answers. A set of pale white stairs beckon him. Except they agreed to go back...

Echo leans in. "We actually figured out the password."

Without Flora. Without Chase.

River slips his hand into Echo's and they look at each other. Even in the dark, he knows she's come to the same conclusion he has. "If we find out what's in there, we'll have more to report to Flora and Chase," he offers.

"Exactly." Echo's hand tightens around his. "They'd probably wonder why we didn't go in."

The decision made, River slips into the opening, Echo right behind him. He pauses. "We should close the door. Just in case."

Echo reaches up and brings the hatch with her as she descends, cutting off the faint light. River didn't think it amounted to much until the door thuds closed and plunges them into darkness the color of black ink.

He's just reaching out for Echo when the tunnel they're in is bathed in light.

"The only working lights in the entirety of the Dead Zone," Echo mutters.

River hates that she's right. He looks around, trying to get his bearings. The stairs rapidly descend then level out ahead. The walls are white. The steps are white.

"It reminds me of the LaB," Echo says.

River's mouth turns down. "It reminds me of the Restricted Area."

If they find another Hive...

Carefully, they creep down, each footstep sounding way too loud. River has to keep reminding himself they're alone.

They reach the bottom step and more lights come on ahead. River and Echo slow as they cautiously continue forward. The walls fall away as the area opens out. The space is so much larger than River expected and in the center is the first answer—how this bunker got its name.

The Alphadome.

River looks one way, then the other, trying to process what he's seeing.

"River, this is—"

There's a faint thud, then the sound of footsteps, freezing them both to the white-tiled floor. Someone's coming!

"Quick," Echo hisses, grabbing his sleeve and dragging him to the nearest hiding place. The opening turns out to be another tunnel, although the lights don't turn on when they enter it. There's no time to wonder at the good fortune as they press themselves against the wall in the shadows. Not when voices are trickling into the room.

One thought pounds through River's mind as his heart hammers so hard it hurts.

If they're caught, no one knows they're here.

CHAPTER SEVEN

The wall of the tunnel is cool against Echo's back. But it's nothing compared to the icy chill sliding through her veins as she sees who the approaching voices belong to.

Oren and Tuff have entered the Alphadome. And Tuff is carrying a limp body in his arms that's covered in slime.

River slips his hand into Echo's and she's reminded of the time they stood in Oren's office and watched these same two men in the Hive. She can only hope this time things don't end in the same way. She couldn't bear to be put back in that wall of fear. If whatever these two men are up to has anything to do with the tunnel they're hiding in, their cover will be blown.

She draws in a deep breath in a failed attempt to stop her limbs from shaking, and a foul odor fills her nostrils. It's both familiar and foreign all at once and she wonders if it's coming from the earthen walls of the tunnel that have been left bare. Or is it coming from wherever the tunnel leads? She squints into the darkness, startling when she thinks she sees a shadow move. River squeezes her hand, warning her to remain still.

Shifting her gaze from the terror of what she can't see,

Echo focuses instead on what she can. There's a glass prism in the center of the main room—the hexagonal structure she assumes must have given Alphadome its name. It gives her the horrors just looking at it, the palpable feeling of fear reflecting off its transparent walls. Large enough to hold two or three people, it currently contains nothing more than a chair with long straps dangling from its white, metal frame.

Oren strides to one of the glass walls of the prism and pulls on a handle. The wall swings out like a door, and he holds it open. Tuff enters, and the person he's carrying stirs in his arms, almost as if whoever it is can sense the danger they're in. He sets them down in the chair and slime drips onto the glass floor, revealing it's a girl with a dark braid hanging down her back. Echo feels like she may have seen her somewhere before, but her face is too obscured to be sure. Tuff straps her tightly into the chair, then steps out, wiping his sticky hands on his trousers with a grunt.

River shudders and Echo knows he's experiencing the same anguish she's working hard to contain. Chase and Flora said people were led willingly to the Alphadome, walking with Oren as they talked about the test. Somehow, Oren must have convinced them they were the Sovereign. Either that, or they had no idea the test is deadly if failed.

But there's nothing consensual about what's happening to this girl. Which makes it all kinds of next level wrong.

Both Echo and River remain where they are, knowing that to save this girl would mean sacrificing the lives of everyone they've ever known. A fat tear rolls down Echo's face and her tongue darts out to catch it, the salty tang distracting her from the harsh reality of what she's about to witness.

Because if Echo is the Sovereign, there's no way this girl can be. Which means...

No, she can't think about that right now.

Oren nods at Tuff, seeming pleased with himself, and Echo bites down on her lip, stopping herself from shouting out the questions that are trying to erupt from her throat. Why is Oren testing this girl if he believes Echo's the Sovereign? Had he found something in Echo's harvest that told him his search was not yet over?

"I'll get the queen." Oren walks toward a glass hexagonal column at the side of the room that stretches from the tiled floor right up to the roof. It's exactly like the columns in the LaB that are used to house endangered plants or bees. This one contains only one of the deadly creatures. And from what Oren just said, this one is a queen—the most lethal of them all.

As soon as Oren has his back turned, Tuff turns to the girl strapped to the chair and his face fills with sorrow. Echo's certain a few more lines crease his already wrinkled forehead as the guilt of what he's doing sinks in.

Echo tugs on River's hand, unable to help feeling that witnessing this crime makes them just as responsible as Tuff.

River presses his mouth to Echo's ear.

"We can't," he whispers on a gentle breath of frustration.

She nods in the darkness, knowing he's right. Wishing he were wrong.

Oren presses a button on the side of the glass column and a hexagonal floor and roof begin to slide toward each other within the enclosure. The queen's movements become agitated as she realizes her available space is being compressed. When there are only a couple of inches between the two platforms, a hatch in the top one opens, and a small glass prism emerges on the end of a robotic arm. It moves with expertise, quickly capturing the angry queen and sealing her inside.

"Hello, my queen," says Oren proudly as he opens a small door on the side of the column and retrieves the prism.

Echo scowls in the darkness. He wouldn't be so smarmy if the queen weren't so safely locked away.

Oren walks back to the Alphadome and holds the smaller prism up to the larger one.

Two glass jail cells.

One large. One small.

Both containing an innocent female.

And neither of them providing their consent.

Oren inserts the prism through a small rubber opening on the side of the Alphadome and it lands on the floor with a plink. The sides fold open until the prism is nothing more than a flat shape and the disgruntled queen flies free.

Echo swallows, holding River's hand like her own life depends on it. He may be the one to make her heart feel whole, but right now it's shattering into a million pieces at the thought of what this poor girl is about to endure. The only consolation is that she's still unconscious, so hopefully won't feel a thing.

There's another terrifying thought tapping at Echo's own consciousness that she's desperately trying to ignore. And failing. Because as she's watching this evil test unfold, she can't help but be aware that if they're going to find out if she's the Sovereign, she'll need to endure exactly the same thing.

The girl in the chair groans and stirs. Tuff's eyes fly open in panic. Clearly, this wasn't part of the plan. But he quickly quashes his surprise as he nods at Oren.

"There's nothing to fear," Oren calls through the glass, smiling broadly. "If you're the Sovereign, like we believe you to be, you'll be fine. Just fine. Be in peace."

The girl's eyes open, but there's too much slime stuck to her face and no matter how much she tries to blink it away, she can't seem to find her focus. She thrashes at her bindings, but Tuff has strapped her far too tightly to the chair for her to budge an inch. Her head rolls around, the only part of her that has any range of motion.

"No!" she cries as the queen buzzes around her face, spurred on by her panicked movements.

The solitary tear that had rolled down Echo's face is now joined by a stream. She can't watch this. *She can't!* But she has to. It's too late for this girl, but it's not too late to save every last life in both colonies. This just gives them even more reason to make sure they succeed in finding the Sovereign before Oren does.

"You can't fight it, Echo!" Oren booms.

She gasps, her heart rate ratcheting up several notches, only to realize the Green Zone leader is staring directly at the girl strapped to the chair in the dome.

Over the next several agonizing moments, the reality of the situation slides over Echo with heartbreaking clarity.

Tuff has sacrificed an innocent girl to fool Oren into thinking she's Echo. That's why the girl seems familiar. Not because Echo has met her, but because she's so much like herself.

And now not only is she about to witness her die, she's about to witness her die in Echo's place. She can't stand by and watch this!

Echo lurches forward, but two things happen.

River pins her to the wall with a strength she didn't know he possessed.

And the girl's chair tips backward, sending her crashing to the floor.

Echo muffles a cry, knowing she's too late. The queen is in an unstoppable frenzy, landing on the girl's face while she violently moves her head from side to side in the only way she can defend herself.

A scream that will haunt Echo for the rest of her days

rattles inside the Alphadome as the queen stings the girl over and over. It feels like she's stinging Echo directly in her chest as her heart aches with the injustice of it all. If it weren't for River's arm pinning her to the wall, she'd surely collapse.

Then the girl's thrashing stops and a deep wheeze erupts from her lungs. It's a hurricane compared to the labored breaths Echo's heard River take in the Green Zone. Each rattle is a throe of death, and eventually the girl falls silent.

River releases his hold on Echo, and she slips her hand back into his, trying to let him know how sorry she is.

"She's not the Sovereign," says Tuff, his voice even more gravelly than the last time Echo had heard it. "She's dead."

"She's not dead." Oren is practically pressing his nose against the glass of the dome in his desperation to see the girl he believes to be Echo survive. "Just give her a moment to recover."

Echo strains her eyes, hoping Oren can see something she can't. From where she's standing in the tunnel, the girl looks unmistakably dead.

The room becomes quiet as they wait. Too quiet. Echo has to work hard to control her breathing, certain the pounding of her heart is vibrating off the walls and giving their position away. The foul smell invades her nostrils again and she sniffs at it, trying to place it.

The queen bee crawls over the face of the girl, the creature's tiny legs seeming unaffected by the sticky slime as it walks across her lifeless eyeball. When the girl doesn't so much as blink, Oren pulls back from the glass and hangs his head in his hands.

"I was so sure it was her." He lets out a disappointed sigh.

The queen bee lifts into the air and flies around the dome a few times, landing on a few surfaces before returning with curiosity to the flat piece of glass that was the prism it had arrived in. It snaps closed, encasing the queen once more.

Tuff opens the Alphadome and fetches the queen, handing her to Oren who inserts her back into the glass column.

"I can finish up here," says Tuff.

"I'll wait." Oren stays beside the column, watching the queen feed on a small dish of nectar, replenishing her reserves for her next victim.

Who will likely be Echo...

Tuff unties the girl from the chair and scoops her up. More slime oozes from her face, revealing features that while very much like Echo's, are also different. Her nose is wider. Her lips fuller. Her skin pinker. Tuff subtly turns her head into his chest and stands up, walking directly toward Echo and River. They press themselves so hard into the wall they almost become part of it.

He walks directly past them and it's hard to tell in the darkness if he sees them or not. A golden glow filters to life as he reaches whatever is at the end of the tunnel and there's a humming.

Then a metallic clacking.

And, finally, a tap, tap, tap.

Echo trembles, wanting nothing more than to run as fast and far away from this place as her legs will take her.

A few minutes later Tuff emerges into the tunnel alone. He shoots River and Echo a stern glance as he passes, but he doesn't give them away.

Echo lets out a long breath, her lungs aching for fresh air.

The golden glow extinguishes, and Oren and Tuff leave the Alphadome, plunging Echo and River into darkness.

"We have to see what's in there," River whispers as he pulls her to his chest.

"No," says Echo. "We already know."

There's another Hive. With another mechanical Worker bee. And Echo realizes with a jolt what's familiar about the foul odor wafting down the tunnel.

It's the smell of decaying bodies.

This Worker doesn't feast on fear.

It's death that she's after.

CHAPTER
EIGHT

RIVER

"We have to know for sure," River insists, even as the same urge to run tugs at every muscle fiber.

Echo nods, but he can see the fear multiply in her eyes, even in the near-black they're now standing in. "We need to know."

Does Oren have more than one Hive?

Which means more than one Worker bee...

Their hands are clasped so tightly it almost hurts as they make their way down the tunnel, staying close to the wall. River's breath is frozen in his lungs as they approach the other end, knowing the lights will be triggered and come on any second.

Revealing what's on the other side.

Memories of the pain they endured in the Sting, in what they assumed was the only Hive, flash through his veins like flares. Whispers of agony quickly follow, taking his breath away. They seem to cling along each nerve ending, refusing to fade.

Walking toward the possibility of being caught and forced

to suffer that all over again feels like one of the stupidest things he's ever done—and he once trusted Oren. But River doesn't slow or stop. Neither does Echo.

They need to know exactly how big this is.

The next step has pale light blooming like a new dawn. River and Echo still, eyes growing wide, but not in wonder.

Horror freezes them to the cement floor. They don't move. Don't blink. Hold their breath as the faint smell becomes an overwhelming stench.

Just like before, the area opens out into a chamber. Except the walls are dark gray, not white. The room is round, almost like a womb.

And the walls are lined with large shelves, like bunk beds. Most of them are holding a body in a different stage of decay. Some are nothing but skeletons. Others are withered corpses, skin like parchment and as gray as the walls. The ones closest to the entrance are the...most recent. They're sunken and decomposing, but they still have eyes, hair, lips. They're still recognizable as the person who once breathed and worked in the Green Zone.

Echo grips River's hand impossibly tighter, as if her knees just went weak. They're not looking at a womb. A place that holds life.

This is a giant tomb.

A graveyard.

For every soul who's died in the search for the Sovereign.

A violent retch scorches through River, shooting bile up his throat. His only saving grace is there's nothing in his stomach to empty onto the floor.

"There's no..." Although Echo doesn't finish her sentence, River knows what she's talking about.

The room is empty apart from the rows of corpses. There's no robotic bee inside the tomb, meaning their imaginations got away from them. Why would there? There's nothing to harvest here. Every soul failed Oren. They didn't have what he was looking for.

They weren't the Sovereign.

River's lashes flutter as he realizes something else. His feet unglue from the floor as he takes an unconscious step forward. "I knew him," he breathes, taking another involuntary step toward the shelf on his left. "Koa. His mother was never the same after she was told he died in the processing center."

His eyes roam to the shelf above, then sting with tears. "Breeze. She was Forgotten. No one ever knew why."

"River," Echo chokes, her arms now wrapped around her middle. "We need to go. We've seen everything we need to."

She's gazing at the shelf below Koa's, even though it's empty, her face stricken and pale. When River realizes why, he almost vomits again.

If Oren captures Echo and she fails, it's her body that will be lying there.

"No," he growls, the single word reverberating through his chest. "We're not—"

Echo shakes her head. "Let's not talk about this here." Her eyes flicker to the newest addition to the tomb, the girl who just died lost her life because Oren believed she was Echo. The Sovereign. "Let's get out of here."

River nods, his heart jammed in his throat. He can't watch Echo go through what he just witnessed. He *won't*.

He turns back to glance at Koa, then Breeze, no longer shying away from their gray complexion or withered skin. Echo will never look like this, he vows to himself. He even lifts a hand, wondering if he can bring himself to touch the lifeless bodies. "We'll figure—"

There's a whoosh, then two sounds River hoped he'd never hear again.

A whirring. Followed by rapid tap, tap, tapping.

"River!" Echo cries, covering the few feet between them to glue herself to his side. "It's another one!"

The robotic bee exiting from a hatch in the floor—River will never call her the Sovereign again—looks just like the one back in the Hive. The one Flora had called the Worker. Shiny silver body, black wings whose expanse almost eclipse the width of the tomb, flashing eyes. And the strange, glowing circle on her back that's only visible because of the liquid light that shines from it.

River has to tilt his head back to gaze into her metallic face, his blood turning to ice when her jaws snap open and shut and her antennae point at them like lasers.

The deadly machine has her target.

River's mind stutters on a loop. The bee is bigger, faster, stronger than them. Not that it matters. There's nowhere to run or hide.

The Worker goes from stationary to moving before the thought can repeat, throwing her jaw open on a screech so loud it hurts River's ears. He and Echo reel back, slamming into the shelves behind them. The smell of death and decay mixes with the scent of their own fear. It coats River's tongue with a sickening tang.

Echo glances around frantically, and River realizes she's looking for a weapon. Something to defend themselves with. But the room contains nothing but shelves and corpses.

And a predator programmed to kill them.

"Run!" Echo screams, grabbing River's hand.

He does as he's told, realizing Echo's survival instinct is far stronger than his. She knows just as much as he does that running is futile.

But she's doing it anyway.

The Worker's wings snap out as she half-flies, half runs

after them, her metallic legs clacking even faster than River's out of control pulse. He and Echo sprint for the tunnel, the distance that was only a few feet minutes ago now feeling like miles. Every inch is a moment they'll be caught. Trapped by those legs, snapped within the metallic jaws, pierced with the deadly antennae.

Miraculously, they reach the mouth of the tunnel, and Echo has the courage to glance over her shoulder. Her eyes widen, making River's stomach bottom out. The Worker must be right behind them.

Except Echo stumbles to a stop. "River!" she gasps.

He yanks on her hand. "Don't give up now. Come on!"

Echo pulls back. "No. Look!"

He spins around, still yanking Echo back so she's further away from the room of death. Then stops, registering what Echo has.

The Worker is no longer chasing them. In fact, she's climbing up the shelves, her front legs and antennae roaming over Breeze's body, then Koa's like a mother checking her children when they're safely tucked in bed. The eerie whirring sound that River now associates with the machine being happy hums through the tomb.

"She's protecting the dead bodies," Echo gasps.

"They're her brood?" River asks, disgusted.

"I think more like her food," Echo says, looking a little green as well as pale. "That's why all the bodies are so...dried out."

River decides that's even worse.

The Worker turns to look at them, jaw opening to let out another spine-clawing screech, and they instinctively take a step back. She doesn't bother to follow them, her legs moving independently one after the other as she attaches herself to the shelves more securely.

"This is our chance, River," Echo whispers.

They continue to retreat, walking backward steadily but swiftly. The Worker remains beside Koa, antennae twitching with agitation.

As River turns away, she crouches closer to Koa, antennae curling toward him. River yanks his gaze forward, not wanting to see what's going to happen next. A harvesting, just like in the Hive.

But of death, not fear.

River can't believe his father used the code for *peace* for this place.

The moment they're a few feet within the tunnel, River and Echo break into a run. The light of the tomb quickly fades, then the room with the Alphadome blazes to life. River doesn't look at the hexagonal glass structure in the center as they run past it. He refuses to consider that someone else will be forced to go in there.

Especially not Echo.

They reach the stairs and take them two at a time, their harsh breathing bouncing off the enclosed space. They only stop when they reach the hatch, chests pumping in and out.

River lifts his finger to his lips and Echo nods. He reaches up and grips the handle. He's not sure exactly how long his father and Tuff have been gone, but surely it's enough time for them to be back in the Green Zone.

Still, River would be holding his breath if he wasn't panting so hard after their frantic run. The thought of getting caught now, with everything they know, makes his heart beat even harder.

The tomb held dozens more reasons why they need to stop this.

He twists the handle and there's a faint click, then the circular hatch pops open. Echo is a statue beside them as they listen intently. If someone approaches, they'll have to close themselves in again. Maybe try to hide.

Alongside who knows how many dead bodies and a Worker.

But there's nothing.

River pushes the hatch open completely and they quickly scramble out. The moment Echo's beside him he closes it, scraping the dirt back to cover it over, deciding they won't be going back into that pit of death again.

They're going to have to find another way to figure out whether Echo's the Sovereign.

"Come on," Echo says quietly. "Let's get back."

River tugs her to him. "That won't be you," he promises fiercely.

"You can't guarantee that, River," she says, her voice heavy. "Everyone's lives depend on finding the Sovereign."

He tightens his jaw so hard his teeth grind. "I'm not—"

They both freeze as a faint scraping sound tickles the air. Simultaneously, they separate, bodies tense as they prepare to run. They can't get caught, not now. Not with everything they've learned.

River peers into the night, blinking rapidly when his head swims from lack of food. He can't falter now. If Oren and Tuff are approaching, they'll be dragged straight back into the Alphadome.

River's promise to keep Echo out of there will be broken minutes after the words were said.

Two figures appear from behind the boulder nearby and River digs his feet into the dirt, deciding he'll fight before flight. It'll give Echo a chance to escape.

"River," whispers a voice that sends relief cascading through him. "It's me, Flora."

The outline beside her straightens a little more. "And Chase."

River's brow slams down, the relief cut short by annoyance. Does that guy always have to be glued to his twin?

Flora rushes over, Chase right behind her. She throws her arms wide with agitation. "Did you just come out of the Alphadome?" she hisses.

River nods, then realizes she probably can't see the action. "We wanted to see if we could crack the combination."

"And we did," Echo adds. "First try."

Flora takes a small step back. "I can't believe you went in without me," she says, sounding hurt.

River frowns in the dark, deciding he won't point out that Flora kept far bigger secrets from him. For far longer than he could've imagined.

Echo huffs. "It hurts when someone you love and trust doesn't include you. Who would've figured?"

The sound of Flora's mouth snapping shut is audible in the quiet night. River almost finds himself smiling. Echo just defended him, actually sounding a little annoyed on his behalf. The thought shoots warmth straight through his chest.

Chase moves his arm, looking as if he's rubbing Flora's back. "We need to remember we're all working toward the same goal."

River snorts quietly. Chase lied to Echo as much as Flora lied to him.

"That's why we came here earlier," Echo says, lifting her chin. "Getting inside the Alphadome was important."

"What did you find?" Chase asks.

Echo falls silent, and River instinctively moves closer to her. "Oren and Tuff came in while we were there."

Flora gasps. "What?"

"We weren't seen," he assures her. "But we did see someone get tested for the Sovereign."

"They're stung by a queen bee," Echo adds, subdued. "The girl didn't make it."

The girl Oren thought was her.

River clears his throat. "We discovered why no one comes out after. There's a room, an underground graveyard, full of bodies."

Flora recoils, seeming to draw into herself at the image in her mind, even though River doubts it would do the horrifying sight justice. He's about to mention the Worker bee when Chase draws in a sharp breath.

"Echo..." he says softly.

She stiffens, and River is struck that it turns out he and Chase have something in common—they both care for Echo.

River tugs Echo into his side. "We're not putting Echo through that. There has to be another way."

"A sting by a queen bee makes sense," Flora says thoughtfully. "They're the most venomous."

"It doesn't matter. We'll find some other way. Surely there's a blood test we can do."

Flora shakes her head. "The gene that indicates someone is the Sovereign is a silent one, which is why it's been so hard to find. Venom must be what activates it. It's how it's expressed."

"River—" Echo starts, resting a hand on his chest.

"No!" He quickly modulates his voice as the word fires off louder than he intended, glancing around. "There *has* to be another way." He knows he's repeating himself, but he won't consider the possibility of losing Echo.

"Do you know how many lives depend on finding out?" Chase asks, his voice soft but steely.

Anger flares through River, and he almost steps in front of

Echo protectively. Chase may care for Echo, but that won't stop him sacrificing her.

"No," he snaps. "Echo's not going in the Alphadome."

Silence falls, feeling suffocating and oppressive, yet River refuses to back down. Echo's hand presses harder into his chest, and he has no idea what that means. Chase looks as if his hands are clenching and unclenching, and River doesn't really care what that means.

"You chose *her* to love hard?" Flora whispers.

River stiffens, flushes, then slices his hand through the air. "Don't you see? This is bigger than that. Sacrificing in the name of finding answers needs to stop."

Flora hunches her shoulders, and River knows her well enough to know she's chewing her lip. "There might be something we can do."

He rounds on her, gripping her arms. "What? What is it?"

"I don't know if it would work," his twin says, eyes darting to Echo. "It's just an idea."

River waits, already deciding whatever it is, they'll do it.

"We get our hands on as much adrenacure as we can," Flora says with a shrug. "And use it if Echo reacts to being stung by the queen bee."

River's hands fall away, his mind whirring as he turns to find Echo just as wide-eyed as he is. It's entirely logical that massive doses of adrenacure could save her.

It could actually work!

Chase frowns. "But that means..."

River blinks, realizing what Chase is thinking. It means they have to go back to the Sting.

CHAPTER

NINE

ECHO

E cho knows she should be tired. But her racing mind
seems to need far less sleep than her exhausted body.
Which is just as well. If they're going to break into the Sting,
they need to do it while it's still dark. Waiting until tomorrow
night would cost them another day. And if they only have one
week to find the Sovereign, each day is painfully precious.

The time to move is now.

"We can't all go," says Flora, glancing at Echo in the dim
light of the stars. "One of us should stay behind, just in case
things don't go to plan."

Echo jams her hands on her hips. "Why are you looking
at me?"

"I'm sorry," Flora says quickly. "It's just that you..."

"Might be the Sovereign," Chase finishes. "Flora's right. We
can't risk you. You need to stay behind."

River lets out an amused huff.

"What?" Chase snaps.

"Nothing." River holds up his hands. "It's just that...well,
you're supposed to know Echo."

"I do." Chase seems confused. "What's your point?"

"Have you ever known her to stay behind when she's asked?" River lets his hands fall.

"She never once followed me into the Green Zone on a raid," Chase retorts.

"That was the old Echo," says River. "I'm not sure you've met the new one. Following people is her specialty."

Echo rolls her eyes, even though what River says is accurate. Chase has no idea about the person she became the moment she was declared an Immune. If they try to leave her behind, she'll most definitely follow. She's not letting River go without her. What if he has another one-off breathing episode?

"I can hear you." Echo crosses her arms and scowls. "You don't have to talk about me like I'm not here."

"Echo and I will both stay behind," says Flora. "Chase knows how to get through the Betadome without being seen. And River knows his way around the Sting."

"Great," says Echo. "Looks like Flora's volunteered to stay here. Which means I'll be going. Saves me having to follow you, so that suits me." She pokes out her tongue at River and sees Chase bristle.

Somehow, River resists the urge to say he told him so.

"I just wanted to keep you safe." Flora sounds bruised and Echo feels immediately guilty.

"I know," she says more softly. "And I appreciate that. But I can look after myself. If anyone is going to risk themselves, it has to be me. I'm the one the adrenacure is for. I can't just sit here and wait while the only two people I love put themselves in danger."

An awkward silence hangs in the night air and Echo instantly regrets her words. She just said she loves River and Chase. In front of everyone. And it came out all wrong. Because while she does love both of them, it's in very different ways. Let alone the fact she's never said that word to either of them...

Flora slips her hand into Chase's. "Looks like I'm on my own then. Perhaps you should bring one of the Razers with you? For protection."

River shakes his head. "We don't need—"

"Good idea," says Chase. "I'll bring Trid."

"No way!" River throws out his hands. "Isn't he the guy who attacked me when I first came here? You're not bringing him."

Echo puts a steadying hand on River's arm. "It's a good idea. You saw for yourself what an experienced fighter Trid is. We could use someone like him on our side. Like Flora said... just in case."

"Well, he'd better stay away from me then," River grumbles.

"You're on the same side now," she soothes, pleased to have his agreement, no matter how reluctant he is.

Chase takes a step away. "I'll walk Flora back and get Trid."

"Be quick," says Echo, aware of how much of the night has already slipped away.

"Make sure you wait for us this time," says Chase.

"Then make sure you don't take too long," River snaps back.

Flora goes to her brother and gives him a quick kiss on the cheek, then whispers something in his ear. Echo doesn't need to hear it to know that she's asking him to give Chase a chance. It's not easy when the two people you love most are at odds with each other.

Echo should know. As she just told them all...

Chase and Flora's silhouettes disappear in the direction of the Dead Zone. The colony's outline is barely visible, but Echo knows each misshapen line and shadow of the place she grew up. In a strange way, she'd missed it while she'd been in the Green Zone. Home is always home, no matter how brutal a place it is to live.

River wraps his arms around Echo, and she nestles into him, drawing in his warmth. He's taller than her but there's something about his shape that seems to fit her own, like they're part of a puzzle made with only two pieces.

"River," she says, enjoying the sound of his name on her lips. Although, not quite as much as she'd enjoyed having his mouth pressed against them.

"You don't need to explain," he says, seeming to know exactly what she wants to clear up. "I get it. You don't know who your heart belongs to."

"I already told you who it belongs to." She pulls back, wishing she could see the intensity of his green eyes in the darkness. "You're the one who makes my heart full. Not Chase."

River tenses. "You don't have to say that."

"But it's true." Echo slides her hands from his waist and loops them around his neck. "I thought I was in love with Chase for the longest time. But that was only because I didn't know what real love was. I hadn't met you..."

"But you said you loved us both." River grimaces. "Just before. You said it."

"And I do." Echo shakes her head, wanting to find the perfect words. "You love Flora, right?"

River nods.

"And do you want to do this to her?" Echo pushes up on her toes and kisses River chastely on the lips.

"Most definitely not," he says as she breaks away.

"How about this?" Echo kisses him again, but this time it's like all the stars shoot across the sky at once as passion explodes between them. Lips caress. Tongues tangle. Fingertips seek and claw. Bodies press impossibly closer as soft moans float into the night, sparking the Dead Zone to life.

Echo's hands find the hem of River's tattered shirt and she slides her palms up the smooth expanse of his bare back. It's hard to believe she ever thought this guy was her enemy. He's proven to her that his soul is full of warmth and kindness. He's brave and loyal and willing to fight for what's right. And...he sure knows how to kiss.

River kicks the kiss up into a territory she never knew existed and Echo's stomach flips so hard she lets out a gasp. Now she understands why Vulnerables fall pregnant when they really can't afford to. The feeling of wanting to be with River is morphing very quickly from something she wants, to something she *needs*.

She pulls back, overwhelmed at the depth of her feelings. Panting hard, she rests her forehead on his chest and tries to find the part of herself she lost in that moment. Although, the time for that is gone. Because she didn't lose it.

She gave it away. To River. It could only be him.

"I'm sorry," he says, breathing heavily through his frown. "Was that too much?"

"No." She shakes her head and looks up at him. "It wasn't enough."

"Oh." His frown tips into a smile and he runs a fingertip down her jawline. "And to answer your question, there's no way I'd ever want to do anything like that with my sister."

Echo laughs. "Well, that's how I feel about Chase. Do you get it now? He's like a brother to me."

"And what am I to you?" he asks, clearly fishing for more.

"You?" She tilts her head. "You're my guy, River."

He seems to like this answer as he goes to give her another kiss but seems to change his mind when he remembers where that got them last time, and he hugs her instead.

"And you're my girl," he says into her hair. "Which is why I can't lose you."

She wants to tell him that will never happen, but the only thing she can think of is the image of that poor girl lying in the Worker's crypt in the Alphadome.

"Flora's smart," she whispers. "Her idea will work. We'll get the adrenacure, then no matter what happens I'll be okay."

River goes to say something then stops himself.

"What is it?" she asks.

"It's just...well, why hasn't Oren tried the adrenacure before?" he asks. "He must have thought of it himself."

Echo nods, having already turned this over in her mind when Flora suggested it. "I don't think he wants to save the people he tests."

"But why?" River seems genuinely perplexed, which reminds Echo even more why she fell so hard for this guy. He's so good that he simply can't see the bad until it's right before his nose.

"Think about it," she says. "Once someone's been tested, they know about the Alphadome. And the Sovereign. Oren can't risk them telling anyone. There'd be mass panic. Let alone all the questions it would raise. Once Oren knows they're not the Sovereign, it's far easier to just let them die."

"But that's outrageous!" River steps back and rakes his hands through his hair. It doesn't seem to matter how much he finds out about the extent of his father's evil, it still rocks him to his core.

Chase's shadow appears in the distance along with a lankier one that must be Trid.

"They're here," Echo says, wanting to give River a chance to pull himself together.

He takes her hand and starts walking briskly toward the Betadome.

"Are you okay?" she asks quietly.

He nods. "Let's just get this over and done with. We have to beat my father to finding the Sovereign. I'm not going to watch anyone else die. I swear it. I'm not."

Echo couldn't agree more. She's just not sure it's entirely in their hands.

They reach the door of the Betadome and Chase points at his companion. "This is Trid."

"We've already met," says River, still not seeming to be able to let go of his animosity.

"Yeah." Trid has the decency to look embarrassed. "Sorry about that day."

"Stick behind me," says Chase, moving on. "Walk where I walk. *Exactly* where I walk, and the cameras won't see you. Got it?"

Echo nods. "Got it."

"Trid, you take the rear," says Chase. "Echo, get behind me and stay close."

"River will go first." Echo pushes him forward and he shoots her a grateful glance. She may have told him she sees Chase like a brother but River's not ready to see her cozied up to him in the darkness just yet.

Chase enters the Betadome and smoke cloaks them even though the bees are all tucked away in their hives at night. He ducks low and takes a sharp right turn, dropping to his stomach and pulling himself across the soft grass with his hands and knees. River is close behind him and Echo mimics the movements, hearing Trid grunting behind as he does the same.

There's a pause and Chase gets to his feet, pressing his back against a section of the netted dome and shuffles several yards before squatting again. River copies him, looking back at Echo every now and then to make sure she's okay. This really was far easier when Tuff turned the cameras off.

They crawl forward until they reach a tree bursting with fruit and Chase picks an apple and eats it, motioning for River to do the same. Echo smiles, not having expected a snack break as part of this.

"We don't want our growling stomachs to give us away when we get to the Sting," says Chase. "All around this tree is a black zone for the cameras."

"How many can we take?" asks Trid with his mouth full.

"Just one for now," Chase says. "We need to keep moving. You can pick some more on your way out later."

River and Echo take an apple each. As Echo bites into the sweet flesh of the fruit, she thinks of Nola and the apple she'd saved for her but never got to deliver. If only she could have held on for a few more days, Echo would have had the chance to say goodbye to her old friend. But the scurge is like that. It sneaks up on you and steals your life when you least expect it. Much like Oren...

"What are you thinking?" River asks.

She shrugs, not wanting to share her last thought. Then her eyes widen to see Trid taking a second apple. He has to reach higher up in the branches to get to it and a thousand leaves rustle in response.

"Chase said one," Echo admonishes. "We have to keep moving."

"I'm hungry," says Trid, already biting into it, juice dribbling from the corners of his mouth.

"Nobody move!" River's eyes are wide. "There's a bee."

"You woke it up." Echo scowls at Trid as she instinctively freezes, even though she's the only one here safe from that tiny creature's venom.

The bee flies around above their heads in a circle, almost as a warning. But it's either sleepy or not feeling threatened as it doesn't come any closer.

For now.

"Let's get out of here." Chase stuffs the apple core into his mouth and chews on it as he steps back near the net, taking a very specific path. "Follow my steps."

River is right behind him. Echo waits a few moments for Trid to finish his second apple, eventually giving up and following River. If Trid wants to get stung, that's on him. He was the one who disturbed the deadly creature.

"Chase!" River half whispers, half shrieks. "Stop. Don't move."

Chase comes to a halt. "What is it?"

"It's on the back of your neck," says River, seeming to be trying to get control of his panic. "Don't move. It might fly away."

A chill runs down Echo's spine. They all know it's not going to fly away. It's just like their Confirmation. Once a bee has its target in sight, there's no stopping it.

Chase raises his hand slowly and uncurls his fingers. "Where is it exactly?"

"You can't kill it!" says River, trying to keep his voice low. "We don't kill the bees."

"River, it's going to kill him!" Echo's feet are desperate to break into a run so she can get the bee away from Chase, but she knows the movement will infuriate it more. Which will also put River at risk.

Damn it! Why couldn't she have done as Chase suggested and walked behind him? If anyone can safely dispense of that bee, it's her. This rivalry between River and Chase is potentially going to cost one of them their lives!

Chase pulls his hand back and readies himself. He's got one chance to slap this bee and kill it. If he misses, he's dead. And it's a task made so much harder because he can't see what he's doing.

"I think I can feel where it is," says Chase calmly. "Don't anyone move. One. Two—"

River darts forward and slaps the back of Chase's neck, sending an almighty crack into the midnight air.

Everyone stands perfectly still for several beats of their racing hearts as they wait to see the result of what just happened. Eventually, River's hand falls back to his side and Chase turns to him and grins. Echo lets out a deep breath, realizing River just saved Chase's life.

"Maybe Flora's right," says Chase. "You do like me."

"I told Echo I don't want to see anyone else die," says River through gritted teeth. "I suppose that includes you."

"Not sure about the bee, though." Chase kicks at the small creature on the ground. "Oh, and thanks for that."

"Don't mention it." River looks back at Echo and she gives him a grateful smile. He just killed a bee to save the life of a human who he doesn't like all that much. He really has adapted to life in the Dead Zone.

"I'm proud of you," she mouths, falling even more in love with him than she'd been before.

River nods to show he heard her, but Chase is already walking on, so he turns and follows. Echo checks to see Trid ambling behind her like he wasn't in any way responsible for what just happened. If he hadn't reached for that second apple...

She shakes her head. There's no point assigning blame now. The four of them need to work as a team if they're going to get in and out of the Sting unnoticed.

Chase weaves them through the Betadome until they reach the green door.

"How are we going to do this?" Echo hisses. She knows

there's a camera pointed at this door. Oren showed them the footage when she'd followed River into the Dead Zone.

Chase drops to the grass. "It doesn't capture the very bottom section."

"But Oren will see the door open." River sinks to his knees, preparing to flatten himself against the hard ground.

"Only if he's watching for it." Chase winks. "He can't review all the footage from all the cameras at every moment of the day. If we stay low and open the door only just enough to get through, he won't notice. Well, he hasn't in all the times I've been through."

Echo looks at River with a frown to see if he's buying this story.

"Oren told me he didn't know how the rebels were getting in," says River.

"We're Razers, not rebels," growls Trid.

"Whatever you call yourselves, Chase is right," says River. "Oren's never seen him come through the door."

"Wow," says Chase, his gaze still fixed on River. "First you save my life, then you agree I'm right. Told you that you liked me."

Before River has a chance for a rebuttal, Chase has cracked open the green door and is sliding himself along the ground.

"Stay as low as you can," he says. "When you get out, turn right. Trid can close the door."

Chase moves with the expertise of someone who's used to moving in this unnatural way. It reminds Echo of a lizard she saw once when she was a child. Belly and head close to the ground. Arms and legs pushed out to the sides to propel the torso forward. She can still taste that lizard now from the portion she'd been given after Chase had trapped and roasted it.

River follows with a bit more difficulty and Echo keeps

close behind him. Her elbows quickly begin to feel like they're rubbing raw, but somehow, they don't hurt. Which is no wonder, really. Adrenaline must be spiking through her body with the cocktail of fear and excitement that's threatening to overwhelm her. She'd be ripe for harvesting right now if Oren got his filthy hands on her.

After what feels like an eternity, Chase rises to his feet, warning the rest of them not to do the same until they're beside him. River groans as he stands, immediately reaching out a hand to help Echo up.

"Thank you." Her skin tingles as a completely different chemical races into her veins at the contact. If only the world would disappear so she could wrap her arms around him again and kiss him until the earth runs out of time.

"Move forward," grunts Trid from the ground.

"Oh." Echo snaps back to reality and takes a step toward Chase, clearing the way for Trid to get to his feet.

"I can get us to the Sting." Chase spits out an apple seed onto the grass. "But after that, it's all on River. I've never been inside."

"I can do that." River pulls back his shoulders and nods. It's a relief to see these two working together at last. The incident with the bee might just turn out to be the best thing that ever happened to them.

Chase takes off at a jog, taking various twists and turns through the grounds of the Green Zone in much the same way he had in the Betadome. Except, thankfully for Echo's elbows, this time there's no need to crawl.

River's breathing quickly becomes labored, and Echo runs beside him, trying not to make it obvious she's monitoring him.

"I'm okay," he says, equally aware of her as she is of him. "Once we're in the Sting, I'll be fine."

She nods, saving her energy for her legs instead of her words.

"In here." River points to an inconspicuous building off to the side of the Sting. "It's the laundry room. We need to blend in."

"Good thinking." Chase looks down at his tattered clothes.

River leads them into a large, dark room that smells of lemon and bleach, two scents that Echo was completely unfamiliar with before she was declared Immune. Dim lights glow from a long wall of machines with circular doors that Echo can only assume are used to wash the crisp, white suits of the Immunes. This place must hum with activity during the day, but thankfully nobody seems to be working at night.

"Where are the clean suits?" Trid asks. "I reckon white's my color."

"I've never been in here," says River, shrugging. "I'm not sure."

"Over here!" Chase marches to the rear of the room and the rest of them follow.

As Echo gets closer, she sees lines of racks with white suits of all sizes. They dive on them, rifling through to find one in their size. Echo chooses one and holds it up to check it.

"I'm going over here," she calls over her shoulder, heading for a dark corner of the room. "A girl needs her privacy."

There's a small sink and she finds a cloth, using it to wash herself down before she dresses, thinking yet again about Nola with a stab of grief. Echo had cared for many people with the scurge over the years, but her abrasive and grumbling friend had managed to find a special place in her heart.

Once on, the white suit feels familiar, leaving Echo ashamed of how quickly she'd adjusted to the brief life of luxury she'd lived in the Green Zone. It didn't seem like Nola had ever adjusted, no matter how long she'd lived in her falling down hut.

Echo's three male companions dress in haste and they stash their old clothes in the bottom of a cupboard. Chase and Trid look downright strange in their suits as they brush them down, trying to make them fit comfortably, but River looks like he's stepped into a second skin. The white brings out the green of his eyes and his hair is mussed, making him seem like he only just woke up.

There's a familiar flutter in Echo's stomach and she tears her eyes from River. Now isn't the time to allow her mind to wander to all the places it's desperate to go.

They head back toward the exit and this time, Echo is the first to step outside. She glances from left to right, knowing they only have a few hours of darkness left to get in and out of the Sting. At least now they're dressed for the occasion, so should hopefully be able to move about with ease.

Echo steps forward and gasps to see a shadow leap from the darkness. Warm hands grip her around the neck, and she's thrown to the ground with a thud.

Pain slices her skull, and she winces as her hands instinctively fly to her throat. Her airway is cut off. She tries to cry out for help but no words can make their way out. Dazed and confused, she struggles to figure out what's happening. And how she can get herself out of it.

A heavy weight sits on her chest.

She needs oxygen.

Now.

TEN

RIVER

The strangled, gasping sounds coming from Echo send terror and adrenaline shooting through River. There's no time to process that they've been found already. That the attempt to secure adrenacure is over before they even got into the Sting.

Not when Echo's desperate attempts to draw in air stop.

River leaps on the shadowy pile where Echo dropped, bowled over by the body that streaked toward her as he followed her out. Blindly, he scrabbles for something to grip, wrapping his hand around a shoulder, then another. Using all the thundering energy firing through his veins, he twists his fists into the material of their suit and yanks.

The person is lighter than he expected, and they're hauled into the air with a shocked gasp of their own. A female gasp.

Not letting go of his furious grip, River drags the woman a few feet away, conscious he needs to neutralize her somehow. Whoever she is, she knows Echo and River are here. He can't let her be awake long enough to raise the alarm.

His stomach clenching painfully, conscious he's never knocked anyone unconscious before, and desperately hoping he doesn't do more than that, he pulls back his fist. The woman must sense that something's coming, even though they're little more than shadows to each other, because she becomes a flurry of movement as she tries to extricate herself from his grip.

But River can't let her do that. If she gets away, then Oren will know Echo's still alive.

"Stay still," he growls, conscious the words sound more like a plea than a demand. He tightens his fist as he hardens his resolve.

The woman stills. "River?" she whispers.

His hand hangs midair, shock rendering him just as frozen. "Clover?"

"You're alive?" she gasps. "I can't believe it, you're alive!"

Moving before he has a chance to blink, Clover throws her arms around him, knocking him back a few steps. River instinctively hugs her back, trying to understand what this is going to mean.

And why she thinks he's dead.

"Oh River, I never thought I'd feel your arms around me again," Clover whispers brokenly.

He stiffens, then quickly tries to disentangle himself. "As you can see, I'm most definitely alive."

"He's been with me," snaps Echo, her voice annoyed but croaky.

Clover spins around to face her. "You!" she hisses. "Oren said you attacked him! That's why you were Forgotten."

"Clearly he was lying," Echo says, an eye roll apparent in her voice.

River moves around Clover, giving her a wide berth as he joins Echo's side. "Are you okay?" he asks in a low voice.

Echo snorts, then draws in a sharp breath as if it hurts. "Mostly just pissed."

River can't blame her. His own anger is still a slow simmer in his gut.

"How dare you," Clover says. "You...you..." She pauses, her head swinging one way and then the other. "What are you doing here?"

"Refusing to be dead and Forgotten," Echo snaps.

River places a gentle hand on Echo's arm. "We snuck in alone," he says, hoping Chase and Trid have hidden themselves. "We were hungry."

Clover recoils. "You've been in the Dead Zone?"

River bristles at how aghast Clover sounds, and he quickly realizes he's becoming defensive. As if the Dead Zone is his to defend. "I ran away, wanting to find Flora. Echo followed me. Oren must've come up with that story to explain why we'd disappeared."

"He must've," Clover says thoughtfully. "So we wouldn't worry about you."

It's River's turn to roll his eyes. Was he as naïve as that? Just as willing to believe whatever he was told?

Clover takes a step closer to River, making Echo stiffen. "But you've come back? Surely you've realized this is your home."

"And rise from the dead?" Echo asks incredulously.

"The last I heard, he was in the infirmary," Clover says defensively. "When there weren't any updates, I assumed the worst. Especially when I found you sneaking back in."

River knows he has to choose his words carefully. "Clover, I—"

She steps in closer and a hand presses to his chest. "I know things were really mixed up for you after the Confirmation," she says earnestly. "I understand that you'd question...things.

But you've seen what the alternative is. There's no life in the Dead Zone."

Except Clover's wrong.

The Dead Zone is alive with everything the human spirit is capable of. Fierce determination. Dogged resilience.

And the seeds of rebellion.

River takes a step back, meaning Clover's hand falls away. "I'm not going back. Not yet."

Not ever, but Clover doesn't need to know that.

"I see," she says, her shadowy outline contracting as if she's drawing into herself. "You've lost your way."

Actually, he's found it.

A faint sound behind him reminds River that Chase and Trid are hiding somewhere. That they need to keep moving.

It's also a reminder that two Dead Borns are listening to this. That maybe they won't be as comfortable with letting Clover live as River is hoping.

He raises his voice above a whisper. "You can't tell anyone we were here, Clover. Including Oren. We'll go back to the Dead Zone. Coming here was a mistake."

Clover falls silent for long seconds. "You want me to keep this a secret? From my colony?"

"Yes." River winces internally as the next words form on his lips. "For me."

"Okay," she whispers, and the guilt stabs even deeper. He's using Clover's feelings for him. It's the only way he can think of to keep everyone here safe.

"But you can't take anything," she adds. "Stealing is wrong, River."

He quickly grabs Echo's hand before she says anything in response to Clover's comment. Yes, it's patronizing, but also clueless. The Green Zone commits far more heinous acts than anyone in the Dead Zone.

"Of course," he says, trying to sound contrite, but not sure he pulled it off seeing as his teeth are gritted. "Thank you, Clover."

Pulling Echo with him, River makes his way back through the laundry and closes the door. He hastily makes his way to the exit, noting two silent shadows falling in behind them. They leave the laundry room, moving quickly. The moment they're out in the open, River's lungs constrict, but he ignores it. They're going to have to go the long way around.

They've only taken a few steps when a hand clamps on his shoulder. "We're just gonna leave her there?" Trid hisses.

"Yes, we are," River says, keeping his voice low and steady.

"How do you know she ain't gonna blab?"

River doesn't. "Killing her would raise far more suspicion," he snaps, shaking off Trid's grip.

"He's right," Chase says, surprising River. "But now it's even more important that we're quick."

Trid huffs. "He's probably planning on runnin' straight back to the Dead Zone so he can keep his word to his sweetheart."

Echo steps between River and Trid. "You're being as blind as Clover. River has no intention of going back."

His chest inflates at the faith she's showing him, glad it's not misplaced. Of course he's not going back. They need the adrenacure.

River spins on his heel. "We'll need to enter another way."

The soft sounds of rustling leaves and rhythmic crickets follow them as River leads them around the Sting. Although he focuses on keeping his breath steady and shallow, scents he'd always taken for granted invade his senses. Lush vegetation, moist air, the hint of rose and lavender and honeysuckle. They trigger a kaleidoscope of emotions. Home sickness. Regret. A rush of pleasure.

A hint of repulsion.

The beauty of the Green Zone can only be experienced by a select few. People who are just as Vulnerable as those living in the Dead Zone.

"I know where we're going," Echo whispers beside him.

River squeezes her hand. They're going back to where it all started.

The glass dome of the hexagonal atrium seems to glow softly in the dark, inviting them to come closer. They creep along the path, keeping to the curved shadows the shrubbery creates.

"This way," River whispers, leading them to one of the large windows on the side. It's been propped open at the base, which is done every night while the bees are asleep. The atrium is kept closed during the day, apart from Confirmation day.

River assumed it was to stop bees from entering the Sting seeing as there's no airlock from the atrium.

But it's to keep the ignorant Green Borns safe.

"Climb in," he says, lifting the window higher.

Echo scrambles through, quickly followed by Chase, then Trid. River's the last to climb in, finding that Chase and Trid haven't got very far. They're standing stock still only a few feet away, taking in the atrium with slow sweeps of their heads.

Light from the Sting on the other side illuminates it gently, making it look almost ethereal. Dwarf fruit trees circle the space, all perfectly pruned. It's a contrast to the verdant climbers creating fascinating, meandering patterns above them. Splashes of citrus orange and luscious berry look as beautiful as they smell.

"This is how you live?" Chase asks, the words clipped.

River finds himself flushing. "The atrium is more...manicured than the gardens in the Green Zone."

"Selfish bastards," Trid growls, stalking forward. "How can you sleep at night?"

This time, the shame feels like it starts from the inside, born of seventeen years of never questioning anything.

Echo moves close enough to press her side against his. "You didn't know," she whispers. "And when you learned otherwise, you didn't bury your head in the sand like Clover just did."

River nudges her. "You really don't like her, do you?"

She huffs. "Heck no."

"Probably for the same reasons I don't like Chase."

Echo weaves her fingers through his. "You have nothing to worry about with him."

"Same with Clover," River says huskily. In fact, he never even considered a relationship with her. He was as blind to that as he was everything else.

Trid reaches out and grabs some fruit hanging from a bent branch and bites into it, letting out a low moan. "Now I get it. Whatever this thing is, it could make me forget my own mother."

River doesn't point out that that would make him as bad as a Green Born.

"Come on," Echo says, tugging him forward. "We need to get to the LaB."

They weave their way down the path, Chase and Trid falling back to pluck fruit and eat it as fast as they can. River picks a peach and passes it to Echo, his stomach already cramping at the thought of food. Echo takes it, then pauses as she glances past his shoulder.

River turns, seeing the table at the head of the room where they'd sat on their Confirmation. It feels like a lifetime ago. Even then, he'd been drawn to Echo, yet determined not to admit it. So many misunderstandings had existed between them.

So many truths had been waiting to be uncovered.

Echo shakes her head. "Oren probably rigged the Selection. Me for the LaB to keep me close, you for Eden to keep you close to Clover."

River shakes his head. Oren's been manipulating them all for a very long time. "And yet it didn't work. You didn't fall for the lies of the Green Zone." He brushes her arm. "And I didn't fall for Clover."

Echo lets out a breath. "I'm glad."

River pulls her in close to press a quick kiss on her hair. "Me, too."

A sound interrupts the sweet emotion welling through his chest. The smooth whoosh of a door opening. Light spills into the atrium, outlining a figure.

"Hide!" Echo hisses, yanking River behind a shrub and down low.

Chase leaps behind the podium, moving so fast River can't help but be impressed. Trid does the same, darting behind a banner proudly printed with the symbol of a bee, snatching a plum on the way. If River wasn't frozen with fear, he'd shake his head at the man's foolish greed.

The woman in the doorway enters, and for a moment River thinks that Clover followed them after all, only to realize it's Daphne entering the atrium. She walks forward, calm and relaxed, smiling serenely as if she's out for a midnight walk. Reveling in the gifts of the Green Zone, probably keen to share her thoughts in the morning's announcements.

River barely breathes as she passes the podium obscuring Chase. She stops beside Trid's hiding place, reaches out, and steadies a branch. The branch that's still twitching ever so slightly after Trid plucked the plum.

Which means Daphne knows—

With one swift move, she kicks out, her foot powering into Trid's face. He falls back with a groan, pulling the banner down with him.

Daphne stands over him, her lip curled. "Filthy Dead Borns. You think you can steal from us?"

She pulls something out that River's never seen before. It's small and dark and metal, shaped like the adrenacure cylinders.

Yet this one is black.

And there's a handle beneath it, shaping the device like an L.

Daphne points it at Trid, her face so carved in stone, River wonders if all the times he'd seen her serene smile were an illusion.

She squeezes the handle. There's a faint pop.

Trid writhes on the floor, gripping his chest as he cries out. The desperate sound is quickly cut off, constricting to nothing more than a painful wheeze. Even from their hiding spot, River sees the man's face turn blue. His throat balloon to the size of his head.

His body still even before it's finished swelling.

Daphne just shot Trid with bee venom.

She just killed him in cold blood.

CHAPTER

ELEVEN

ECHO

E cho stifles a whimper. She's stuck in a recurring
nightmare. First, she saw Vern being tortured in the
Hive. Then that poor girl killed in the Alphadome. And now
Trid being shot by Daphne. And each time she's been hiding
beside River with neither of them able to do a single thing
about it.

River pulls her closer from their position behind the shrub
and presses his lips to her ear.

"Greater good," he whispers so quietly she barely hears.

It was a risk to speak at all, but she'd needed to hear those
two words. Every cell in her body is ready to leap from the
shadows and run toward Daphne. Because while Oren might
believe he's acting for the greater good, they both know he
isn't. Their own cause is for the true greater good. One that
respects the lives of those not just in the Green Zone, but the
Dead Zone, too. Although, she knows she must stay put. It's
bad enough Clover knows she's alive. If Daphne finds out, it's
as good as going directly to Oren herself.

They must stick to the plan.

Get the adrenacure.

Confirm that she's the Sovereign.

Put an end to this madness.

Daphne steps back from Trid and glances around. She looks like a different person to the one who'd taken a shell-shocked Echo from the Betadome to the Sting after her Confirmation. Back then she'd seemed angelic. Serene. Filled with peace and light. Right now, she's shimmering with heartless menace. It's clear she doesn't care about the life she just took. After all, Trid had been nothing more than a *filthy Dead Born*. At least Echo now knows what Daphne really thought about her.

"Are there any more of you in here?" Daphne's expressionless veneer cracks as she marches toward the podium that Chase had ducked behind. "You can't hide from me."

Echo turns to River, waves of nausea flooding through her. She might not love Chase in the way she thought she had, but she cares about him an awful lot. She can't sit by and watch yet another death, no matter how important the cause. Especially when the whole reason Chase is here is to get the adrenacure to keep Echo safe.

She can just make out the curved shape of Chase's back, hunched behind the podium. Only a few more steps and Daphne will be able to see him, too.

Wrenching herself free from River, Echo shoots to her feet, revealing the upper half of her torso above the shrub. But Daphne is too distracted by her gut feeling that there's someone behind the podium. A feeling that's terrifyingly correct. It's no wonder Oren chose her as his trusted advisor.

Just as Echo's about to shout out to Daphne, Oren marches through the door.

"Who's here?" he asks in his way of shouting without raising his voice.

Daphne pauses and turns. "It's Daphne. Be in peace, Oren. I was just exterminating some vermin."

River tugs on Echo's shirt and she instantly squats back down, her heart beating fast as she realizes how close she came to blowing this whole mission. Which would mean Trid died for nothing. She can't let that happen.

Oren walks calmly toward the banner that Trid pulled down when Daphne landed that agonizing kick in his face. He's lying on the ground, swollen and still. Clearly dead.

Echo tucks her hand in the crook of River's arm. She can hear a crackle in his breathing. No doubt the stress of the situation is taking its toll on his one-off breathing issue.

Oren nudges Trid with the tip of his shiny white shoe, then turns to Daphne and nods his approval.

Echo isn't sure why, but her heart sinks. She knows how evil Oren is, yet somehow, a small part of her must have been hoping that River would get to witness at least one redeeming feature in his father.

"Was he alone?" Oren asks.

"I don't think so." Daphne turns back to the podium and marches forward. Her weapon is pointed out, ready to fire another deadly shot.

Echo resists the urge to squeeze her eyes closed, reminding herself that Chase knows how to fight. He can overpower Daphne and wrestle her weapon from her hand. He's a better fighter than Trid. Or anyone she's ever seen. He'll be okay.

Daphne reaches the podium and comes to an abrupt stop. She turns around, scanning the rest of the stage, then lowers her weapon.

"I must have been mistaken," she says to Oren. "There's nobody here."

Echo lets out a slow breath as she looks to River. He raises his eyebrows, and she shrugs in response. Nobody had seen

Chase move from his hiding place, including them. It seems he not only knows how to fight, but also how to use a brief moment of distraction to get himself out of danger.

"We need to be vigilant," says Oren, returning his attention to Trid. "Unusual for them to infiltrate alone. There could be more."

Daphne joins Oren at Trid's side. "They're getting more desperate. I've never seen one of them so close to the Sting."

"Or dressed like us." Oren scratches at his chin. "You did well to identify him as a Vulnerable."

Daphne laughs in her high-pitched way that sounds more like a small bell tinkling. "Look at him. He's filthy! The smell alone was enough to tip me off. He doesn't need a suit to disguise himself. He needs a long, hot shower."

Oren nods. "True. Although, Vernon was a Green Born and he wasn't exactly known for his hygiene."

"With respect, I disagree," says Daphne, holding her nose. "He was very well known for his hygiene. Or lack of it, rather."

Oren's deep laugh is a contrast to Daphne's but it sets Echo's nerves equally on edge. River bristles beside her.

"I'll get Tuff to clean up this mess." Oren reaches into his pocket for the paging device he'd used to summon River when they were hiding in the Restricted Area.

The anger and fear that had been coursing through Echo's veins are replaced with sadness at Oren's words. Trid is not a mess to clean up. He was a human being with a family and needs and dreams just like anyone who lives on this side of the net. The only thing that gave him away was him being unable to resist picking one more piece of fruit, which any starving person could understand. And that most decidedly does not include Oren.

Tuff arrives moments later, almost like he'd been expecting

Oren's call. It's no wonder he's aged beyond his years with the heinous tasks his master has him perform. His life would have been far happier as a Vulnerable. And that's saying something!

Echo peers out from behind the leaves of the shrub, noticing the way Oren simply tilts his head in the direction of Trid's body, not seeing the need to explain. After all, Tuff is nothing more to Oren than a filthy Dead Born.

River puts a hand on her back, sensing her anger. She knows he feels it, too. Anybody with a heart would. And River's heart is more generous than most.

"Let's talk more in my office," Oren says to Daphne.

She nods, giving him the same smile she'd graced Echo with after Confirmation, only now Echo knows it's only skin deep. Tuff goes to Trid's body and squats beside it while Daphne practically floats out of the room beside her beloved leader. Echo doubts either of them will think of Trid again, despite being responsible for his death.

When Echo is sure they're gone, she stands. River rises beside her and Chase steps out from behind a leafy lime tree. Tuff has proven more than once that they can trust him, even if he makes himself extremely difficult to like.

Tuff doesn't notice them. He's still bent over Trid. His shoulders are shaking and he has one hand pressed to Trid's chest as if checking for any sign of life.

"Tuff," says Echo moving briskly toward him. "Are you okay?"

He startles but his eyes remain on Trid. "What are you doing here?"

"Did you know him?" Echo asks gently, avoiding his question.

Tuff clears his throat to get his voice working. "You shouldn't be here."

"Was he your friend?" she asks, already well aware that she's breaking all the rules.

Tuff nods. "When we were boys."

"I'm sorry." Echo reaches out for Tuff but withdraws her hand. Tuff isn't the sort to be soothed by touch.

"He was happy when I was confirmed as Immune," says Tuff. "Thought I could make a difference."

"You are making a difference," says River from beside Echo.

"Not to Trid." Tuff scoops up his friend with ease. His frame is frail from years of malnutrition and the white suit hangs off him despite it being one of the smaller sizes.

"Where will you take him?" Chase steps forward.

"Crematorium," says Tuff.

Chase shakes his head. "Let me take him home. Please? I'll return him to his family. They deserve that much."

Tuff considers this for a beat, then carefully passes Trid over. Chase takes his weight with similar ease, and Echo regrets begrudging him that extra apple he'd taken in the Betadome, even if it had almost had catastrophic consequences.

"Go back now," grunts Tuff. "I'll put the cameras on a loop."

"We need to get to the LaB first," says Echo, hopping on her toes with eagerness to get moving.

"Oren thinks you're dead," Tuff barks. "He'll see you. Go back now. It's not safe."

"But we're looking for answers," says River. "Like you asked us to."

"They're not in the LaB." Tuff grunts, seeming to have maxed out his quota of words for the day. He turns to leave.

"We think we've found the Sovereign," says Echo, neglecting to mention it might be her.

This news has Tuff's steps pausing.

"All we need is some adrenacure so we can be sure," River adds. "That's why we're here."

"That won't do nothing," says Tuff. "Queen bees are deadly."

Chase shifts Trid's weight in his arms. "Have you ever tried using adrenacure in the Alphadome? Flora thinks it will work."

"Oren said it won't work," Tuff says.

"Oren's said a lot of things that aren't true." Echo gives Tuff an encouraging smile. "If we can just get some adrenacure, we'll be straight out of here."

"LaB's too risky," he replies curtly. "Oren can see from his office."

Echo tries to hold in her frustration. "I helped Reed make adrenacure in the LaB. We have to go there."

"I think I made a mistake letting you out of the Hive," Tuff says. "There's somewhere else you can look."

"Where?" Echo asks.

Tuff shakes his head. "Figure it out for yourself. You're not worthy of finding the Sovereign if you can't do that much."

He stomps out of the atrium and Echo and River look at each other blankly.

Chase shifts Trid's weight again, seeming to find a more comfortable way of holding him.

Echo sighs. "Chase, why don't you take Trid back home while the cameras aren't working? We'll be right behind you."

"You don't even know where you're looking!" Chase protests. "We need to stick together."

"No," says River firmly. "You need to get Trid back to his family like you promised. He's sacrificed enough."

Chase stares at River for a few seconds and Echo hopes he's remembering how River saved his life in the Betadome.

"Fine," says Chase. "But only because I need to do it while the cameras aren't working, not because you told me to."

River laughs gently, the crackle in his breathing becoming more obvious.

"Be careful," says Echo as Chase heads for the open window.

"It's one of my middle names," Chase calls over his shoulder as he swings one leg out of the window, being careful not to bump Trid's head.

"What's the other one?" she asks, taking the bait.

"Figure it out for yourself," he says, quoting Tuff. "Otherwise you're not worthy of knowing."

"I think I know what his other name is," River mumbles as he disappears into the darkness. "Smart—"

"That's right," says Echo, not allowing him to finish that thought. "Smart. I'm pleased to see you two are getting along better."

River smirks at her before letting out a gentle cough.

"You need to watch your breathing," she says, growing more concerned. "There's a lot of pollen here. Remember, deep breaths in. Deep breaths out."

River nods, taking her advice and drawing in some air. "Last thing I need is to end up in the infirmary."

"Which is exactly where everyone thinks you already are," says Echo. "I can't believe that was the story Oren came up with. I tried to kill you, so I was Forgotten and you went to the—"

"Infirmary!" he says. "That's it, Echo. The infirmary. Reed makes the adrenacure in the LaB and then sends it to the infirmary for the medics to access. That's what Tuff meant! We can get what we need without going anywhere near the LaB."

"You're a genius." She uses the excuse to drop a kiss on his cheek.

"A genius would have thought of it in the first place," he corrects. "Come on. We need to move quickly."

He takes her hand and leads her out of the atrium into the dimly lit corridor. Scurrying toward the lift, Echo hopes Tuff's had enough time to put the cameras on a loop. River presses the hexagonal button to go up and the door opens almost immediately. Thankfully, it's empty. She'd half expected to see Daphne in there.

"Second floor." River hits the number two, and the lift takes off, barely able to pick up speed before it comes to a stop again.

River leads the way out and Echo concentrates on her own breathing, aware her fear is starting to take over. This is riskier than going to the atrium but far less than a trip to the LaB. Tuff had been right to warn them. Although, surely, it wouldn't have killed him to have told them directly where to go. He would have to be one of the most frustrating people she's ever met.

Pushing open a set of double doors, River walks quietly inside.

"What if we see someone?" she whispers, right behind him.

River presses a button at a second set of doors and a medical face mask ejects from a slot. He takes it and presses the button again.

"Put this on," he says, passing her the mask and taking the second for himself. "It's required here. Also, very convenient for not being recognized."

The second set of doors open to reveal a large room with a dozen beds lined along each of the walls. A sterile smell hits Echo's nostrils through the mask, and she blinks in the bright light. She's never seen a place so...white. And that's saying something given she's spent time in other parts of the Sting. There are crisp white sheets, white curtains, and white tiles lining the floor and walls. The beds that are occupied contain patients dressed in white robes and there's a nurse roaming the room dressed in a white suit, wearing a white face mask and cap.

"Act normal," River whispers, and Echo wonders how one acts normally in a strange room like this. Nothing like this exists in the Dead Zone. If you get sick, you die at home in your bed. Simple. This is like something out of a science fiction story.

The nurse looks up at them in surprise. "No visitors allowed."

"Reed sent us," says River. "The last batch of adrenacure he gave you was faulty. He asked us to collect it immediately so he can replace it."

"Of course." The nurse's eyes smile above her mask, and she marches over to a supply cupboard, not thinking to question them further. Oren's trained his people to accept everything they're told. "Luckily, we haven't used any from this batch yet."

"Great news," says Echo, as she takes the small basket the nurse holds out. "We'll get this straight back to Reed."

It's only now as she holds the basket that she thinks of the ramifications of what they're doing. Taking these canisters leaves innocent Green Borns at risk if they get stung. Then she reminds herself that the water they're drinking in this colony is protecting them. They're far safer than the Vulnerables taking shelter underneath a net.

"Thank you," says River, nodding at the nurse.

"My pleasure," she replies, her brow furrowing as she looks more closely at his face. "You know, you look a little bit like Oren's son."

River waves a hand at her and laughs. "I get that all the time! Must be the color of my eyes. Thankfully, he's handsome."

The nurse giggles. "He is. Or should I say, was."

Echo tugs on River's shirt. They need to get out of here.

"Was?" River asks, not seeming to be able to resist. "I was told he was in here somewhere?"

The nurse's eyes dart around, and she lowers her voice. "Well, I was told if anyone asks, to say that he's here in the infirmary. But the truth is he was Forgotten."

Echo's jaw falls open. Perhaps Oren should have focused a little less on getting his people to believe everything they're told, and more on the importance of not spreading gossip.

"Wow." River nods. "At least I won't get mistaken for him now if he's no longer here."

Echo clears her throat. "We need to get these to Reed. Thanks for your help."

"Yes. Thank you," says River, taking a step back.

The nurse's eyes smile again, fixed decidedly on River. "Be in peace, ummm. What was your name?"

"Rocky," he says confidently.

"And you?" the nurse asks, shifting her gaze to Echo.

"Clover," she says without missing a beat.

"I'll pop that in my record book." The nurse smooths out a wrinkle on her skirt. "My name's Avon. Be in peace, Rocky and Clover."

"Be in peace, Avon," they reply, heading away as fast as they're able without raising suspicion.

"Hold on," calls Avon when they reach the door. "Doesn't Clover work in Eden? I remember her sister. Cascade. I thought they were both blonde."

Echo looks back over her shoulder. "We have the same name."

"Nobody here has the same name," River whispers on a groan.

Avon glances toward a big red button on her wall, and

River dives for the double doors, pushing them open and dragging Echo through. They just make it to the second set of doors when a soft alarm filters through the speakers of the Sting.

They got what they came here for.

Now it's time to run.

CHAPTER
TWELVE
RIVER

The moment they sprint out of the Sting, River knows he's not going to make it. One frantic inhale as the shouts in the airlock behind them feel far too close and his lungs constrict. They feel as if they have halved in size in the space of a heartbeat.

"We just need to get through the Betadome," Echo pants as she takes his hand.

River realizes his breath is a sharp, wheezy staccato. Echo knows he's struggling.

But not how much.

Still, he focuses everything on keeping up with her. They move away from the faint glow of the pod waiting to whizz someone deeper into the Green Zone, and off the path that's far too exposed. Amongst the shrubs and trees are shadows to blend into. Darkness to hide them.

And more pollen to draw into River's shrinking lungs.

"They'll head to the Betadome!" someone cries behind them.

"Dirty Dead Borns," another man growls. "Daphne said

one attacked her when she tried to stop them from stealing all the plums."

Echo tugs River around a tree, and he follows her blindly as he tries not to stumble. It's hard to tell how close the voices are over the roaring in his ears, but the intent is clear. End the threat to their precious Green Zone.

The very Zone that is strangling River with grim determination.

They reach a shadowy stand of trees that River knows are walnuts. The acre block is a point of pride for the Green Zone, after the precious, nutritious nut almost went extinct. He also suspects being in a dense area of trees is the last thing he needs right now.

"Straight through," he croaks. "It's quicker."

Echo hesitates, but another shout punctures the night air somewhere to their left.

"Hurry," he urges her. She needs to think of the adrenacure.

Of their chance to save every last life that has no idea depends on them.

If they can keep running like this, they'll beat the Green Borns and slip through the Betadome first.

Well, Echo will.

Her hand tightens around his as she plows between the trunks. "Almost there," she whispers.

River doesn't answer. He can't. As they're enveloped by thicker layers of darkness, he's suddenly surrounded by pendulous sprays of flowers. Each one feels like another fist to his throat. Another band around his chest.

All he can do is blindly follow as Echo guides him around the trees. If she pulls right, he steps right. If she tugs left, he does too, hoping to hell he doesn't stumble.

A particularly swift move has one foot crashing into the other. River reaches out with his free hand and pushes off a trunk, simultaneously regaining his balance and maintaining his momentum. A branch slaps across his face and he's faintly aware of petals and leaves exploding around him. For long seconds, his throat feels the size of a reed.

"River?" Echo whispers, and even in the haze of pain he can hear the concern.

He focuses on using what little air he has to say two words. "Keep....going."

"We're close," Echo assures him, the look she throws him so bright with panic that he's scared it'll be a beacon to those chasing them.

They burst out of the grove of walnut trees, freeing them of the extra layers of cloaking darkness, but not freeing River of the suffocating pain. The relief he was hoping for doesn't course through him. The air he desperately needs doesn't make its way into his body.

"There it is," Echo pants. "We're so close, River."

His sight is constricting as ruthlessly as this throat, meaning the Betadome is a shining orb at the end of a dark tunnel. It could be right in front of them. It could be yards away.

It doesn't matter.

One knee gives out, then the other. River releases Echo's hand as he crashes to the ground. He's vaguely aware of the impact squeezing the trapped air out of his lungs, even as he knows his ability to refill them is dying.

Just like he is.

"River," Echo gasps.

"Go," he croaks.

What's left of his lungs feel like they're full of water. He's drowning from the inside out. There's no way to escape the rising tide.

"Not happening," she mutters.

Then hands are slipping under his arms and he's being dragged across leafy ground. Echo thinks she can drag him the whole way to the Dead Zone? They'll be caught for sure! Yet he can't stop her. Can't tell her to save herself one more time.

His arms and legs are little more than numb extremities, but River's vaguely aware she's pulling him away from the Betadome. She pants a little and he knows he's a dead weight, but no matter how much he wishes he could help, it's as if his mind is slowly disconnecting from his body. As his airway is being cut off, so is the rest of him.

They stop and Echo draws him in close. A flicker of his eyelids and he realizes they're tucked behind a pod, probably the only thing big enough to hide them this close to the Betadome. Yet it also emits a pale light, faintly illuminating them if anyone were to think to look here.

It also reveals Echo's stricken face as her gaze roams over him. He wonders if his lips are as blue as Trid's were. "River," she mouths.

"Go," he tries again. He wishes he could remind her why they're here in the first place.

Humanity needs the Sovereign.

It needs her.

"Save your breath, River," Echo mutters back.

A faint flicker of humor sparks somewhere amongst the agony at her choice of words. He has no breath to save.

What's left of it is a wheeze. One that's far too loud in the near silence of the night. All he can hope is the sounds of the breeze and crickets are enough to hide them.

It's clear Echo refuses to leave him.

In his last moments, he admits he's glad. As his life is slowly strangled, it's not the Green Zone he wants to see. It's her beautiful features.

The face that changed everything for him.

The sounds of running steps have Echo stiffening. "Quick!" a Green Born calls out. "They must've already gone into the Betadome!"

"Those bastards aren't escaping with our adrenacure," a woman shouts. "They're all as good as dead, anyway."

The footsteps fade away, then are abruptly cut off as the green door closes.

Echo leans over River, her hands clasping his face. "Focus on me, River. Breathe in and out. Just like we have before."

His lashes flutter. He can barely feel her warm palms. His skin is numb. His body is carved of stone, cracking, disintegrating. And it hurts so bad.

"River!" Echo hisses, now sounding panicked. "Look at me!"

Except he can't. His oxygen-starved body doesn't even have the strength to do that. His eyelids are too heavy. The agony is too overwhelming.

He focuses on his lips, hoping that he can make them work, even if no air is getting past them. "I...love..."

"Sh." Echo's voice cracks. "Tell me later. When we're safely back in the Dead Zone."

Although he knows he'll never get that chance, River can't finish the sentence. Darkness is closing in. He intuitively knows relief is coming, too.

Suddenly, Echo shoots to her feet. "Touch him and you die," she growls.

Alarm grips River just as tightly as death's first throes. Someone's here! Echo needs to run!

"Right now, I'm the only one who can save him."

Clover?

Echo sinks back beside him. "He can't breathe," she chokes.

Faint footsteps shuffle on his other side. "Asthma worsened by an allergic reaction to pollen. His mother suffered from it, too. It was my mother who helped her manage it."

River tries to understand what Clover's saying, why she's here, but he's floating on a sea of semi-consciousness. Pain holds him in an agonizing grip. Yet it's somewhere far away and it's unable to reach him.

"Can you help him?" Echo asks desperately.

"That's why I followed you. I noticed River's breathing outside the laundry. I suspected he may need my help."

Except River doesn't want Clover's help. He just wants Echo.

Echo draws in a sharp breath. "Did you tell Daphne we were here?"

"Of course not! Why would I do that?" Clover huffs. "Now, move aside. I need to help River."

River wishes he could grab Echo's hand. He wants her close by. To his relief, she tightens her grip and even shuffles closer. "You can reach him from there."

Clover huffs again. "River," her voice is closer. "You need to chew on these."

His jaw is pulled down and something sprinkles on his tongue. Seeds? He tries to chew. He really does.

But the darkness beckons. His body has had enough.

"Chew, River," Echo says firmly, her grip replacing Clover's, then working his jaw.

The seeds work their way around his mouth, several getting caught between his teeth and grinding loudly. He instinctively swallows, even though his throat doesn't feel like it can accommodate even that.

"That's it," Echo coos. "Again."

River dredges up a burst of strength and does as he's told. More of the gritty seeds make their way in. But that one movement drains the last of his reserves. His body goes limp.

His mind slowly detaches. A part of him welcomes the promise of peace, even as he fights it. He mustn't completely lose consciousness, because he hears Clover let out a breath.

"My mom told me they work fast."

"They'd better," Echo mutters. "What did you give him?"

"Serpentwood seeds. They helped his mother, so I knew they'd do the same for him."

There's a pause. "Thank you."

Echo's words hold no animosity. Only gratitude.

"I didn't do it for you."

"Then why?" Echo says softly. "Why are you doing this? River will go back to the Dead Zone."

"He's lost," Clover says as if it's simple. "And I'll be here when he realizes and comes home."

"You don't know that."

"I do. River and I grew up together. I've loved him since we were children." The confession jolts awareness through River. History he wasn't aware of is being uncovered.

"I know losing his mother cut him deep. Losing Flora sliced even deeper. I know how it messed him up. I know *him*."

As Clover's words filter through, River realizes he can breathe. His airway is expanding, his lungs are loosening.

He's going to make it.

There's the almost imperceptible sound of a door opening. "They must still be in the Sting," a man spits. "Or somewhere in the Green Zone."

"Hiding like the vermin they are," growls another.

"Stealing anything they can get their hands on."

Footsteps trudge past accompanied by more disgruntled muttering and promises to protect the Green Zone at all costs. River's hand twitches as disgust fills the spaces slowly opening up in his chest. Each one of those Green Borns sounds like Oren.

Echo gasps. "He's waking up!"

River's eyes flutter open to see her concerned face hovering above him, only for it to be shoved out of the way as Clover presses in close. "Thank goodness," she gushes, her hands fluttering over his face. "I wasn't too late."

He blinks as more of his surroundings come into focus. Beyond Clover's worried face is Echo, sitting back and chewing her lip. He wishes he could go to her, thank her for trying to keep him safe. Except it's Clover who saved his life...

"Thank you," he croaks.

Clover's face softens. "Anything for you, River."

He struggles to his feet before she can embrace him, even though his muscles feel like water. Stumbling, he finds Clover under one arm, with Echo under the other. Being caught between the two is almost as uncomfortable as his breathing attack.

Asthma. Triggered by pollen.

He's essentially allergic to the Green Zone.

Clover smiles up at him as she slips a small pouch into his pocket. "Just take these when you come back. You won't have an attack like that again."

"But serpentwood..." His voice fades away as his lungs still struggle to function.

Serpentwood is a vulnerable species they're still working hard to bring back from the brink of extinction.

And it's essential for creating adrenacure.

Clover shakes her head. "We have enough from the last Harvest Day. It was a particularly bountiful one."

River's gut clenches. He and Echo were a part of that Harvest.

The torture, the agony, are forever imprinted in his memory.

Yet, it's the lingering pain that infuses some strength into his body. The depths of the pain reminds him exactly what they're fighting for.

"We have to get back," he croaks, noting the way Clover's eyes dim. "While we can."

Before the Green Borns hunting them come back.

She frowns and opens her mouth just as Echo fits herself better under River's arm. "A few minutes and we'll be back to safety."

River turns back to Clover. "I'm sorry," he says through a tight throat that has nothing to do with an extreme reaction to the Green Zone.

He's sorry he can't find a way to say thank you properly.

He's sorry this is all so messed up.

And he's sorry he can't give Clover what she so clearly wants.

A tremulous smile hovers on her lips. "We'll talk when you come back. I'll be waiting."

She hugs him and he wishes she didn't press all of her body against him so intimately. Everything is feeling so much more complicated.

He pulls away and Echo starts to walk them toward the Betadome. River turns his focus to walking beside her. His body aches with exhaustion. His mind is whirling, torn between a past growing up with a girl who saw their friendship far differently to him, a present that involves more than one brush with death, and a future that's coming at him faster than he'd like.

Now that they have the adrenacure, it's time they focus on discovering whether Echo's the Sovereign.

River's vaguely aware that Echo leads him through the green door, through the Betadome, then the black door. His shallow, relieved breathing doesn't change. The scent of honey that's an unmistakable warning there are bees nearby doesn't trigger his alarm system.

His body doesn't have the capacity to do anything but refill his oxygen reserves.

They've just started trekking toward the Dead Zone colony when Echo's footsteps pause. "River..."

He looks down at her, wondering at the hitch in her voice. She's been silent since the exchange with Clover, no doubt as deep in thought as he's been. He needs to reassure her that none of that mattered, he just hasn't found the words to convince himself, let alone her.

But Echo's staring straight ahead, her eyebrows pulled down low. He follows her line of sight, and his own feet falter.

Several bodies are approaching from the village. All striding toward them with purpose.

Each one of them taut and tense.

Each of them suggesting the fight to get through this alive isn't over.

THIRTEEN

ECHO

Echo narrows her eyes at the group of Dead Borns approaching from the colony in the early morning light.

River balls his hands into fists even though he's in no state to fight. He's still leaning on Echo for support. But at least he's started to breathe smoothly again. "What do they want?"

"Blood." Echo's seen looks like that on her people's faces before. They're angry. And it's directed at the two of them.

She sets the small basket of adrenacure between her feet and holds up her palms to show this isn't a fight she wants. River takes her lead and does the same, his fingers uncurling as if against their own will.

There are a dozen men and women. There's even a young boy. Echo knows all their faces. Some of their names. As they get closer, she realizes she knows one of them a little better than that. Jupiter is marching at the rear, and Echo feels slight relief. Because while the last time Echo had seen Jupiter they'd lost all hope with the world, she knows they have a kind heart. That had been more than obvious at Confirmation.

"I'm a Dead Born," Echo calls when the mob gets any

closer. "And my friend's a Vulnerable. Don't be fooled by our suits."

"We know exactly who you are." A man with a scruffy beard draws to a stop. "And him."

"Then you'll know we're on your side," says River, his voice little more than a croak.

"You're not on our side," a woman with a wild mane of blonde hair says. Echo thinks she remembers her name is Fray. "You're nothing more than a selfish Green Born. The Razers lost one of our own because of you."

"You're the Razers?" Echo's brows shoot up in surprise and a little relief.

The young boy steps forward. "Too right we are."

"We're friends of Chase," Echo says quickly.

"Chase was the one who told us what you did." The bearded man seizes River by the arm, not seeming to care about any connections they might have. "You killed Trid."

"We didn't! That wasn't us." Echo tries in vain to get the man to release River and instead finds herself in the grip of another set of hairy arms.

"Hold still," a deep voice growls in her ear, his hold on her a painful vice-like grip.

She kicks out as Fray picks up the adrenacure. "Hey! Leave that. We need it."

"We need it more." Fray clutches the basket to her chest.

"Did Chase tell you why we need it?" Echo struggles to get her words out. It feels like she has a steel band across her chest. "It's for the good of everyone. In both colonies."

"We don't care about the Green Borns," the bearded man spits out, his grip on River seeming to be all that's holding him up. "We've been raiding them for years, the selfish bastards. We'd all be dead without the extra food we've managed to pilfer. It's our time now. Let them suffer like we have."

"So, Chase didn't explain?" Echo's eyes remain glued on the basket in Fray's dirt-stained hands.

"Chase didn't tell us anything," says Jupiter, stepping forward. "Sledge saw him carrying Trid's body back to his family and called the Razers together. He made the assumption that—"

"I don't make unfounded assumptions!" The bearded man whose name must be Sledge points at Jupiter with his free hand. "I never liked this one. She's no Razer."

Anger fuels in Jupiter's eyes, but they don't correct Sledge on his choice of pronoun. There are bigger arguments to be had right now.

"Chase invited me to be a Razer," says Jupiter calmly. "And for what it's worth, I don't think these two killed Trid. You saw them in the Betadome on Confirmation. They don't have it in them."

"We really don't," says River, his words even more believable given how haggard he looks.

"It's gotta be someone's fault," Fray says. "Trid didn't exactly kill himself. And he was wearing one of those white suits."

Echo stops fighting against the Dead Born holding her, relieved when he loosens his grip a little in response. It's no wonder the Razers haven't been able to make much traction in the Green Zone. They can't even get organised within their own ranks, let alone overthrow another colony.

"If you could just let go of us, we could explain," says Echo, aware of the pleading tone to her voice.

"You'll run," Sledge says, keeping a tight grip on River.

"Where to?" Echo points her chin at the sky. "It's too light now to go back into the Betadome. Nowhere to go inside this net. Let me go so I can talk."

The arms holding her release and Echo stumbles forward,

trying to keep her eyes on Fray. Sledge seems to strengthen his hold on River, which is possibly a good thing. He looks like he might fall over at any moment. He needs rest after his recent ordeal, not an interrogation.

"We went with Chase and Trid into the Green Zone to get some adrenacure," says Echo cautiously. "We're trying to find Immunity. For everyone."

"That doesn't exist," says Sledge. "You're lying."

A man from the back of the group moves into view. Echo's brows raise to see it's Tuff's brother, Ruff.

"She's telling the truth," he says. "There's word of a cure. Tuff told me."

"Not a cure exactly," Echo corrects. "But a way to make everyone Immune."

"That doesn't explain what happened to Trid." Fray clutches the basket so hard her knuckles turn white. "Sledge said Trid's face was all blown up like he'd been stung. Couldn't you have used some of your precious adrenacure on him? Or didn't you want to waste it on the likes of a Dead Born?"

"You keep forgetting I *am* a Dead Born." Echo shakes her head.

"Maybe because you don't act like one," the boy pipes up. "Or dress like one."

Echo holds up her palms. "The suits were so that we could blend in. And Trid died before we got the adrenacure. Of course, we would have saved him if we could have. He was shot with bee venom. He died almost instantly."

"How come they didn't shoot the rest of you?" Sledge raises a brow.

"They didn't see us," says Echo. "Trid was taking a plum from a tree and a Green Born saw the movement of the leaves."

"Trid wanted to bring food back for all of you," River adds.

Echo isn't sure this is strictly true, but she likes what

River's doing—preserving Trid's memory as one of a hero, not a desperate, hungry man. After all, he'd died on a mission to retrieve something with the sole purpose of keeping Echo safe.

"He was very brave," says Echo. "Please don't let his actions have been for nothing. Let us go so we can continue our work. It's what Trid would've wanted."

"We don't trust you," Fray narrows her eyes.

"I do," says Jupiter.

"I kind of do," says the boy.

"I don't," says Sledge. "But I'd like to see what you can find out."

Fray lets out a gasp.

"It's worth a shot, isn't it?" Sledge shrugs at her. "The Razers have been able to bring back food, but we need a better solution. Something bigger than what we've been doing. Something more...long term."

He lets go of River and Echo darts forward to slip an arm around him before he falls.

"Five days," she says to Sledge, seeing their chance to get away. "That's all we have left to figure this out. If we don't, the Green Borns will kill us themselves."

Sledge nods. "We've waited this long. We can wait another five days."

Fray leans in. "But if Trid died for nothing, we'll kill you ourselves."

Echo nods, prizing the adrenacure out of Fray's bony fingers. The stakes just got raised impossibly higher. Because now they're not safe in the Green Zone and they're not safe in the Dead Zone either. If they don't find the Sovereign, they may have to think about the possibility of life in the Extinction Zone. And the name of that place speaks for itself...

River steadies himself on his feet and raises his chin. He takes Echo's free hand and they walk toward the colony.

"Five days!" Fray calls after them. "Or we'll rip your guts out!"

"Pleasant thought," River murmurs.

"They won't actually rip our guts out," Echo says. "But...I wouldn't rule out them capturing a bee and killing us in the same way Trid died."

"An eye for an eye." River seems unimpressed.

"Chase will calm them down," she says. "They're just upset about Trid. Let's not worry about them for now."

"Hmm." River walks on, clearly not as easily able to set aside the threat of the Razers as she is.

"How are you feeling now?" Echo asks, certain she'll never take his breathing for granted again.

"I'm okay." He smiles gently despite the dark rings under his eyes.

"You need to rest," she says. "We'll go back to the hut so you can sleep."

"I'm not going to say no to that."

As they turn the corner to the crooked road of the hut Echo grew up in, a flash of movement runs toward them.

"It's Flora." River shakes his head. "She should've known I'd be okay."

"You nearly weren't," Echo reminds him. "No wonder she's worried."

Flora runs the length of the road and throws herself at River, embracing him tightly.

"You scared me!" she admonishes. "When I heard Chase had come back without you, I thought the worst."

"I'm fine." He tries to release himself from her grip, then gives up. "Echo's fine, too."

Flora finally lets go of him, shoots Echo a warm smile, then returns her gaze to River, noticing his pale complexion.

"River!" Her hands fly to her twin's face, making Echo feel

like she's intruding on a private moment. "You look terrible! What happened?"

"I just need a little rest," he tells her. "I had a bit of an issue with my breathing, but I'm totally fine now."

Echo straightens her spine. "Flora, why don't you take River back to the hut and he can tell you all about what happened?"

River tilts his head. "Why? Where are you going?"

Echo's mind spins as she tries to come up with something. The truth is that she wants to give River some time with Flora. Plus it's obvious that as soon as he finishes telling his twin what happened, he's going to fall straight to sleep. She's too highly strung right now to rest.

"I want to go to Nola's hut," she says, coming up with the one thing she's been meaning to do and hasn't had the chance. She never got to mourn her friend. Visiting her home seems the best way to do that. "I'd like to see for myself that she's really gone."

River nods, realizing this is important to her.

"Take this." She hands the basket of adrenacure to Flora. "I won't be long."

Flora has a quick look at the canisters, seeming impressed with the number they managed to get. She loops her free hand into the crook of River's arm and smiles. "I'll take good care of him."

"I know." Echo gives River a quick kiss on the cheek and leaves him with his sister, noticing how similar yet different the two of them look with their short dark hair and brilliant green eyes. It will be good for them to have some time alone. Everything feels like it's been running on fast forward since they escaped the Hive.

Echo winds her way through the Dead Zone, glad it's early morning. She should probably have changed her clothes as the few people she sees all stop and stare at the crisp whiteness of her suit. She might have to take one of Nola's dresses to wear for the walk back.

Tears sting at her eyes to think of her friend. There are so many conversations she wishes they had. She never got to find out about Nola's life growing up in the Green Zone. She'd love to be able to talk to her about how she felt walking into a world so foreign to everything she'd ever known. But it's too late now. She can no longer talk to Nola, just like she can no longer talk to her dad.

A sharp pain stabs at Echo's chest and she reaches for the locket that hangs around her neck. The last thing her father ever gave her. And it contains nothing more than a handful of strange seeds.

Kicking at the dust, Echo remembers the promise she made herself to plant the seeds in the Dead Zone. But the dirt beneath her feet can't possibly support life. The seeds will have to wait. Perhaps she should give the locket to River before she gets tested to see if she's the Sovereign? To let these seeds die with her seems like a betrayal to her father. She needs to make sure they get the chance to sprout.

She reaches Nola's hut and stares at it for a few moments. While it looks the same as always from the outside, it also looks different without Nola inside. It's like a body without a soul.

Crouching down, Echo pushes the half-sized door open, noticing there are no longer any rags jammed in the gaps. It swings open freely and she crawls through, leaving it open behind her to let in more light.

She stands and looks around. The thick curtain that used to act as a second door is missing along with all of Nola's possessions. While it seems that nobody had wanted to claim her falling down hut as their own, they'd pilfered everything else.

There's only one thing remaining and the sight of it sends a trail of stubborn tears running down Echo's cheeks.

Nola's battered armchair is in the center of the empty room. Either too heavy or too old, it seems nobody had any use for it.

"Oh, Nola." Echo sighs. "Why couldn't you have held on? Just a little longer."

She sits down in the chair and wipes away her tears, almost able to hear Nola's voice in her ear telling her to stop making such a ridiculous fuss. She'd been cantankerous, but Echo had a soft spot for her all the same. Maybe it was because Nola had nobody else. Or maybe it was because Echo always knew how much she appreciated everything she did for her. Her words may have been brisk but there was no mistaking the affection in Nola's eyes.

Echo scans the hut, not having seen it from the perspective of Nola's chair. She notices the way it's pointed at the door instead of the grubby window and realizes that Echo's daily visits had meant more to Nola than her view of the sky. If only the scurge hadn't taken hold of her, her life would've been filled with so much more. None of this seems fair, but that's a sentiment Echo has had to get used to recently.

Something small and yellow catches Echo's eye on the highest part of the wall above the door, right up near the ceiling. She hauls herself out of the chair to get a better look at it.

Returning to the chair, she pushes it to the doorframe and climbs up on it. Stretching out her arm, she takes hold of the object and pulls on it. It slides out from between the two sheets of tin and Echo gasps to see it's a piece of yellowing paper filled with scrawled writing. She squints at it, collapsing back into the chair when she sees the word at the top of the note.

Echo.

It's addressed to her! Somehow, Nola had known she'd

return here and sit in her chair. Which is odd given as far as Nola was aware Echo was supposed to spend the rest of her days eating oranges in the Green Zone.

She ignores the thumping of her heart as she reads on, sounding out each word one at a time just like her father taught her.

I hope you can read. I will try to use small words and write in a way only you will understand.

Echo rolls her eyes at Nola's bluntness, even though she's grateful Nola has taken her limited literacy skills into account. And the need for secrecy.

I was told where you are.

Echo's hands start shaking so hard she nearly drops the paper. How could Nola have possibly learned that Echo was in the Hive? Nobody visits her. Nobody! Who would have told her that?

I have been given the chance to take your place. You know I am dying. I have nothing to lose. I want to protect the person I love the most. I said yes.

The pain in Echo's heart worsens as she lets out a whimper. She can't bear to think of her friend suspended in time in the horrors of the Hive. And all because of her.

"I love you, too, Nola," she whispers.

If you are reading this, you have returned. I have one thing to ask of you.

"Anything," Echo murmurs, knowing she'll never be able to repay Nola's ultimate act of sacrifice.

Save my chair. Don't let anybody take it. It holds important memories.

Echo lets out an almost hysterical laugh. Of all the things to ask! This is typical Nola. She loved this chair, no matter how many times Echo tried to convince her to get out of it.

Love from Nola

Echo stares at that last line for several minutes until there's a sound at the door. Getting to her feet, she shoves the note in her pocket.

"Who's there?" she asks.

"It's only me," says Chase, crawling through the door. "Flora said I could find you here."

Echo pats her pocket, making sure the note is hidden. She's not ready to share it yet.

"How's River?" she asks.

"So fast asleep Flora's checking for a pulse every two minutes." He grins and she notices he's changed out of his white suit into his more familiar ripped jeans and tee-shirt. "I decided to leave her to it."

Echo nods. "Did she tell you what happened with the Razers?"

Chase runs his hand through his blond curls. "I'm so sorry about that. Sledge and Fray have a tendency to get a little carried away."

"You can say that again," Echo huffs. "If it weren't for Jupiter and that boy standing up for us, we'd both be dead."

"I'm going to talk to them." Chase shakes his head. "They listen to me. What they did isn't okay."

"I hope so." She waves her hand to show it's no longer an issue. "How's Trid's family?"

Chase's eyes fill with sadness. "As you'd expect."

She nods.

"Are you okay?" Chase puts a hand on her arm and looks at her in the same concerned way Flora had looked at River. "I know you cared about Nola."

"What do you know about how she died?" Echo asks, testing him.

"I already told you." He looks down at the floor. "The scurge took her. You know how sick she was."

"Chase." Now it's Echo's turn to put her hand on his arm. "Tell me the truth. Please. You lied to me about the pollen at my Confirmation. And who knows what else. I need the truth now. What happened to Nola?"

He lets out a long sigh, a war seeming to rage behind his temples. "Ruff took her. Tuff needed someone to replace you in the Hive. I was going to tell you, I swear it. But I knew you'd have that look in your eye."

"What look?" She pulls back and blinks at him in the dim light.

"That one." His voice cracks with concern. "Like you're responsible for what happened. But it made sense, Echo. She wanted to take your place. I swear it. She was already in pain. Her life had no more meaning after you left. She wanted to give you a chance."

Echo clenches her fists and Chase pulls her to his chest. She pushes him away, not liking he'd kept yet another secret from her. Doesn't he see after everything that's happened that they're on the same side?

"She wanted to do it," he says, not seeming fazed by her rebuff. "To say thank you for everything you did for her."

Echo crosses her arms. "I didn't do it to be thanked."

"Which made it even more honorable." He goes to reach for her then thinks better of it and lets his hand fall.

"We have to find the Sovereign," she says, deciding to keep the note private for now. If Chase keeps secrets from her, maybe it's time for her to start doing the same. "Then we can get Nola out of there."

He nods. "Well, we have the adrenacure, so that's the first step."

Echo swallows. They both know what the next step is. And the risk to Echo's life that it poses.

"Will you help me with something?" Echo asks.

"Sure." Chase's face lights up.

"Will you help me carry this chair home?" she asks.

His eyes flare as he looks down at the ancient piece of furniture covered in stains. "Echo, you do realize why nobody's taken it already, don't you?"

"Too dirty?" she suggests.

He shakes his head. "It's twice as big as the door. I have no idea how Nola got it in here in the first place. She must've built her hut around it."

"Oh." Echo's brow furrows to see what he says is true. Flopping down in the chair, she looks up at him. "Seems like I'm staying here for now then. I have to say that four was becoming quite the crowd back home, anyway."

"Are you serious?" he asks. "This chair means that much to you?"

"Do I look like I'm joking?" She frowns. Looking after this chair was literally the one thing Nola asked of her, but she's not going to tell Chase that. And given she can't take it home with her, staying with it is the only thing that makes sense.

"I agree on one condition," he says.

"Not sure I need your permission, but okay..." She tilts her head, waiting for him to elaborate.

"Take River with you."

"Deal." She wholeheartedly agrees with this suggestion. Chase and River may have come a long way in their relationship but asking them to live together was stretching things too far. Actually, asking herself to live with Chase after yet another one of his lies is stretching it now. This will be a good thing. Somewhere neutral for Echo to stay with the one person she truly trusts while they figure things out.

That is, if she lives long enough to pass the next step.

FOURTEEN

RIVER

The light is muted and peaceful when River wakes up. For a moment, he thinks it must still be early morning, but there's little activity beyond the walls of the hut. That and the heaviness in his limbs, as if they've barely moved for hours, tells him otherwise.

It's evening, meaning he slept the whole day.

He blinks, looking around the barely-lit space, his mind already awake and racing. They got back from the Green Zone with the adrenacure. Then the Razers were furious and out for blood, but they managed to talk them down with a promise of finding Immunity.

Which means Echo needs to be tested to find out whether she's the Sovereign.

"Hey, sleepy head."

River sits up, finding his sister sitting beside him and smiling. He scratches the back of his head. "Where's Echo?"

"She just checked in on you, but when she saw you're still asleep, she went off with Chase to help someone with the collapsed wall of their hut."

River suppresses a frown as he brings himself to a sitting position. He trusts Echo. But he doesn't trust Chase...

Flora's gaze sparks with humor. "Chase never had feelings for Echo."

"That's not what Echo believed at the time," River mutters. "He lied to her, just like everything else."

Flora sighs. "I don't think we've ever disagreed on something before."

He realizes she's right. There was always an understanding between the two of them that they're on the same page. United.

Except Flora lied to him, just like Chase lied to Echo. Even though she's his twin.

Even though River trusted her with every fiber of his being.

He sighs too, nudging her with his shoulder. "I miss those days."

"Me, too," she says, her smile small and soft.

"How did you fail Confirmation, Flora?" he asks. There are still unanswered questions. So much they haven't had a chance to talk about.

"Oren stops adding the immunity to the water for anyone taking part in the Confirmation, one month before. Just enough time for it to wear off. Except, I knew he was still adding it to the bottles delivered to our rooms. So, I tipped mine out and hydrated myself with fruit instead. Sometimes I took Cascade's or Willow's water. Then on the day I had some pollen, for extra insurance."

River nods, suspecting as much. Flora knew how to ensure she was Vulnerable, while he stayed Immune.

He thinks of Vernon and how his immunity had waned when he'd insisted on drinking kasi instead of water. This makes sense now.

Opening his mouth, River hesitates, then asks the question

that lies beneath them all. The one that he hasn't been able to fathom an answer to. "Why didn't you tell me?"

This time, it's Flora's turn to sigh. She shuffles over, then leans against him. "I wanted to, River. I almost did, even on Confirmation day. But I couldn't do that to you. You were so excited to do your part for the Green Zone."

He was, but now that he thinks back on it, he was excited to be part of something bigger than him. Something important. Something that would mean a future for humankind.

Flora failed to tell him that the Green Zone isn't it.

River slips his arm around his twin's shoulders. He doesn't want this coming between them. "Well, it's done now, and we're here, together. That's what matters."

Flora rests her head on his shoulder, reminding him of the hours they used to spend in the Sting, sitting in the lifts and just riding them up and down as they stared out at the Green Zone. People got used to seeing Oren's children in there. They'd smile indulgently as they wished them peace.

River thinks of everyone being drawn into this vortex of lies and secrets. Himself, Echo, Flora, Chase. Even the Razers. Each holding a piece of the puzzle. A fragment of truth that's only part of the solution.

He frowns, pulling back to look at his sister. "You know that everyone in the Green Zone is Vulnerable."

She nods. "Discovering that is why I decided I couldn't stay there after Confirmation."

"Have you told Chase?"

The Dead Borns knowing the Green Borns are no different to them, yet get to live surrounded by plenty, will mean chaos.

It will mean war.

Flora stills as she gazes up at him. For a second, he wonders if she's going to tell him the truth. Whether they're really in this together. "I tell Chase everything. I love him."

River is just as frozen. "Then the Razers know?"

"No," she says, shaking her head. "If they knew the truth, they'd storm the Green Zone. It would be a bloodbath seeing as the Green Borns would think they're making it all up as an excuse to attack. They're too strong."

River lets out a breath, his back curving with relief. "I'm glad he realizes that."

"That's why Chase is recruiting Razers. And training them. Once they're a force to be reckoned with, he'll tell them."

The breath that River draws in is so sharp, it stabs the back of his throat. "But..."

Chase will give the Razers what they need to finally act. The knowledge they've been lied to as they've been left to starve and die will be a grenade to their fury.

And he can't blame them.

"Surely, there's another way," he finds himself saying.

The way Flora regards him confirms the answer that's already leaped in his mind. There *is* another way.

The Sovereign.

She can save everyone, irrespective of which Zone she's been cast into.

Yet that solution is as palatable as war. That solution means testing Echo.

And hoping the adrenacure saves her if she's not the one who can save them all.

River's chest suddenly feels too full, but not with warmth and light. Everything inside him just turned to stone. Jagged and heavy. Cold and grating.

Flora turns to press a hand to his chest. "You really love her, don't you?"

River opens his mouth to deny that, but he can't be upset with Flora for lying to him if he does the same to her. Except that means being truthful with himself. That means admitting he's fallen for the girl who he first thought was his enemy, and was totally wrong.

It means he's fallen for a girl who may not survive confirmation of who she actually is.

He's not sure how to reconcile the beauty of the first admission, and the bone-gripping fear of the second.

Flora's palm presses against his chest with more pressure. "You don't need to speak," she murmurs. "I just got my answer."

"What answer?" asks Echo as she enters the hut.

River leaps to his feet, finding Flora beside him. "Hey," he says, his voice somewhere between normal and a whisper.

Echo's smile grows, seeming to fill the dusky air with light. "We had a thunderstorm earlier. You slept right through it."

He rubs the back of his head. "I had a busy night," he says sheepishly.

"You really did." Echo's voice dips, as if emotion just drew it down.

Flora slips toward the door, her gaze jumping between the two of them. "I'm going to talk to Chase." She pauses. "We'll need to get going as soon as it's dark."

River nods, his eyes not leaving Echo. He tries not to feel as if he's memorizing her features, even as he commits each one to memory.

She moves toward him the moment they're alone. "How do you feel?"

"Fine." He takes her hands. "I didn't mean to sleep for so long."

"I'm just glad you're alive."

River doesn't want to think about Clover and the serpent-wood seeds that saved him. Not when they're about to go back to the Alphadome.

The place where Echo could die.

"Echo..." he starts.

One step and she banishes the space between them. "River, we don't have much time, and I'd really rather not spend it talking."

She presses her lips to his, wraps her arms around his neck, and kisses him. River's arms clamp around her back, unsure whether he's steadying himself or her as mouths open and tongues explore. There's a heated, rushed tone to their hungry movements. A wild need to feel everything.

As the kiss inevitably deepens, River tastes Echo's passion and desire. But also the desperation and fear that's trying to claw its way up. He suddenly understands her words. Why Echo didn't want to talk.

In their last moments of privacy, Echo wants to lose herself to this. And if that's what he can give her, that's what he'll do.

Hauling her up against him, he lifts Echo until her feet are off the ground, then loses himself in the beauty of their connection. Of her. He kisses her mouth, her cheeks, her eyelids. He strokes her hair with his free hand, then cups her jaw, reveling in the sound of her soft gasp.

He gives her all that he has, as if they can brand this moment with what they feel. Maybe stop time so that this can be their future.

"Echo," Chase calls, his voice coming closer. "Echo, oh—"

They don't pull apart quickly. Instead, they rest their foreheads against the other, breathing hard. Echo's eyes glisten in the gloom, and River's not sure what emotion is overwhelming her.

What they just experienced.

Or the fact they may never have it again.

"River," Flora says quietly. "We need to go. I have the adrenacure."

That lifeline is the only way he's able to step away from

Echo. She squeezes his hands then leads the way out of the hut, her shoulders high. River tells himself she looks strong and determined.

Not like a sacrificial lamb making her way to the altar, just like every other soul in the Sovereign graveyard.

It's a silent group of four who make their way out of the village and into the expanse of the Dead Zone. Unlike the Green Zone with its biodiversity of sounds, all that breaks the silence is their squelching steps in the mud after the rain and the slumbering hum of the Betadome. River wonders if everyone can hear his heart beating louder and harder the closer they get to their destination.

Echo tugs on his arm as they walk behind Flora and Chase. "When we get back, we're moving into Nola's hut," she whispers.

When we get back. Echo, with her strong will and soul-deep determination, is talking about surviving this.

"I'm not sleeping in that chair," he whispers back.

A snuffled snort of laughter escapes her, loud enough for Chase to glance over his shoulder. Flora yanks on his arm and he stumbles, forcing him to focus forward again. River's grateful to his twin. She knows he needs this time with Echo.

He glances down at her, finding her smiling as she gazes at him. He smiles back, wishing they could kiss one more time. But then promising that's exactly what they'll do after they leave the Alphadome.

He won't consider that Echo could die. They can't afford to think of failure.

Echo failing will spark a domino of deadly events. The Razers will follow through with their promise and kill River, then wage war on the Green Zone.

And yet, without the Sovereign, none of it will matter.

Without the Sovereign, humanity is doomed.

The boulder that sits not far from the hidden hatch appears ahead, silent and still. River draws in a deep breath, finding that it rattles around his chest like it just became a cavern.

He has no idea how he's going to stand by and watch this unfold.

Whether Echo will live or die.

All he knows is that he has to.

CHAPTER
FIFTEEN
ECHO

Echo takes the stairs into the Alphadome feeling like she's walking straight into the pit of hell. The last time she'd been in here, she'd fled for her life. It's hard to believe she's come back of her own free will.

"Why do we have to do the test here?" River asks, a step or two behind her. "There's got to be a better way."

"Do you know anywhere else we can get a queen bee?" Flora asks gently.

"There are lots of them in the Betadome." His voice is full of defeat.

Flora doesn't bother to respond. What River says is true, but they all know extracting a queen from the Betadome would be highly dangerous. They're putting themselves at enough risk already. Echo especially.

"What if Oren comes here?" River asks as they step into the expanse of the room and the bright lights blink on. He glances around as if he expects his father to pop out from behind the ominous glass dome in the center.

136

"I talked to Ruff," Chase says. "He got word out to Tuff. He'll warn us if Oren decides to come here."

River doesn't seem satisfied with that answer. Echo puts a hand on his back. His questions are coming from a place of concern for her wellbeing. She suspects he's going to ask plenty more.

"What about that...thing?" River glances toward the dark corridor that leads to the crypt. "The Worker."

"She's not interested in us," says Flora. "Unless one of us di—"

She doesn't need to finish her sentence. They all know what she was going to say. And why she'd changed her mind about saying it. She seems to have finally realized what Echo and River mean to each other. Echo isn't so sure River's caught up to her and noticed just how much his sister loves Chase.

Flora rubs her hands together, keen to move on. "Should we get started?"

"Wait." Echo reaches inside her shirt for her locket. She'd changed back into the more familiar clothes of the Dead Zone when she'd returned home after securing Nola's hut. If she's going to die, she doesn't want to do it dressed like someone she's not. Because as much as she may have been declared an Immune at Confirmation, the blood in her veins will always feel Vulnerable. The Dead Borns are her people. Not the colony responsible for creating this chamber of death. It feels more fitting to die in her tattered clothes than a crisp white suit.

"What are you doing?" River asks as Echo slips her locket from her shirt and over her head.

She holds it out to him. "You know this was a gift from my father. There are seeds inside. I want them planted in the Dead Zone one day. When the soil recovers enough to be able to support life. Will you do that for me?"

River pushes the locket back to her. "You can plant them yourself."

"But..." Tears fill her eyes. This sweet handsome guy doesn't have much time to start facing the facts. "River, please?"

His green eyes moisten in response to her show of emotion, and he nods slowly. Wrapping her outstretched hand in both of his, he takes the locket and holds her gaze. Something passes between them that feels bigger than the sum of them both, and she knows without doubt he's already faced the facts. He realizes how dangerous this is. And the only thing that's allowing him to keep moving forward with it is the knowledge that the lives of everyone in both their colonies depend on it. As much as he may have grown attached to Echo, he can't choose her over the possibility of the rest of humanity losing the ones they love most. That would go against everything that River is.

He loops the locket over his head and Echo reaches up to trail her fingertips down his cheek.

"Thank you," she whispers. "You're the best person I ever met."

"No." He shakes his head. "You are."

This makes her smile. "I didn't meet myself."

He takes her hand from his cheek and moves it to his lips, placing gentle kisses on her knuckles.

"Right," says Chase, seeming to have caught Flora's impatience. "Shall we get on with it?"

Echo looks across at her friend with the tumble of blond curls and remembers the feeling at Confirmation of wanting to slap and hug him at the same time. None of that has changed.

"Chase." She's not sure what she wants to say to him but feels the moment warrants something. "I'm glad you found Flora."

He nods briskly. "Me, too. I'm sorr—"

"It's okay." She doesn't want his apology right now. Not for the way he rejected her, or for the lies he's spun. She *is* glad he found Flora. Because that led to Echo finding River. And that's all that matters right now.

Flora sets down the basket of adrenacure and takes out a canister, holding it up in front of her as she studies it with squinted eyes.

"Have you ever administered adrenacure before?" River asks.

Flora shakes her head. "It's not hard. I've seen the medics do it a thousand times."

River chews on his lip, not seeming convinced.

"Do you have a better option?" Chase cocks a brow at River. "You want to do it?"

"Flora's fine." River turns his attention to the glass dome. "But does Echo really have to go in there?"

Echo decides it's time for her to take charge of this situation. After all, it's her life at stake here.

"I'm going in the dome," she says firmly. "We need to make sure I'm the only one who gets stung. River, we've been through all this before. We agreed on the best plan."

"But what if you need the adrenacure?" River asks. "Bees can sting multiple times. Flora would be at risk if she goes in there to save you."

"And finally he makes a good point." Chase frowns. "He's right, Flora. You can't go in there."

"Then I'll administer it myself." Echo snatches up the basket of adrenacure and opens the door to the glass dome. She steps inside and plonks herself down on the chair, not bothering to strap herself in. It's not like she's going to run away.

Balancing the basket on her lap, she takes out a canister

and studies it. Like Flora said, it's not hard. And while she may not have seen them administered as many times as Flora, she knows what to do. Once she's been stung, the moment she begins to feel unwell she'll jam it down on her thigh and reach for another.

"I'll be right here if you need me." Flora is still clutching her canister of adrenacure. "Just call out if you want help."

"That's not a good idea." Chase secures the door, suddenly far more concerned now that it's Flora's life at risk. "You need to stay out here."

"Not if Echo needs me." Flora goes to the glass column containing the queen before Chase can argue it any further.

"It's the green button on the side." River rushes to Flora. He's the only one other than Echo to have witnessed this test. He's the expert, whether or not he wants to be.

River presses the button and the roof and floor of the column slide toward each other.

"Wow." Flora's voice is muted on the other side of the glass but clear enough for Echo to hear the reverence in her tone. "She's magnificent. Look at her. How can something so beautiful be so deadly?"

Echo winces at that final word. She closes her eyes, not needing to catch sight of the creature that's very possibly about to end her life.

Or begin it...

She concentrates on slowing her breathing, hoping it will calm the rapid beating of her heart. She's about to be injected with deadly venom. The worst thing right now would be for her blood to be racing through her veins. She needs time to administer the adrenacure. That is, if she needs it. Is it really possible she won't?

Of course, it is. She'd hardly be sitting here right now if she didn't believe that to be the most likely outcome. She reminds herself of what led the four of them to believe she's the Sovereign.

Oren's been rigging the Confirmation for years.

Because nobody in either colony is a true Immune.

Except Echo.

She hadn't been drinking the Green Zone's water before her Confirmation. She tried everything she could to provoke the bees and they weren't the slightest bit interested. Then when she'd comforted Avid as he'd died, she'd been unmistakably stung on the thumb. And the same venom that had killed her terrified friend had barely even left a mark on her.

It has to be her.

She's the Sovereign.

There's a click from the glass column and Echo's eyes pop open to see Flora passing River the small glass prism that she knows contains the queen.

This is it.

It's really happening. All efforts to still her breathing and heart rate are lost as both skyrocket into a rhythm she has no hope of controlling. It doesn't matter how much she might believe she's the Sovereign, she can't fight the nagging thought that's hammering her senses.

What if she's not?

"Are you ready?" River holds the small prism up to the rubber opening of the much larger one.

"I'm ready," she says, even though this isn't something that anyone could possibly be ready for.

River grimaces then pushes the prism against the opening.

"Don't look away," she pleads, before he drops it. "Please. I need to see your eyes."

River nods. His face is pale, torment burning in his eyes.

She holds steady on the green depths of his irises as she tries to blink away her fear. River's watching over her, even if

TAMAR SLOAN & HEIDI CATHERINE

there's nothing he can do to help. This feels important. If she's about to die, she wants to be with this selfless guy who was embraced by his colony only to discover he's allergic to it. Which has never seemed to matter to him because he's adopted both Echo and her home like that's where he belongs.

River lets go of the prism and it lands with a tiny yet terrifying plink. The sides fold open to reveal what's inside.

The time has come to find out.

Echo's either the Sovereign...

Or she's dead.

CHAPTER
SIXTEEN
RIVER

River isn't sure whether the tear tracking its way from the corner of his eye and down his cheek is because his eyes are stinging from being open too long, or because his heart is slowly, painfully cracking.

Either way, he doesn't blink.

Echo asked him to not look away, and if that's what he can give her during these seconds where her life hangs in the balance, then he will. With the total commitment the moment deserves.

Even as the moment stretches out to feel like a lifetime.

Even as the burning sensation intensifies, both over the surface of eyes and deep in his chest, fueling a matching line of moisture down the other cheek.

Even as Chase draws in a sharp gasp.

The queen bee must be getting close. Flashes of the last time River watched this stab, unwanted and unrelenting, through his mind. The queen in a furious frenzy once she realized she wasn't alone. That a threat was inside the Alphadome with her. The brutal, swift attack as she targeted the girl's face, her most open and vulnerable area.

The instant red welts. The immediate swelling.

The scream that was drenched with terror, then abruptly cut off by a bloated throat.

Oren had thought the girl was Echo.

And now it's really her, possibly about to endure the same thing.

River locks his muscles. Despite what Flora agreed to, there's no way he's standing here and watching once Echo's stung. She may react too fast to be able to administer the adrenacure herself. At the first sting, he's going in, ready to jam as many of those canisters into Echo as needed.

"She's dead!" Chase cries.

This time River blinks, wondering if his mind has been firmly gripped by denial. Maybe he's only seeing what he wants to see. Except Echo's staring back at him, terrified and stoic, most definitely alive.

One bat of his eyelids and the burning lessens. A second and it's gone, revealing Echo's still there. Surely Chase isn't being so callous as to play out the worst-case scenario. While Echo can still hear...

Chase drops to his knees, his hands pressing against a hexagonal pane of glass. "No," he moans.

And that's when River sees it.

The glass case that holds the queen bee lies on the floor flat and open. And in the center lies the queen bee herself.

Lifeless.

Dead.

Echo bolts to her feet, having registered the same thing. "What the..."

All it takes is two steps and she's beside it, jolting River's heart into an unsteady canter. The queen may just be stunned, or even resting. Echo's inviting death far more completely than she did just by stepping into the Alphadome herself.

But the queen doesn't move. A closer inspection reveals one translucent, laced wing is slightly askew.

"What happened?" Flora cries out, darting to River's side as she stares at the queen in horror.

"She's dead," Chase repeats, looking stunned. "How?"

River replays the moments after the queen was caught, ready to travel the short distance from the cylinder to the Alphadome. He barely glanced at her or the prism she was encased in. All his focus was on Echo, and honoring what may have been their last moments together. He heard the prism drop but he didn't see it open.

"She must've died in the container," he says quietly. The queen was very much alive in the cylinder.

A sob bursts from Flora and she clamps a hand over her mouth. "We must've missed a step." She stills, then turns to River. "But it also means..."

River turns back to Echo, his eyes now wide. The loss of the queen means they won't be finding out whether Echo's the Sovereign. Not today.

Echo's out of the Alphadome before River can blink, although he's already moving toward her. He discovered how optional the need to blink is when it comes to this strong, beautiful girl.

They crash into each other's arms, holding tightly. River buries his face in Echo's hair. She digs her fingers into his back, as if she's fastening herself to him. They stay like that, possibly for as long as Echo was in the Alphadome. It's as if they're erasing those terrifying moments, rewriting them so that they're defined by their hearts only inches apart, slowly reaching a matching rhythm, rather than separated by glass and not knowing if they'll ever be the same again.

Or maybe they're pretending this is what it would be like if Echo was stung. And she survived.

Chase clears his throat. "Although I know this is a relief, it's also not the greatest outcome."

River and Echo pull apart, although she remains tucked into his side. Flora is still beside the queen, staring at her dead body through the glass. "Maybe they don't survive very long without a colony."

River's still stunned at the timing. The queen died seconds before Echo was to be tested.

Echo sighs. "But now we still don't know if I'm the Sovereign."

Chase glances around the large room, his hands on his hips. "What do we do now? Oren wouldn't have queen bees just lying around. We've all seen that those girls are crazy aggressive."

Flora frowns. "He probably raises them himself. A queen is simply a worker who's fed royal jelly."

"And how long does it take to raise one?" River tenses, unsure what he wants the answer to be.

If it's less than a week, then they'll be doing this again very soon. If it's longer...

"Sixteen days," Flora says. "We don't have that kind of time."

They only have four days before they have to be back in the Hive.

Chase crosses his arms. "We'll have to catch one."

River's about to say that would be a suicide mission when Echo speaks first. "It's the only way." She glances up at him. "And I'm Immune."

"You're going to enter the Betadome and pluck one from a hive?" River asks incredulously. "The worker bees aren't just going to let you take *their* sovereign."

146

Echo doesn't answer, simply gazing at him with dark eyes that say it all.

They don't have a choice.

Flora huffs, then stalks into the Alphadome, scoops up the flattened prism holding the queen, and stalks back to the cylinder that houses her. "All you've done is put off the inevitable," she mutters, tipping the bee back in.

The queen slips from the glass and tumbles onto the floor. River takes some satisfaction from knowing the next time Oren returns with another unsuspecting innocent to test, that no one will be dying in the Alphadome that day.

They'll be safe just like Echo was.

For now.

Echo sighs. "Come on, let's get out of here. We can plan our next steps in the morning."

She sounds so weary that River tightens his arm around her shoulder. "Good idea."

The four of them make their way out, leaving behind the dead queen, the empty Alphadome, and the Sovereign crypt, thankfully without one more body added to it. River suppresses a shudder at the thought. He would never allow anyone he knows to be entombed in there with the Worker.

Outside, the air smells of wet soil, although not the rich, earthy scent of the Green Zone, but a dusty scent closer to ash. The moment the hatch closes, they're surrounded by darkness, and River guesses it's close to midnight. Silently, they make their way back to the village, Chase and Flora holding hands as she carries the adrenacure they never got to use, River and Echo a few steps behind.

As they near the Betadome, the same tension that had wound through River's muscles in the Alphadome once more tangles through him. It never occurred to him that this could get *more* dangerous. The Alphadome was deadly and it only held one queen bee.

The Betadome is alive with the aggressive insects they'll have to get past just to get their hands on a queen. One the workers will do anything to protect.

And Echo's the only one who's Immune.

River's mouth twists. And here he thought watching Echo go into the Alphadome shredded him from the inside out.

Both domes hold the key to survival. And the promise of death.

Echo wraps herself around his arm. "It's funny how you can feel both relieved and disappointed at the same time," she murmurs.

He huffs an agreement. "We've dodged a bullet, only to realize a cannon is now pointed at us."

"Then we'll have to duck real fast," Echo says, a smile in her voice.

River finds his own smile creeping up his face. "Always coming up with a solution, huh?"

She giggles. "Trying to stay alive is great motivation."

River's not sure whether to smile broader as they manage to find humor in a moment such as this, or to let it drop under the weight of the reality they're trying to lighten.

He doesn't get a chance to do either.

"There they are!" A female voice stabs through the darkness.

A female voice River recognizes, even though the first time he heard it he was working hard just to stay conscious.

Fray strides forward, separating from the group of people who materialize, eyes scanning the four of them. She glosses over Flora, her lip twitching, then it curls when she sees River. Her eyes widen to reveal more white when they fall on Echo.

"She's alive!" Fray gasps.

Chase quickly steps forward. "We weren't able to test her," he says hurriedly.

Echo turns to him. "You told them what we were doing?"

"Of course, I did," Chase says indignantly. "The Razers are a vital part of this fight."

River crosses his arms, conscious that Chase is drip feeding the Razers information. When he and Echo returned from the Green Zone, the Razers thought Immunity was a myth. More of a legend.

Now they know the Sovereign exists.

And that Echo might be the one who can save them all.

River's not sure how he feels about that.

Sledge steps up beside Fray, his nose twitching with enough agitation that his beard tics, too. "Why wasn't she tested?" he demands.

Chase lifts his hand in a conciliatory gesture. "We were going to, but the queen bee died. We're not sure how, but it's possible we missed a step in the process."

Fray lifts a skinny arm and points at Flora. "She did it! She killed the bee!"

"She did not!" River says, jumping in between the accusing finger and his sister. "You can't throw accusations around like that."

"I don't trust her," Fray spits. "She *chose* to come to the Dead Zone. Who does that?"

Sledge grunts. "Unless they got a real good reason."

"She did," River says, keeping his voice even. "She—"

"Enough! You're the guy who rejected Ruff's girl, Navy," growls Sledge. "Like you're too good for her."

"I wasn't willing to barter her body and her future," River growls back.

Chase steps in between Fray and River, creating another

buffer. "Flora came here because she learned about the Sovereign."

River steps up beside him, not needing to be protected. "She came here to help you."

Fray sneers at him. "Of course you'd defend her. You're probably a spy, just like she is."

River pushes his face close to hers, ignoring the tang of her breath. He bites out each word. "I will never align myself with my father and what he stands for."

Fray's gaze slides away as she subtly leans back. "I don't trust either of you. Never will, either."

Echo slips beside River. "Then you're just like the Green Borns," she says quietly.

Fray gasps as a rumble ripples through Sledge. The other Razers shuffle, and River's not sure if they're getting ready for a fight, or whether they're uncomfortable with the truth Echo just spoke.

"Okay, okay," Chase says, his voice as smooth as the inside of the Alphadome. "We need to focus on moving forward. We're going to get another queen and try again. Tomorrow."

"You're going to catch a queen?" one of the Razers gasps. River thinks their name's Jupiter.

"We don't have a choice," Echo says, her voice steady. "We have to find the Sovereign."

Jupiter looks at Echo for long moments. "But that means—"

"We know," River finishes, not really wanting to hear it said aloud. He can feel the Betadome's presence behind him. Waiting.

Because they're going to go to it, knowing the thousands of lethal weapons it holds.

Jupiter nods then spins on his or her heel, River's not entirely sure. The quiet yet thoughtful teen seems to have an identity that's neither and both. "I'm going back to get some sleep," they say. "The best thing we can do is wait."

"Jupiter's right," says Chase. "Rest. There's no fight here tonight."

For long seconds, River wonders if the Razers will follow Chase's direction. Is his role as leader respected considering the mistrust clearly stamped on several faces?

Ruff is the first to follow Jupiter, then several more. Fray and Sledge are the last, and not before they cast threatening glances at Flora, then River. Although they follow Chase's order, their look promises there's most definitely a fight coming.

River turns to Flora to make sure she's okay, sad that she was attacked so personally just because she's a Green Born. Except his twin is beaming as she wraps herself around Chase.

"Thanks for sticking up for me," she purrs.

Chase presses a kiss to her forehead. "They'll see you're on our side," he promises. He glances back at River and Echo. "Come on, I don't know about you guys, but I'm ready to hit the mat."

River falls into step beside Echo as they follow Chase and Flora back to the village, trying not to let his thoughts wander too far. Chase may be sure that the Razers are going to accept Flora, but he can't help wondering... What if they don't?

They reach Echo's old hut and Chase and Flora disappear inside after whispered goodbyes. It's clear they can't get away quickly enough. River tells himself it's sweet to see his sister so happy. In fact, he doesn't remember her ever beaming like that back in the Green Zone.

Echo leads River to Nola's hut and as they crawl through the strange half-door, River realizes he's also ready to "hit the mat," as Chase said. It's been an exhausting rollercoaster of a night.

And tomorrow is going to be an even more terrifying ride.

It's dark inside, but River can still make out that Echo's already set up a sleeping mat in the corner of the room opposite to the chair. One large enough for the two of them.

The sight of the flat length of woven scraps of material has his heart stuttering.

Then bursting into a gallop.

Echo's alive. Here with him. They have what he thought was about to be taken away from them.

More time.

Not only that, it's time *alone*.

CHAPTER
SEVENTEEN

ECHO

E cho surveys Nola's hut in the dark shadows. She spent the afternoon collecting water from the stream, cleaning down the walls and sweeping the dirt floor. Chase had scavenged her a few necessities like a sleeping mat, blanket and water jug. Echo knows he did it so he can have alone time with Flora, but she hadn't complained. The things he'd brought had been exactly what she and River had needed.

Even Jupiter had turned up with a string of flowers they'd made from scraps of colorful plastic. They'd helped Echo to hang it from one corner of the ceiling to the other to brighten up the hut. Echo suspects Jupiter was feeling guilty about the way the Razers had treated Echo and River when they'd returned from the Green Zone. But Jupiter hadn't needed to worry. Echo knows it wasn't their fault. If anything, it had been Jupiter who'd led the charge in their defense. Chase had been smart to recruit Jupiter to his army of rebels. He needs more Jupiters and far fewer Frays and Sledges if he's going to succeed.

It had taken hours, but Echo's satisfied she created a place she and River can call their own until Nola returns. Because Echo's determined that will happen. And she can't have her friend returning to an abandoned hut filled with nothing but dust and her beloved old chair.

"Are you sure this is the same place?" River asks.

"You can't even see it in the dark." Echo punches him playfully. He catches her fist and unravels it, threading his fingers through her own.

"But I can feel it. I can certainly smell it." She hears him take in a few deep sniffs. "As long as I don't get too close to that chair."

"Stop it." She laughs. "You know I'm looking after it for Nola."

On the walk here, she'd filled River in on the note she'd found, aware that while she hadn't been willing to share that information with Chase, it had tumbled from her lips the moment she'd been alone with River. Which tells her almost as much as the note itself.

"That chair's a whole zone in itself," River says. "The Bacteria Zone."

She laughs against her will. "I said stop it! Besides, we're sleeping over here."

Pulling on his hand, she guides him down to the sleeping mat and they stretch out. He lies on his back, and she snuggles into him, resting her head on his chest while he wraps an arm around her. While she'd gotten changed into her Dead Zone clothes, he remains in the white suit he'd taken from the Green Zone. She knows she's not supposed to like anything from the enemy side of the net, but she can't help but admire the way that suit clings to him. Certain parts of him in particular...

"Echo," he whispers.

"Yes," she replies quickly, hoping he doesn't ask what she was just thinking.

"I was so relieved when the queen was dead." He pulls her a little closer to him. "But now...it's even worse. You can't go into the Betadome. There has to be another way."

Echo closes her eyes in the darkness. She doesn't want to talk about any of this right now. Because she was also relieved when she saw the tiny dead bee in the prism, even though it was a huge setback in their quest to find the Sovereign.

River draws breath to speak again, and Echo leans up on an elbow and presses her lips to his, stopping his words before he can form them. She's tired of talking. Tired of worrying. Tired of carrying the weight of two colonies on their shoulders.

He freezes beneath her for one surprised moment, then melts into her kiss. His hands slide up to the back of her head and he pulls her closer, moaning softly as their passion ignites.

"Better," she murmurs.

He doesn't need to stop to ask her what she means. He knows. He always does. Tonight isn't about rehashing the past or shaping the future. It's not about finding Sovereigns or making Immunity. It's about the two of them in this moment. They've spent too long feeling worried and frightened and confused and brave. Here, alone in the darkness of this hut, all they need to be is...Echo and River.

They kiss with desperation, pouring a thousand promises into each brush of their lips, each gentle exploration of their tongues.

When Echo had been inside that glass dome, she'd thought she was about to die. And now she's never felt more alive. Not knowing how much time they have together, she decides not to waste another second. She undoes River's shirt and he slides out of it, shaking it off like an unwanted husk. Running her palms down his chest, her breath catches in her throat. She pulls back from his kiss, wanting to take in the smooth feel of his skin, along with the smattering of hair growing in a line down the center of his chest. She follows the trail, heading lower, not knowing exactly what it is she wants, but knowing it's something more. A lot more.

She reaches the waistband of his trousers, and he moans.

"Echo," he breathes. "Are you s——"

She smothers his words with another kiss. She's sure. She's never been more sure.

River fiddles with a button on her shirt and she slips it over her head, saving him the trouble, then wriggles out of her trousers. Pressing herself to him, she revels in the sensation of chest against chest. Their breathing morphs into desperate panting and River gently flips Echo onto her back. He runs his hand from her collar bone down her curves, over her hip, then to the softness of her inner thigh.

"Take these off," she whispers, tugging at the waistband of his trousers.

He quickly complies and she can only wish there was more light so she could appreciate him in all his natural beauty.

Instead, she sees him with her hands. In her mind. With her soul.

"I love you," he says. This time she doesn't smother his words. She glories in them, letting each spectacular syllable soak into her core. "Always."

"I love you, too. Always." She runs her hands to his lower back and gasps as he seals their pledge to each other.

No longer Green Born and Dead Born. Right now, they are simply born.

Born into a place made from love and tenderness.

Born into a world of longing and pleasure.

Born into a life woven from the fabric of everything that brought them together, knowing it's impossible to tear them apart.

And there in that falling down hut in the middle of a sea of desperation and misery, River makes Echo the happiest person to draw breath in this struggling world.

She has everything she ever wanted. Which was nothing she ever knew existed...until she met River and he opened her eyes, just like she opened his. She needs him and he needs her.

And now the world needs them both.

Her body takes over from her mind and soon Echo is gasping, her fingernails clawing River's back as she looks up at the shadow of the string of flowers above them. She can die tomorrow. She can die today. None of it seems to matter. Because right now, she's drowning in River.

She's drowning in pure and utter bliss.

CHAPTER
EIGHTEEN

RIVER

River slowly wakes up, lashes fluttering as his brow scrunches. As consciousness surfaces he realizes it's because so much is different compared to how he's woken most days of his life. There's no gentle music piping into his room. His stomach is empty in ways he didn't know were possible. The mat beneath him is hard and unyielding, a far cry from his old, comfortable mattress.

And there's a warm, delicious body tucked into his side.

A smile lights up River's face as he lets that sensation sink in. Echo's soft, even breathing is all the music he needs. Her presence fills his soul in a way his stomach will never experience. And her living, breathing curves give him comfort just by existing.

Memories of last night curl through his mind, igniting his blood all over again. During those passionate, blazing moments, anything had seemed possible. It wasn't just a union of Green Born and Dead Born. It was the merging of two hearts who no longer cared what their past had dictated.

They were forging a new tomorrow.

Yet now, with the first rays of light breaching through the cracks of Nola's hut, River acknowledges that although those moments rocked his world, the yards and miles beyond these walls remain unchanged.

The fact they're in this hut is proof of that.

Nola sacrificed herself for Echo. The one she loved, just so Echo could escape the Hive. It's thanks to Nola that Echo's in his arms right now. It's a stark reminder of how much has to change.

That without the Sovereign, those sacrifices would've been for nothing.

Echo sighs in her sleep and buries in closer to River. His heart swells as his chest tightens, yet he doesn't have the heart to wake her.

Not with what they'll be facing today.

Shuffling footsteps sound outside, telling River the people of the Dead Zone are already awake and moving around, probably to collect water. It's not like they have much else to do. There are no crops to tend to. No cloth to weave, no fruit to be dried, no bread to bake. A baby cries and River winces. Just hungry mouths to feed.

"Did you hear the news?" one woman says in a hushed voice just loud enough for River to hear through the thin walls of the hut. She shuffles a little faster and the baby quietens.

"Yeah, the old wretch didn't even have a sleeping mat. Even if we could get that chair out, no one would've wanted it."

"No, not Nola," the first woman says, sounding like she's rolling her eyes. "Fray lost another one."

The second woman gasps. "Another?"

"Yeah, this would have to be the fourth." The woman clucks in sympathy. "She got real excited about this one, too. Got much further than the others."

159

"I know. Sledge was already saying they were going to name it Von if it were a boy. It means hope."

River stills, realizing too many things at once. Fray and Sledge are a couple. A couple who have tragically lost several babies.

No wonder they're so filled with hatred for Green Borns.

The first woman clucks again. "I heard Sledge took the stone where they'd been recording all the losses and threw it as hard as he could into the creek."

River has to stop his hands from clenching as he imagines the bearded man trying to rid himself of the grief and loss, even as he knows it won't work.

"So sad. Surely they're not going to try again. Fray ain't got nothing left to give."

The first woman snorts. "That's what we said about her aunt, and look what happened to her."

The baby lets out a thin wail, and there are more shuffling sounds. "The chance to have another mouth to feed ain't worth dying for."

The women's voices fade away, leaving River with the final, bitter words. He blinks up at the roof, his chest aching at all the pain shrouded under the anger and disappointment in the Dead Zone. Echo shifts beside him and he glances down, registering that she's awake.

"You heard that?"

She nods. "I didn't know that about Fray and Sledge."

They stare mutely at each other, a silent understanding growing in the space between them, here in the hut that Nola built.

An understanding born of suffering. Loss. Sacrifice.

And if that's what it takes to find the Sovereign, that's what they have to do.

They move simultaneously, River bending down, Echo

moving up, and meld their mouths together. This kiss is slow, almost aching in its tenderness. They cup each other's faces. They squeeze their eyes tightly closed.

They even smile as they pull apart.

"Look at it this way," Echo whispers, her eyes glittering with moisture. "I might get to hold Fray's son one day."

River strokes her cheek. "And I might get to say I made out with the Sovereign."

She huffs out a husky laugh. "I say we go find Chase and Flora and coordinate to meet tonight, when the bees are at their quietest." She snuggles a little closer. "Then we come back here for more alone time."

River's blood heats and ices over all at once, but he decides to honor their unspoken agreement and focuses on the anticipation her words kindle. "I like the sound of that."

They dress quickly and crawl out of the half-door, blinking in the blinding light even though it's barely morning. River's not sure he'll ever get used to the glaring nakedness that is the Dead Zone. No shade. Little color. No way to hide the desolation.

River and Echo clasp hands as she leads him through the village. Every hut is a different size, the paths and streets are different widths, yet the faces they pass are all painted with the same grime and bitterness. River finds himself scanning for Fray or Sledge, even as he wonders what he would say to them. That he's sorry? Sledge will probably punch him in the face. And River can't blame him.

They've just turned a corner that River recognizes isn't far from Echo's old hut when they see Chase and Flora approaching. They're holding hands, and for the first time, River doesn't begrudge them that. He thinks he finally understands his sister's choices.

He'd choose Echo and the Dead Zone a million times over.

Flora waves when she sees them and Chase indicates that they should slip into a small alley which is mostly just dust. River can feel Flora watching them as they turn to face each other and he instinctively moves closer to Echo.

Flora leans into Chase. "I told you they would," she whispers with a cheeky smile.

Chase rolls his eyes. "And I told you I didn't want to even think about it."

River finds his cheeks getting hot as Echo clears her throat. "We go to the Betadome tonight," she says in a low voice. "And get a queen."

Flora holds her hand up, revealing a small, glass prism. "I borrowed one of these from the Alphadome." She squeezes it and it flattens on her palm. "One press on the base and it opens and closes. Quite clever, really."

Nausea tumbles through River's gut. They're all talking about this like it's straightforward.

Not a suicide mission.

"And the adrenacure?" he asks tightly, even though he doesn't want to consider what happens if they need to use it in the Betadome.

That means less adrenacure for when they actually test Echo.

"I made a satchel to carry it," Flora says proudly. "Using the material from the Green Zone suit."

Chase squeezes her hand, then returns his focus to Echo. "Once we have the queen, we go straight back to the Alphadome."

She nods soberly. "It's the safest place to release a queen. We don't want anyone else getting stung."

The nausea climbs further up and lodges in River's throat. It'll be safe for everyone but Echo.

Flora reaches over to squeeze his arm. "Everything's going to be okay."

He can't help but arch a brow. There's no way his sister can promise that.

Echo slips an arm around his waist. "Then it's agreed. We'll meet at your hut just after dark. We'll go to the Betadome from there." She tightens her hold. "Until then, River and I are going to rest up in our hut."

Our hut. He likes the sound of that. That is, until his twin's sly smile returns. "*Resting* sounds like a great idea," Flora says, her eyes twinkling.

Chase groans in disgust. "We'll see you then."

River decides to ignore both responses. He has the day with Echo to spend alone in Nola's hut. That's a gift he won't be taking for granted. He smiles down at her, his heart tripping when the same look of barely-veiled anticipation lights up Echo's face.

They're going to make today count.

"Okay, we'll see you later." Chase has just stepped out from the alley when he's bowled back by a small ball of movement.

The child disentangles himself as Chase steadies him. River is sure he's the same boy who was with the Razers when they came back to the Dead Zone.

"There you are, Chase!" the boy says. "I've been looking everywhere."

"Makk?" Flora asks. "What are you doing here?"

The boy, possibly around nine or ten years old, although it's hard to judge in the Dead Zone, rolls his eyes. "I just told you. I've been looking everywhere. I went to your hut, then Sledge's—that was a mistake—then the other Razers, then back to your hut in case you went for water or something, then wondered if you were at that old woman's hut." Makk draws in a breath as he throws his skinny arms out wide. "And here I am."

Makk's still panting hard, but River's not sure if it's because of the run, or that lengthy explanation.

Chase tugs Makk back into the alley. "What's so urgent?"

Flora glances at River, then Echo. "Makk hangs around the Betadome in case Tuff has a message for us."

Makk puffs out his chest. "That's me. The Razers' messenger. I can remember anything you tell me, doesn't matter how long it is. You could have enough words to fill up a hut, and I'd still remember them. Maybe even the whole Dead Zone. Or the—"

"Makk?" Chase asks. "Did you get the message through?"

"Oh, yeah." The little boy deflates. He furrows his brow, as if he's choosing his words. "Oren's getting suspicious after Trid got so close to the Sting. He's watching the cameras extra close. Putting them on a loop isn't safe anymore."

Chase frowns. "Did you tell him we need to get into the Betadome?"

"Of course I did," Makk says, indignant. He taps his forehead as he mimics Chase's voice. "Tell Tuff he was right about Echo, but the queen in the Alphadome is dead. Time's running out. We need to get one from the Betadome."

Echo stiffens and River can't blame her. Tuff already suspected she was the Sovereign. No wonder he was willing to risk himself to let her out of the Hive.

Flora presses her fingers to her temples. "How are we going to do it now? Oren will be watching the Betadome like a hawk."

"We can't go in there," River says, his body unwinding for the first time. "We'll be caught."

And then Oren will not only know Echo's alive, but he'll have his hands on the potential Sovereign.

Makk puts his hands on his hips. "I haven't finished." He straightens, clearly preparing to relay another message, word for word. "I thought you might need to get in," he says in a low, rough voice that sounds unerringly like Tuff. "I told Oren the cameras will be down for ten minutes today so I can address the glitches he's been noticing. After that, they can't be tampered with again."

Dread replaces the nausea in River's gut, black and heavy. "When?" he asks, not wanting to know the answer.

Makk reaches into a satchel by his side and brings out an hourglass. Half the sand has already poured through to the bottom. "When this runs out, the cameras will go off for ten minutes."

River turns to Echo, registering she's as pale as he feels.

Their day together has just drastically altered course. It won't be spent safe and content in their hut. In fact, River can almost hear the Betadome calling to them, alive with the sounds and movements of thousands of tiny beings.

Bees.

Deadly, aggressive, terrifying superbees.

And they have to capture one of their queens.

Now.

CHAPTER
NINETEEN

ECHO

T he sand in Makk's hourglass seemed to slip through in double time as Echo scrambled to gather everything she's going to need to snatch a queen bee from the Betadome. But now as she stands outside the ominous black door, it feels like the sand has come to a standstill.

She's ready. Her heart is racing. She has so much adrenaline in her veins, she's surprised there's room for any blood.

"Nearly time," says Makk proudly.

Echo wasn't surprised to learn Makk is the Razers' messenger. She's often seen him trailing around the Dead Zone finding excuses to talk to Chase. He's a cute kid with a mane of black hair that sticks up like a permanent halo and a smattering of freckles across his nose. She just hopes Chase hasn't been putting him in any danger. From what she's seen since he turned up today, he'd be willing to do anything to impress Chase.

"You need to promise me you'll be careful in there." River pulls Echo to his chest and her locket digs into her. He'd returned it after their failed attempt in the Alphadome, but now she's wondering if she should've asked him to hold onto it. Because she's even less sure she's going to survive what today holds for her than she had been in that underground chamber of death.

"I have a plan," she says against his familiar warmth, trying to sound more confident than she feels.

"We have plenty of adrenacure if you need me to bring it in." He drops a kiss on her forehead.

"You can't go in there, River," Flora admonishes. "If the bees are agitated, none of us can. You know that. Echo is the only Immune."

"I can administer it myself if I need it." Echo pats the small bag of items she'd thrown together. She packed one shot of adrenacure, knowing if it doesn't work, she'll be unlikely to be alive to give herself a second or third. Hopefully it's just a precaution anyway. She'd barely felt it when the bee had stung her in Confirmation. All she needs to do is avoid a sting from a queen. Which is where the terrifying part of all this comes in.

"You can do it, Echo." Chase winks at her, despite the fear she sees hidden behind his façade.

For a brief flash, she remembers why she used to think she was in love with him. Then she glances up at River and is reminded of what true love looks like. He squeezes her tighter as if he can read her mind.

"Time!" shouts Makk, waving the hourglass with the sand having completely fallen to the bottom chamber. "You have ten minutes before the cameras are back. Hurry, Echo!" He starts to count under his breath.

Echo pushes away from River with not a moment to spare to say goodbye. This makes her all the more grateful they'd taken their time to revel in each other's presence the night before.

Chase pulls open the black door and practically shoves her

through it. She runs through the smoke without pausing and seeks out the target she'd decided on from the other side of the net. Her chosen hive is of medium size and shaped like an irregular teardrop. But most importantly, it's hanging low in a branch of an enormous apple tree that's bursting with flowers and fruit. And it's not too far from the black door for a fast escape.

"Nine minutes!" shouts Makk.

She stumbles forward, throwing herself to the ground underneath the tree. The humming of the bees is like a siren in her ears as the tiny creatures gather the pollen to bring back to their hive. But she's not ready for them just yet.

Reaching into her bag, she pulls out the flammable scraps River had helped her hurriedly collect, along with the flint and a knife with a long blade that Chase had given her. Working quickly, she builds a nest, being careful to leave space for air between the layers. A few curious bees fly around her, as if to inspect her work.

"What do you think?" she asks them, reminding herself that they can't hurt her, even though the sight of them still terrifies her.

"Eight minutes!" Makk calls, making Echo question if he really is that cute.

"I'm going as fast as I can," she mutters under her breath.

A bee lands on her arm and she resists the urge to swat it away. It flies off on its own accord and she takes a deep breath, knowing if she's to succeed there will be plenty more of them to come.

She picks up the flint and holds it against the nest, using the knife to strike at it. The first attempt produces a few sparks but nothing more, so she tries again, accidentally knocking over her nest.

"Seven minutes!" Makk calls.

"Don't distract her." River sounds frustrated. "She can do it."

"She asked me to tell her the time," Makk huffs.

Which is true. If only Echo realized how annoying it was going to be.

Drawing in a breath, Echo quickly rebuilds her nest, trying again with the flint. But her hands have started shaking, making the action of drawing the knife along the flint impossible.

Seeing a fallen apple on the grass beside her, she picks it up and eats it in hurried bites, knowing she needs the energy if she's going to steady her hands and achieve what she came in here to do.

"Six minutes! No time for a sna—" Makk's shrill shout is abruptly cut off and Echo has no doubt River gave him a death stare to silence him.

The sugar in the fruit does its work and Echo draws in a few deep breaths, trying again with the flint, pleased that her hands seem far more steady. This time, the sparks light into a small flame that catches hold of the nest. Echo smiles broadly, reaching in her bag for the damp piece of timber she'd brought with her and adding it to the fire, coughing when gray smoke billows up.

"Five minutes!" calls Makk.

Satisfied that the first part of her plan has worked, Echo stands and flaps her hands to direct the smoke up to the beehive. She knows the theory of why smoke calms bees is because it interferes with their pheromone sensitivity. But there's another theory she's also banking on. If a bee thinks there's a fire, they'll head into their hive and gorge themselves on honey. Just like Echo with the apple, they know they need sustenance if they're going to survive. And a bee in a sugar coma is far less likely to sting.

The smoke drifts into the hive and the bees instantly react, flying into their honey laden home in droves.

"Echo!" Makk sounds panicked. "Four minutes. Hu—"

"Echo," shouts River this time. "You really do need to hurry." His voice is a lot calmer than Makk's but she can hear the urgency in it. And he's right. She does need to hurry. But catching a queen also takes time.

The smoke builds, getting in Echo's eyes and making them burn. Blinking back the discomfort, she picks up the knife and swings blindly at the hive.

"Harder!" shouts Flora. "You have to hit it hard!"

"I'm trying!" Echo calls back, taking one giant swing and landing it right in the center of the hive.

It crashes to the ground right next to the fire and partially cracks open. More bees desperately try to get into the hive as others try to get out, and Echo can only hope the bulk of them have had enough time to get drunk on their honey, like Vernon with his kasi.

A rogue bee that doesn't seem to want to stick to the script flies at Echo and stings her on the cheek. She winces at the small pinch and swats it away. It comes back at her and she swipes at it with her free hand, making contact and sending it tumbling to the ground.

"Don't kill them!" calls Flora.

"She has to!" River huffs, clearly annoyed.

"It was only one," says Chase.

"Three minutes!" shouts Makk.

Knowing the queen will be somewhere in the very middle of the hive where the other bees can protect her, Echo slams the knife into the fallen hive and it splits wide open. Bees pour out and Echo gasps to realize they're not drunk at all.

They're furious, resembling Oren a lot more than Vern.

Stepping out of the smoke, Echo rubs at her eyes, knowing

she needs to be able to see what she's doing. A queen bee has a long, narrow abdomen with a point at the end. Her wings will be shorter, and her legs splayed. But there are so many squirming and circling black and gold bodies, it's impossible to see any individual one.

Two more fly at Echo. One stings her on the neck three times in quick succession and the other pierces the skin on the back of her hand.

"Put the queen in the prism!" Flora shouts, like it's that easy.

Ignoring the sharp little bites, Echo squats down and uses the knife to poke around the sheets of honeycomb.

This isn't just a hundred times harder than she expected, it's a thousand. She's not sure if numbers go higher than that but if they do then that's what it is. This is impossible.

Then, she sees her.

The queen.

The sovereign of this little colony of deadly bees, and exactly what Echo needs if she's to prove she's the Sovereign of them all.

Quickly grabbing her bag, Echo takes out the prism and the adrenacure. One shot won't be enough if the queen stings her, but it's the best she can do. If only that queen hadn't died in the Alphadome she wouldn't be doing any of this now. But then again, she also wouldn't have had that incredible night with River...

"Echo!" Makk screams, bringing her back to the horror of her reality. "Two minutes!"

Echo drags in her courage and with shaking hands reaches out with the prism to collect the queen, only to find the bees aren't having any part of that.

An impossibly large swarm flies out of the hive like a thick blanket. They coat Echo. She falls backward, squeezing her eyes and mouth closed, and dropping the prism to put her hands over her ears.

They're everywhere! Crawling all over her and stinging her again and again. One or two stings at a time hadn't hurt, but dozens at once is torture.

The adrenacure is useless. If she opens her eyes to find it, they'll sting her eyeballs. If she tries to call out, they'll fly right down her throat.

So, she does the only thing she can do.

She curls herself into a tight ball and tucks her head into her chest. Her lungs scream at her for air as her skin lights on fire.

"One minute!" she hears Makk call over the humming that's become a hurricane. "Time is almost up."

As her lungs struggle for air, she knows Makk's right.

Her time is almost up.

She said she was willing to give her life to find out if she's the Sovereign.

Which is exactly what's going to happen.

Except, now she'll never know.

CHAPTER
TWENTY
RIVER

R iver throws open the black door and bursts into the Betadome, running before it's had time to shut. His pulse is as loud as the furious swarm descending on Echo. It thrums inside him at the same frenzied beat as the wings of the hundreds of deadly superbees.

"Echo!" he shouts, uncaring that the Betadome is the one place where quiet is important.

He's not here to placate the murderous beings.

He's here to save Echo.

She doesn't move from the protective ball she's become, and he's glad. She can't. The moment she does, she'll make herself even more vulnerable. All he wants is for her to know he's coming.

That if she's not the Sovereign, then he's not going to sit by and watch her die.

River leaps over a small shrub, grabbing a spray of flowers from an almond tree above him. He rubs the fistful of blossoms over his chest as he lands, never breaking stride, never breaking focus.

The superbees are about to find a new focus.

"River!" Flora screams and he's glad.

The panicked wail will only agitate the bees further.

"Hey!" he shouts, throwing the word out like a bullet. "I'm coming for you!"

The moving horde crawling over Echo twitches, looking like a midnight monster being poked with a stick. River waves his arms high in the air, gripping two adrenacure canisters in one of his hands.

"Yes, you!" He wishes he had something to throw, but the adrenacure is for Echo. Instead, he swipes at his chest with his other hand, smearing the streaks of yellow pollen. "I'm not letting you take her!"

He steps around the small fire only a few feet away from Echo, noting it's shrinking. Without more fuel, it'll die. The idea was a good one, but they didn't have enough time to let the smoke work its magic.

Or maybe the bees would've reacted this way, regardless. Their hive is destroyed. Their queen is exposed.

This was always going to be a suicide mission.

River hunches his shoulders as he focuses on his goal. This won't be Echo's suicide mission.

The humming increases far sooner than he expected. The bees are already reacting to this new threat. Impossibly, their agitation grows, as if their current level of lethal anger was just the beginning.

The army of bees contract and Echo flinches beneath.

"Take me!" River screams as he throws the two adrenacure canisters so they tumble beside her. A single bee pelts at his face and he claps his hands together, killing it instantly.

The sound, maybe the whiff of the loss of one of their own, has the bees reacting before their dead comrade has hit the ground.

Yet when the black mass lifts, it's far more terrifying than River could've predicted. The relief that Echo's now free is quickly replaced by the reality of what he just invited on himself. The ominous cloud is alive with deadly intent.

Countless tiny wings beat the air, creating an unrelenting hum.

Hundreds of bees compress, moving as one as they arrow for River.

Each carrying a stinger with enough venom to kill a dozen people.

River turns and runs, his breath sawing in and out of his throat. He has no idea whether it's his allergies or plain old terror, but it doesn't matter. He focuses on getting oxygen to every cell, on pumping his legs, and moving the fastest he ever has.

He sees Flora on the other side of the Betadome, Makk beside her. Both their eyes are big enough to be beacons of white. Makk is waving the hourglass. Flora's mouth is working, but River can't hear her.

The humming is practically a roar. The air is vibrating with fury right behind him.

The black door is a short sprint away. A bee whips past his ear, making him duck. Another lands on his neck and he wildly brushes it off. He dares not look back, already knowing what he'll see.

Echo is free.

He's in mortal danger.

His peripheral vision picks up the ominous cloud that's about to encase him as he reaches the black door.

Just as an explosion of smoke pours over him.

River spins around to see the vibrating mass of bees shear away like a knife just cut through the precious inches that were between them, then shoot away. He barely glances at them. His focus is on where he came from. On Echo.

His breath whooshes out when he sees she's standing, looking down at what's left of the hive. She's alive! Her shoulders hunch as the bees advance toward her once again. A quick glance over her shoulder, and she turns back to kick the hive into what's left of her fire. The timber frame that was hung in the tree to encourage bees to build the hive topples and splinters as it hits the trunk of the tree it fell from. Then Echo spins around and breaks into a run, her gaze locking onto his.

"Time is up!" Makk cries out.

The black door opens and River hears Flora behind him. "Did she get the queen? I didn't see!"

River has no idea. He was too busy running for his life. And now Echo is, too.

She takes a wide berth as the swarm shoots toward the hive that's now a smoldering mess, meaning it takes her far longer to reach them than River would like.

His frantic pulse feels as if it's in slow motion as Echo sprints toward him. Her hair streams behind her. She darts around the almond tree that River used to smear pollen on himself. She glances furtively up at another hive that's no doubt agitated.

A breathless eternity later, she leaps into his arms. River grabs Echo, holding her tight as he staggers backward through the black door.

"Thank you," she says, her voice muffled where her face is buried in his neck.

"I couldn't let you hog all the excitement," he says huskily, holding her even tighter. He can't quite believe they both got out of the Betadome alive.

"Did you get it?" Flora asks somewhere behind them. "Did you get the queen?"

Echo pulls back and River reluctantly puts her back on her feet. Makk crowds in as she opens her hand.

Sitting in the middle of her palm is the glass prism, a very angry queen bee trapped inside.

"Once River made himself a target for the bees," she throws him a disgruntled glare and he grins back at her, "I was able to capture her."

"Oh yeah!" whoops Makk. "We did it! And just before the cameras were back on!"

River and Echo glance at each other, wide-eyed and still breathing a little hard. That last minute felt like a lifetime.

Flora takes the queen and carefully slips the prism into her satchel. He can hear the furious buzzing and faint taps as the queen desperately tries to escape. River can only hope she calms down soon. His adrenaline rush is crashing, and the thought of Echo being trapped in the Alphadome with that thing is completely overwhelming. Especially with less adrenacure.

Echo takes his hand. "Let's get back to the village. We need to be as far away from the Betadome as possible."

River's more than happy to oblige. He glances back at the netted dome, glad to put some distance between them...and stills.

"Echo..." he whispers.

Her gaze flies to him, then follows his line of sight. She gasps. "Oh no."

Makk must see it too because he yelps. "That's not good!"

The fire licking up the trunk of the tree is most definitely not good.

"Actually, this is bad," Makk continues, taking a step back. "Like, really, really bad."

The hive is now a melted puddle at the base of the tree, the wooden frame nothing more than charred sticks. But the fire is feasting on new fuel as it crawls over bark and reaches the lower branches. Charcoal colored smoke winds its way up through the leaves, splitting into twisting tendrils.

And the cameras would be recording it all. The flames. The smoke. It's only a matter of time before Oren is here with his men.

And those black guns loaded with venom.

"Back to the village!" River gasps, already pushing Makk in that direction.

"Chase?" Flora's voice spikes with alarm. "Where's Chase?"

River looks around frantically, noting that Echo's doing the same. Except Chase is nowhere to be seen. In the adrenaline-drenched moments escaping the Betadome, even Flora didn't notice he was gone.

CHAPTER
TWENTY-ONE
ECHO

Echo turns in a circle, looking for any sign of Chase. Her breath is coming in gasps and her skin smarts all over from the dozens of tiny stings she received in the Betadome. But she got the queen. And thanks to River, she also got out alive. That's all that matters right now. Well, it would be if Chase hadn't just vanished.

"Maybe he went back to the village." River runs a hand through his dishevelled hair.

Flora moans. "He wouldn't do that. Something terrible must've happened."

Echo scans the nothingness of the Dead Zone's terrain, certain she's missing something. But she's breathing so hard, it's difficult to focus on any one particular point.

"Makk, did you see anything?" River asks.

Echo turns to Chase's self-appointed smaller shadow to see his face crumple.

"I was too busy counting." Makk clutches the hourglass to his chest. "I didn't notice."

"Oh, Chase." Tears track down Flora's cheeks as she looks around in desperation. "Where are you?"

Echo rubs at her arms. It's as if they've caught fire, just like the tree in the Betadome, which is still pouring smoke into the sky. Her breathing isn't returning to normal either. She really has to pull herself together so they can find Chase and get out of here before Oren and his men burst into the Betadome. It feels like Makk has started his timer all over again.

"Are you okay?" River asks.

"I'm itchy." She rubs at her cheeks, then her legs, trying to use her palms to soothe the discomfort instead of her fingernails. The temptation to scratch away the first layer of her skin burns at her, and she rubs harder.

"What are you doing?" Makk asks. "I thought you were an Immune."

"She is," Flora answers for her. "One or two stings won't impact her, but she's had dozens. Not even the Sovereign could walk away from that."

Echo drops to her knees as her breathing develops a crackle, reminding her of River's persistent one-off breathing issue. She rubs more furiously at her arms then neck as River crouches beside her.

"I...can't...brea—" Her words catch in her oxygen-starved throat, and she falls to the hard ground.

"Echo!" River reaches for her, shaking her gently. "Echo!"

She draws in a shallow breath, not able to respond.

"Chase!" Flora whimpers. "River, I see him. He's in the Betadome."

But River is too busy fiddling with something to give any attention to his twin. Echo tries to turn her head to see what he's doing but she's too depleted.

"Oren's in there, too!" Flora cries out. "He's going to see Chase. River! We have to do something."

There's a sharp pain in Echo's thigh and she realizes River
has injected her with adrenacure. There's another stab as he
drives in a second canister.

"Breathe, Echo!" River pleads. "Come on. One breath in,
one breath out. Just like you showed me in the cornfield. You
can do this."

Her airway opens and she sucks in a deep breath, using the
energy it gives her to immediately scratch at her arms, only to
find the itchiness is easing. She stretches out on her back and
looks up at the blue, netted sky, following River's instructions.

"I'm okay," she tells him between gasps.

"I'm going in to get Chase," says Flora. "Oren will kill him if
he finds him in there."

This snaps River's attention away from Echo as he grips
Flora's arm. "You have to stay out here."

"Like you did when Echo was in trouble?" she hisses.

"Get down!" Makk whispers loudly, dropping to his belly.

There's something in the urgency of his young voice that
has River and Flora on the ground in a heartbeat. Echo rolls to
her stomach and leans up on her elbows, concentrating on her
breathing as she lets the adrenacure do its job. She'd been so
focused on not being stung by the queen, she hadn't really
given any thought as to what would happen if she was stung
by a swarm instead. If she hadn't been an Immune, she'd
surely be dead.

This thought has her eyes scanning for Chase.

He's a Vulnerable in a dome filled with bees.

There's a fire that's quickly getting out of control.

And Oren will kill him the moment he sees him.

"Where's Chase?" River whispers to Flora. "I can't see
him."

Flora lifts a shaking hand and points to a tree just beyond
the fire.

Echo squints. It takes a few moments for her to see what Flora has spotted. There in amongst the branches is a hint of the blue shirt Chase had been wearing.

"He must have decided to get some apples," whispers Makk. "While the bees were distracted."

"Why would he do something so stupid?" River is clearly as astonished as Echo.

"He thought I was counting too fast," says Makk quietly. "He must have figured he had more time. But I know how to count properly."

Flora's lips thin. "And he knows how much we need food."

Makk falls silent as Oren stalks through the Betadome, getting dangerously close. Thankfully, his focus is completely on the fire which has now jumped to a neighboring tree. He's completely oblivious to the four sets of eyes watching him from the Dead Zone. And one from the branches of a nearby tree.

"Hurry!" Oren shouts in a way that's not at all peaceful.

Two Green Borns burst into the Betadome dragging a long flexible pipe. Water is pouring from the end, and they wave it about with little control, sending droplets splattering through the silver net. Echo lifts her face, enjoying the cool sensation on her angry skin.

Flames leap up from the trees and her eyes widen to realize the small fire she'd started is quickly becoming an inferno.

"It's going to melt a hole in the net," River gasps.

"Who cares about the net," sobs Flora, her eyes glued to the tree Chase is hiding in.

Makk lets out a stifled cough. "The net keeps us safe. We'd all die without it."

"Chase is the one who's going to die." Flora tries to get up, but River pins her to the ground.

"Oren doesn't know he's there," he whispers fiercely. "Or us. Just lie down."

"Chase won't die," says Makk. "He knows what to do."

Echo remains quiet, concentrating on getting her energy back for whatever is about to come next. She wishes she could be as confident as Makk that Chase will be okay. If he really knew what he was doing, why hadn't he stayed out here? Had he really needed an apple that much? Then she looks at Flora's frail frame being held down so easily by River and she realizes Chase wouldn't have headed into the Betadome for himself. No doubt he wanted to make sure Flora had something decent to eat. If Oren decided to fix the glitches with his cameras, who knows what other measures he's about to take to keep the Dead Borns out of his precious zone. Chase would have been well aware of that. He just hadn't anticipated his path out of the Betadome being blocked by flames.

The two Green Borns get their water pipe close enough to the fire and douse it, working together to control the direction of the spray. Orange and blue flames are replaced by thick gray smoke and Echo holds back a cough as the wind blows it in their direction.

"Look," says Makk, pointing as Daphne rushes into the Betadome, along with Tuff.

Echo presses herself into the hard dirt hoping the slope of the land is giving them enough cover should Oren or Daphne decide to look this way. At least their dirt-stained clothes are camouflaging them. Makk and River lie perfectly still. Even Flora has settled down, accepting her best move right now is to stay quiet and wait.

"What happened?" Daphne cries out as she runs to Oren. "Are you hurt?" She goes to put her arms around Oren, then seems to think twice and lets them hang awkwardly by her sides.

"Must have been a freak lightning strike," says Oren, despite the sky being bright blue as the sun beats down on them. "Flames are out almost now."

"And the cameras?" she asks.

"Back online." Oren smooths down his beard and smiles. "We won't be having any more problems with visibility. I've fixed up those blind spots in here, too."

Echo's stomach drops. Without the blind spots, Chase has no hope of getting out of the Betadome unseen. Although, if he can get back into the Dead Zone, Oren holds no authority over him here. All he needs to do is bide his time and make a run for it as soon as it's safe. Oren can watch his precious camera footage later and realize how close he was standing to one of his enemies.

"Over there," Oren calls to his men with the waterpipe.

The two men nod obediently and redirect the gushing water away from Oren, aiming for the surrounding trees. Anger slides through Echo's core. If it's that easy to transport water, why hasn't the Green Zone set up one of these pipes on the other side of the net? These trees are currently being treated better than half the human population left in this world.

Oren strides to the smouldering tree and plucks a small twig from one of the branches, twirling it in front of him as he admires the tiny flame. The small patch of blue that's in the tree just past him moves and Echo braces herself.

Not now, Chase. Not now! Oren thinks the fire was caused by a freak bolt of lightning. He hasn't seen them watching him yet. They have a queen in their possession. All Chase needs to do is wait a few more moments until Oren leaves and they can get on with the next part of their plan.

Still holding the small flame, Oren goes to Tuff and whispers something to him.

"What's going on, Oren?" Daphne narrows her eyes. "Are we leaving?"

Oren gives her a flirtatious smile, but he doesn't answer her question. Instead, he walks to the tree Chase is hiding in and holds the small flame up to the leaves, laughing as they catch alight.

He looks across at Daphne and winks. "We'll leave in a moment. We just have to flush out some vermin first."

CHAPTER
TWENTY-TWO

RIVER

Seeing his father for the first time since he left the Alphadome has River's head spinning. Everything about his father's smooth, gray hair, his perfect white suit, his regal bearing is familiar. It's the same man River saw every day of his life.

His father is still the same.

Yet River now sees him completely differently.

The man who's watching the flames spread from leaf to leaf is no longer someone River's proud to be related to. The man who shields his eyes as he traces the first branch catching alight isn't someone to look up to.

The man who smiles as the growing smoke makes him squint makes River feel sick.

"No," Flora moans. "He knows Chase is up there."

Daphne frowns at Oren, then looks up into the tree. The leaves are turning to ash as if they're made of paper, leaving the branches exposed.

Leaving Chase exposed.

Daphne's eyes widen, then narrow as disgust fills her

features. Just like Oren, she's nothing but an illusion. Those placid smiles cover a cold heart. Just like the Green Zone hides a sinister secret.

"Another thieving Dead Born," she snarls.

Chase curls his lip straight back at them, then scrambles up a few branches, trying to escape the fire. River admires his fearlessness, even though it's misplaced. Chase is trapped.

Oren slowly circles the tree, holding up his hand when one of the Green Borns gripping the hose steps forward, stopping him with the slightest shake of his head. "In broad daylight. They're getting a little too bold for my liking."

Daphne withdraws one of the black venom guns from her tunic and River realizes she must carry it with her at all times. "Thank you for the clear line to shoot," she mutters, lifting it to point at Chase.

Although River's heart is stuttering at the prospect of what's about to happen, he holds his sister even tighter. Just as he expected, Flora tries to get to her feet, wanting to run to Chase. Gritting his teeth at having to do this, he pulls his twin into his chest, her back to his front, and clamps a hand over her mouth. She bites his fingers but he just winces, never releasing his grip. Flora lets out a helpless moan when she sees he's not letting her go.

"I'm sorry," he whispers. "There's nothing you can do."

Echo glances at them both, nodding at River as if to let him know this is the right thing. Yet her pale cheeks reveal it's not easy for any of them. Even Makk's skin is the color of bleached dust.

Chase slips around the trunk, putting it between him and Daphne. Her face tightens as she moves around, keeping a good distance from the flames illuminating her cold features. Chase moves again, looking as if he's going to play cat and mouse for as long as he can, but it's quickly cut short when he discovers the flames licking at his bare feet.

Flora moans softly against River's hand and he tightens his arms, in part to make sure she stays out of sight, in part to comfort her. He hates that she has to watch this.

Smoke curls around Chase as he looks up, registering that there aren't any other branches strong enough to hold his weight. He glances down, squinting through the haze, then scooting back the way he came as red and gold flickers through the ash and cinders. Straight back into Daphne's line of sight.

He's surrounded.

A calm settles over Daphne as she lines up her target. Her finger tightens around the gun loaded with bee venom. River can feel Flora's tears spilling onto his hand. Echo's fingers dig into the soil as if she's working to keep herself here. Makk is pale as he watches his hero's last moments.

Oren's hand appears above the gun, then he slowly pushes it down. "Not yet," he says in that soft, commanding way of his. "This one could be useful."

Daphne instantly, unquestioningly, lowers the weapon the rest of the way. "Of course."

River's stomach tightens at the mix of blind loyalty and eagerness to please. What's more disgusting is that used to be him.

Oren angles his head to look up at Chase, who now has streams of smoke swallowing him, a harbinger of what the flames will do next. "You can be roasted up there, or come down here and talk."

Flora whimpers and River wonders if she knows that either option is going to involve torture for the man she loves.

Chase makes the decision far quicker than River expects, but then again, the heat is probably just as potent as the smoke in telling him what's coming next. He drops to the ground in a crouch only a few feet from Oren and Daphne. The two men holding the hose instantly leap on him. Tuff quickly picks it up and starts to douse the tree.

Chase fights, but it's short-lived. The well-fed Green Borns quickly subdue him, each grabbing an arm and bringing him to his feet. When Chase still tries to struggle, Daphne steps forward and rams an elbow in his gut. He doubles over with a groan.

"That's better," Daphne spits. "Oren was right. Keeping you alive is much more fun."

Although River already realized Daphne's sweetness was just a veneer when he saw her kick, then kill, Trid, the callous strike and words still shock him. A glance at Echo shows her face now tight with anger. Flora's also tense in his arms, now vibrating with fury rather than fear.

Oren places a hand on Daphne's shoulder. "Thank you," he murmurs. "Now, I'd like to have a word."

Daphne nods and steps back, but Oren doesn't move closer to Chase. In fact, he steps away and turns toward the Dead Zone, his eyes bright and shrewd. "Show yourselves."

Makk ducks down lower, whispering a word that River's never heard before, but knows shouldn't be coming from a child. Echo and Flora are like River—still as statues.

"I know we have an audience," Oren continues. "I know you Dead Borns don't work alone."

Echo shakes her head imperceptibly at River. They have no reason to do what Oren says. At this stage, it's little more than a guess, even if it's true.

"And I saw movement when we arrived just like I saw this rat scurry up the tree," he says, taking a step forward. "Show your faces."

No one moves.

"You're willing to watch your friend be taken captive?" Oren challenges. "Do you have no loyalty at all?"

Echo grabs Makk's hand. "He's just trying to goad us," she whispers.

Oren waits a few tense seconds. "Very well." He turns to Daphne. "Now you can have some fun."

An excited grin spreads across her face and for the first time, River sees a flicker of fear flash across Chase's features. He quickly covers it as he tries to lash out with his foot, but Daphne sidesteps it as if she's a seasoned warrior woman, then delivers a short, sharp punch to his exposed thigh. Then another to his gut. And another to his throat.

Chase's grunts turn to a garbled choke.

"Anyone want to put a stop to this?" Oren calls out. "Take note that she likes to strike in threes."

Flora struggles in River's arms and he quickly tightens them. "We can't," he hisses. "Chase wouldn't want us to."

If Oren knew River isn't in the Hive or that Echo's alive...

Daphne steps back, sizes Chase up, then spins and kicks him in the chest. Chase tries to double over but the two men holding him keep him upright, leaving the pain to twist his features instead. Daphne pulls back her foot, then snaps it out again, striking low over his thighs, then his temple.

"She's quite impressive, isn't she?" Oren calls out, admiration clear in his voice. "And she can do this for hours."

"Don't listen—" Chase's words are cut off by a fist to his jaw. His head snaps back with the impact, then ricochets forward, straight into the second punch, then the third.

"River, please," Flora moans through his hand. "Oren knows I'm here."

Echo's gaze snaps to his. Flora's right. Oren is well aware his daughter is in the Dead Zone. It wouldn't turn everything upside down if she were to stand up and reveal herself.

They could still discover whether Echo's the Sovereign.

Except Oren doesn't take kindly to any threat to his beloved Green Zone. Discovering his own daughter is somehow involved in all this would be dangerous. Who knows what Oren's fury would mean.

Daphne steps back, panting a little and River hopes she needs a few moments to catch her breath.

It turns out that's not enough to stop her.

She strides to the tree and picks up a nearby stick, then indicates for Tuff to turn off the water. He does as he's told, that shuttered look that's becoming familiar stamped across his face. Daphne steps up to the tree and holds the stick high. Against a still-smoldering branch.

And lights it.

Once a merry flame is alive on the tip, she turns back to Chase. This time, her grin is more of a leer. A twisted smirk of anticipation.

"River," Flora moans.

Daphne stalks back to Chase, who visibly shrinks back. The two men holding him jerk him forward, pulling his arms out wide so he forms a cross. Offering him up to be tortured.

"She can't..." Echo whispers.

"You will be an example," Daphne hisses. "Of what happens when you don't stay where you belong."

Oren glances at the Betadome, his gaze focused beyond the metal net, as if he's looking straight at River. As if he's asking him exactly how far he'll go in the search for the Sovereign.

What River will sacrifice? Will he do whatever it takes, just like Oren is?

River's arms loosen around Flora, having no idea what the right choice is.

Let Chase be tortured, probably killed, as they watch?

Or allow his twin to try and save him, no matter the consequences to her?

Oren turns back to Daphne. "Start with his clothes."

Daphne's eyes light up as if she likes that idea. She waves the burning tip in front of Chase's face. Moves it across his chest, leaving a singed streak in its wake.

Then lowers it to the hem of his shirt.

Flora uncoils in River's arms and he doesn't stop her. He would do the same for Echo.

"It was me!" Makk leaps to his feet and scrambles the few feet up the incline so he can be seen. "I was with Chase."

A slow, satisfied smile spreads across Oren's face. He waves a hand toward Daphne, telling her to step down. "And who else was with you, boy?"

Makk plants his hands on his hips. "I don't need no grown up to look after me. Chase said he needed to get some food, so I was his lookout." He puffs out his chest. "Like I always am. I got the best eyesight in all of the Dead Zone. I can see a bee a mile off. I sometimes hang around the Betadome just so I can let anyone know if one of them deadly bastards get through—"

"Enough," Oren snaps. "Bees are our saviors—"

"Not on this side of the net." Makk crosses his arms. "I was the one who told Chase you were coming after that weird lightning hit. I've also got the best hearing in any Zone. I can hear a Green Born fart, which you do a lot of seeing as you eat so much."

River's eyes are so wide they sting. Makk is either extremely brave or extremely foolish, possibly a bit of both. Does he realize exactly who Oren is? What he's capable of?

Oren slices an agitated hand through the air. "Silence!"

"Let Chase go," Makk shoots right back.

Flora gasps and Echo wipes a hand down her face. Makk's intent to save them all is about to backfire. Even Tuff is shaking his head, imperceptibly but furiously as he stands behind Oren and the others.

Oren curls his lip at Makk. "Your Dead Born friend will be coming with us." He slides a glance toward Daphne. "For a longer chat."

Daphne holds up the stick and jabs it into Chase's shoulder, wrenching a cry out of him as the faint hiss of burning flesh fills the air. She yanks it back, notes that the fire's been extinguished, and throws it to the ground. "Some of us will be doing more talking than others."

Oren glances at the men holding Chase. "You know where to take him." The men spin Chase around and march him to the green door, obedient as always. Oren glances at Tuff. "Make sure no one sees him."

For the first time since River met him, Tuff hesitates. His gaze flickers to Makk, but then he spins on his heel and follows. Oren strides to the net of the Betadome, his hard gaze on the young boy. "Use that mouth of yours to tell everyone in your dirty colony to stay away from the Betadome."

Makk jams a hand on his hip. "Or I could use it to tell them you're as much of a monster as bees are."

River buries his face in his hands as he suppresses a groan. He doesn't need to see his father's face to know that sort of insubordination won't be tolerated. Yet when he looks up, Oren is stalking away, ushering Daphne with him.

He leans in to say something and River assumes he won't be able to hear it.

"You were a sight to behold, my dear."

Daphne seems to grow an inch as she sways toward Oren, and River's stomach suddenly feels like it's full of acid. Nothing about his world was what it seemed.

The moment the green door closes behind them, Makk leaps down the incline, grinning. "You're welcome."

River's not sure whether he should hug or shake the boy. He doesn't get to do either because Flora launches herself into his arms. "River, we have to do something! Daphne's going to..."

His gaze connects with Echo's. Neither of them wants to finish that sentence.

"Do you have any idea where they may take him?" Echo asks, although River can already tell she knows the answer.

"The Restricted Area is the safest place in all of the Green Zone." Because it's the most secret.

And a harvest is the ultimate torture.

Echo nods grimly. She turns to Flora. "We can't go there when it's light."

"It's too dangerous," River adds, hoping she'll understand.

Chase is going to spend the day in the Sting. Even though Oren and Daphne are going to try and break him. Even though Chase carries the knowledge that the Dead Zone has its own secrets.

Even though the rebellion could be over before it started.

Flora nods, her face white and tear streaked. "But when the sun goes down?"

River and Echo's gazes connect once more. A second understanding passes between them.

The moment darkness falls, they're returning to the Sting.

And they won't come back without Chase.

CHAPTER
TWENTY-THREE
ECHO

Echo stretches out on the mat in Nola's hut, enjoying the soothing sound of River's rhythmic breathing. He hadn't wanted to leave Flora, but she was exhausted and insisted on returning to her hut alone while they wait for nightfall. They were all in need of a rest. Echo should perhaps be the most exhausted of all after what she went through to collect the queen, but she knows the worry alone will be enough to wipe Flora out for a few hours. Seeing the guy you love being beaten then dragged away is about the worst thing Echo could imagine. Even worse than going through it yourself.

She puts an arm across River's chest and snuggles closer. If it had been River on the receiving end of Daphne's fist, she's not sure anyone could have held her down. Which is how she can understand why Makk jumped out of their hiding place to save Chase, even though he'd risked everything. She'd been so close to doing it herself. The only thing stopping her had been the thought that if she revealed herself to Oren, that poor girl in the crypt would have died for nothing.

"Did you sleep?" River murmurs.

"A little." She lifts her head and leans up on her elbow so she can look at him.

"Your skin is heaps better. I can barely see the stings." He runs his fingertips across her cheek. "How's your breathing?"

"I'm fine," she says. "The adrenacure worked its magic. It's like it never happened."

"But it did." He closes his eyes and shudders. "You were so brave."

"No, that was you." She laughs gently. "I still can't believe you ran in there like that."

"I couldn't let them keep stinging you," he says, turning serious.

"Well, you're my hero." She rests her head beside him and looks up at the chain of plastic flowers Jupiter made for their hut. "You could have died."

"Do you think Chase is dead?" he asks quietly.

"No." She can't possibly believe that to be true. "Oren will want him to talk first. And Chase would rather die than talk."

"Daphne was like a mother to me." His whole body goes rigid with anger. "After my mom died, my whole world fell apart. Daphne was a constant. Always there supporting the three of us. But now I see what she was doing. What she's really like…"

Echo nods as she listens. "You don't mention your mom often."

He shrugs. "You know how it is. You don't mention yours much either. What was your mom like?"

"I'm not really sure," she answers as honestly as she can. "I was only young when the scurge took her. I remember the essence of her more than I actually remember her, if that makes sense."

River slips an arm under her head and pulls her closer. "It does."

"Can I ask how your mom died?" Echo bites down on her bottom lip the moment she's voiced the question, unsure why she's pushing him to talk. It's clear that it's a sensitive topic.

"It was a fire," he says without hesitation. "Which is one of the reasons why Flora was freaking out so much today."

"Oh, River." As if it hadn't been traumatic enough for Flora to watch Oren set fire to the tree. "Should we check on her? Maybe it wasn't a good idea to leave her alone."

"She's tough. And it's almost dark anyway." River sits up and stretches, and Echo can't help but admire his lean strength. "We should head over."

There's a quick knock on their door and it flies open.

"Why is this door so small?" Flora grumbles as she crawls through. "Was your friend very short?"

"No." Echo stands, glad Flora hadn't barged in on a more intimate moment. "Just paranoid. She thought a smaller door would let in fewer bees."

Flora seems confused, no doubt thinking that there aren't any bees in the Dead Zone for Nola to have been worried about. But Nola had never been one to bow to logic.

"We were just going to check on you," says River, giving Flora a quick hug. "How are you?"

"We have to get Chase back," Flora says, ignoring his question. She has dark circles under her bloodshot eyes and clearly didn't get any rest. "We can't leave him in the Sting. He got you two out when you were trapped in there."

"We're getting him back," says Echo firmly. "Nobody's leaving him in there."

"I made disguises." Flora holds up three masks she's fashioned out of scraps of old clothing with holes cut out for their eyes. She pulls one over her face. "We won't be able to get past Oren's cameras in the Betadome, but at least he won't know who we are."

"Good thinking." River takes a mask and hands the other to Echo. "He'll think we're Razers."

The door swings open again and Jupiter hurries in. The hut instantly seems smaller with four of them inside.

"The Razers are on their way here," says Jupiter, panting. "Makk told them what happened. They're furious! They want to go with you to the Sting."

"No!" Flora is aghast. "They'll ruin everything."

"I tried to tell them that." Jupiter runs their hand through their short hair. "But Makk tells a good story. He got them all riled up. They're determined to get involved."

"Chase is their leader," says River on a sigh. "Of course, they want to rescue him."

Flora's jaw falls open. "You think we should let them?"

"I never said that." River goes to the flap at the back of the hut that Nola used to empty her bedpan and opens it.

Echo grins, remembering the last time they used that hatch as an escape and almost landed in Nola's mess. Hopefully it's a much dryer landing today.

"Hold the Razers off as long as you can," River says to Jupiter before pulling on his mask and darting through the hatch.

Needing no encouragement, Flora is right behind him.

"Thanks, Jupiter." Echo gives Jupiter a quick hug before putting on her mask and disappearing through the hatch. She lands on her feet with a thud, pleased to find there's nothing but dust beneath her soles.

"You lead the way, Echo." Flora's green eyes are shining behind her mask. She's more determined than any of them to get Chase back. Which is saying something given Echo's burning with the injustice of what happened to him.

Echo darts through the maze of streets of the Dead Zone, knowing them like she's come to know each line and contour of River's face. Whatever rest they had in the hut is going to have to be enough. Now that night is falling, they have no time to waste.

They leave the village and start making their way up the incline toward the Betadome just as dusk turns to night. When they reach the same place they'd been hiding only hours earlier, Echo crouches down and scans the Betadome. She can still smell the fire, the scent of ash mingling with the dust and despair that permeates the Dead Zone.

River puffs as he jogs up beside Echo, lifting his mask to take in more air.

"Catch your breath," says Flora. "On my signal, we're going straight in. No detours. No dodging cameras. We run straight through the Betadome to the green door and out into the Green Zone. Then we go straight to the Sting. Don't stop for anyone. No matter what."

Echo frowns as a sick feeling winds its way through her stomach. She takes off her mask and tucks it in the back pocket of her ragged jeans.

"What's wrong?" River asks, sensing her hesitation.

"We're making a mistake," she says cautiously. "This plan is never going to work."

"Do you have a better one?" Flora snaps with an uncharacteristically snarky tone. "I agree this is risky, but like I said before, Chase has risked plenty for both of you in the past."

"But he was smart about it." Echo pushes up her mask, her heart breaking for Flora and the stress she must be feeling. "This isn't smart. We're rushing. We're going to end up getting ourselves killed. Then we're no use to anyone. Especially Chase."

"She's right," says River. "Chase wouldn't approve of this. We need to slow down."

"We can't," Flora pleads. "He needs us."

"Getting into the Sting is going to be even harder than last time," says River. "Oren will have locked the laundry room, which means we're going to have to do it dressed as Dead Borns. It's impossible. We're being hasty."

Flora lets out a long sigh. "They could really be hurting him in there. He was already hurt. You saw what Daphne did to him."

"Which is why we need to make sure we succeed when we rescue him," says Echo, glancing in the direction of the Alphadome, an idea sparking to life. "Flora, do you have the queen?"

"I took her to the Alphadome," Flora says, getting impatient as she adjusts her mask. "While you were resting."

"But why?" River asks.

"To keep her safe." Flora shrugs. "Everything the queen needs to survive is inside that glass column. She'd have died if we kept her in that tiny prism too long."

"Oh." River nods. "Good thinking."

Echo is impressed. She hadn't thought of that. If the queen died, everything they went through today would have been a waste. Flora has got to be one of the cleverest people she's ever met. It's no wonder really that River loves her so much. She figured out something was wrong with the Green Zone long before anyone else had thought to raise so much as an eyebrow.

"Why don't we go to the Alphadome now that we know the queen is already there?" Echo suggests cautiously. "You can test me. If I'm the Sovereign—"

"*When* you're the Sovereign," River corrects.

"When I'm the Sovereign," she repeats with slightly less conviction. "Then everything changes anyway."

Flora shakes her head adamantly. "No, we need to get to Chase now. We can't wait."

"We will get him," Echo insists. "The test won't take long. We need to know before we risk ourselves in the Green Zone."

"It's a much smarter plan," says River.

"And what if you're not the Sovereign?" Flora asks cautiously.

"Then you and River go and save Chase." Echo slips her hand into River's. "Don't undo everything we've achieved by insisting on rushing into a plan that's never going to work. Besides, the longer we wait to test me, the more we risk the queen dying like last time."

"She's right, Flora." River squeezes her hand. "We need to do it now."

"Then I'll go to the Green Zone by myself," says Flora, still not giving in.

"Five minutes," says River. "That's all we need to do the test. Then we can stick together."

"Come on, Flora," says Echo. "Be smart."

"Fine." Flora marches off toward the Alphadome. "Hurry up then!"

"I want to save Chase as much as she does," Echo whispers.

"We all want to save him." River pulls her in for a hug. "Flora just has a thing about being ganged up on, that's all. She used to accuse Mom of siding with me, so she's sensitive."

Echo nods. There are so many things she doesn't understand about having a sibling.

"I know we need to get this over with," he says. "But I'm still dreading it."

"Me, too." The sick feeling in Echo's stomach worsens. "Although, I'd rather die at the hands of a queen than Daphne. Really, I'm just taking the coward's way out."

"Hardly." River tightens his embrace and drops a kiss on her forehead. "I love you, Echo."

"I love you, too." She lifts her chin and kisses him, trying to push away the thought that this could be the last time their lips meet. The whole thing seems so unfair, which is a stupid thought given her entire life has been like that. River's has, too. At least Echo wasn't lied to by her parents. That's one consolation she can hold onto.

Breaking away, she loops her locket over her head and puts it around River's neck. No words are needed this time to explain why. He'll take care of it if he needs to. There's nobody she trusts more.

Flora already has the hatch to the Alphadome open by the time they reach it and has disappeared into its eerie depths. Echo takes one long glance around at the dark nothingness that's her home and follows Flora, pleased when the lights blink on.

River closes the door behind them with a thud and seals them in.

"This isn't how it ends," he tells Echo as they descend. "You're the Sovereign. I'm even more sure of it after what happened in the Betadome today. Nobody else could have withstood so many stings. It has to be you."

"She's still alive." Flora points to the glass column where the queen is being stored. "She doesn't look terribly happy, but she's alive."

"Let's do this then." Echo marches straight into the glass dome in the center of the room and closes the door behind her. She can't bear to say goodbye to River again. There have already been way too many farewells between them. It's time to get this over with.

She sits down on the chair and waits for Flora to retrieve the queen.

"Echo!" River's eyes fly open in a panic, and he throws open the door to the dome.

"It's okay!" she protests, holding up her hands. "Let's just get it over with."

"Someone's coming." He grabs her by the wrist and hauls her out of the chair. "I can hear them putting in the code. Flora!"

Flora moves one way then the other, not seeming to know which way to turn. River drags Echo out of the dome, takes Flora's hand and pulls them into the one hiding spot available in the Alphadome.

The dark passageway to the crypt.

They press themselves against the wall and heave oxygen into their lungs, trying to quieten their breathing. The feeling of déjà vu is not a welcome one.

Heavy footsteps clomp down the stairs, and a familiar *tap, tap, tap,* starts up inside the crypt. Both sounds are equally terrifying.

"What are you waiting for, Tuff?" Oren snaps. "Take him to the Worker."

Echo's eyes fly wide open as she dares to peek out and catches a glimpse of Tuff holding a battered Chase in his arms. His face is bruised and bleeding, and his clothes are charred and torn. If they're taking him to the crypt, does that mean he's already dead?

Tuff grunts, but his feet remain still.

"Come on then," Oren says. "I like to tuck my children into bed."

"You don't like it in there." Tuff's voice is quiet, more like a whisper. Echo had almost forgotten that he chooses not to talk to anyone in the Green Zone. And while she's heard him talk to Oren before, it seems he likes to keep his words to the bare minimum.

Oren sneers at him. "I don't like it. But I'll make an exception this time. My Worker won't hurt us. By the time her programming changes take effect, we'll be far away from here."

Programming changes? Echo has no idea what that means. And she really doesn't want to find out.

Realizing they have no other choice, Echo, River and Flora tiptoe along the dark corridor and enter the crypt. The *tap, tap, tap,* gets louder and Echo's heart rate follows suit. She hates knowing she's so close to that creature.

A dim glow lights the room and the giant metallic bee comes to a stop, rubbing its forelegs together and tilting its giant head as it inspects them.

"She only harvests dead people," Echo whispers, more for herself than anyone. "We're not dead."

"There's nowhere to hide," Flora hisses, waving her arms to show the Worker she's most definitely alive.

"Get on a shelf." River pushes Echo and Flora toward the long rack of bodies that line the rear wall. "Hurry!"

Echo climbs into the first empty shelf she sees, while River and Flora do the same. It's not until she's halfway in that she realizes it's not actually empty. Thankfully all that remains are a pile of crumbled bones, but it's enough to send shivers down her spine all the same.

"I'm so sorry," she whispers, hoping whoever those bones belonged to forgives her. Surely, they would understand.

The Worker taps and clacks and lets out a screech, seeming unsure what to do with her three new subjects who are behaving as if they're dead, yet are clearly still alive.

Footsteps clomp down the corridor and Echo freezes, torn between wanting to be as convincing as possible to Oren that she's dead, but not so convincing that she fools the Worker.

"Be quick," says Oren from the doorway. He might have claimed not to be afraid of his Worker but it's clear he doesn't want to get any closer to her than he has to.

There's a low moan that sounds like Chase. Echo lets out a sigh to realize he's still alive. At least not everything has gone wrong with this plan. She dares to open her eyes a crack and sees Tuff settling Chase on the floor at the Worker's agitated feet. He backs away slowly with his palms raised, returning to Oren's side.

The Worker makes a whirring sound and the large circle on her back lights up. She's getting excited, almost as if she can sense Chase's imminent death. Soon, it will be time for her to feed.

"Excellent," says Oren. "Be in peace, Chase. You Dead Born scum."

"How long?" Tuff asks.

"Not very," sneers Oren. "We should have just enough time to get out of here. In a few minutes, our Worker will be switched over to crave the living instead of the dead."

CHAPTER
TWENTY-FOUR
RIVER

River listens to the footsteps receding, each faint thud feeling louder than his own heartbeat.

Each one another thunderous second that passes.

Yet he doesn't move after he can no longer hear Oren or Tuff. They'd be climbing the stairs to the hatch. River's lips move as he silently counts to ten.

Hoping on his dead mother's soul that it's not too short and Oren and Tuff will come running back in, meaning they'll be captured after all.

Praying that it's not too long, and the Worker ends this before it could even begin.

One. Two. Three.

The Worker hasn't moved as she stands over Chase, meaning her programming hasn't switched over.

Four. Five. Six.

A soft sob reaches him from Flora's shelf. River's fingers twitch, silently begging her not to move, not knowing whether he's counting to their escape.

Or their death.

Seven. Eight.

The Worker makes her whirring sound, launching River's heart into his throat. Above him, Echo shifts and there's the unmistakable rattle of bones.

There's a clack, then another as the Worker's legs ripple and rearrange, but she doesn't make another move.

Nine.

Another groan wrenches out of Chase, and River has no idea whether the sound will save his life. Right now, the Worker has no interest in him because he's alive. The moment some programmed switch flicks, being alive will be his greatest vulnerability.

Ten.

"Now," River hisses.

Echo's already leapt to the ground before he's finished. Wordlessly, they split up and run to opposite sides of the crypt, dividing around the Worker. Flora stumbles from her shelf, looking at them with eyes the size of Nola's half-door.

The Worker draws herself up, now on alert. Her massive head twitches from side to side, those glass eyes watching River and Echo as they converge in front of her. She rears up as she lets out a furious screech, her wings snapping out, blocking River's view of his terrified sister.

"We have to grab Chase!" Echo shouts as she dives to her knees and skids the remaining distance.

Right in front of the Worker.

Just as the mechanical bee's forelegs crash back onto the floor, framing Chase.

It feels like there's nothing but adrenaline rushing through River's veins as he leaps to join Echo. Simultaneously, they grab Chase under the arms as his head lolls. His eyes are closed, for which River's glad.

Seeing the Worker this close is the most terrifying sight he's ever seen.

A faint glow frames her thanks to the panel on her back, illuminating black and silver steel. Smooth, impenetrable armor. And a seamless, soulless machine designed to kill.

The Worker's jaws open wide and a piercing screech sends fear straight to River's marrow. She bears down, antennae pointed at them with deadly accuracy. Her legs hitting the tiled floor feel like a crack of lightning.

The need to run threatens to consume River's mind.

He yanks his gaze away to focus on Chase. The one they're trying to save rather than themselves. He and Echo haul at his lifeless body.

It doesn't budge.

"He's trapped," Echo says desperately.

River sees what she means. A part of Chase's shirt is pinned beneath one of the Worker's legs.

"River!" Echo screams.

He rolls out of the way a blink before another of the Worker's legs impale where he was just kneeling. There's no second strike, though, because the mechanical bee turns to Echo, her antenna poised like spears. Echo scrambles back at the last second, clearly hating leaving Chase where he is. The Worker screeches again, her glass eyes flickering between Chase lying prone before her, and River and Echo a few feet away, breathing hard.

Yet the Worker doesn't want any of them.

She just wants to protect her brood. Her food source.

Which gives River an idea.

He runs to the nearest shelf, instantly attracting the Worker's attention. Her head twists sharply, her focus now completely on him.

"Drag Chase out," River shouts, as he reaches out blindly,

his hand connecting with what feels like soft paper. "Now! Flora!"

His words do two things. They snap his sister out of her stupor and she darts to help Echo.

And the Worker becomes a blur of movement.

River doesn't get a chance to see whether Echo and Flora succeed because he has only a handful of seconds. He grabs the body on the shelf, disgust injecting through the adrenaline as he sees what felt like paper is parched, gray skin. Not giving himself time to think, he shoves the body, blanching when the arm dislocates at the shoulder as the mummified skeleton caves in on itself.

The Worker screeches again, this time far louder and longer. The sound grates over River's ear drums. Scrapes down his spine. And claws at his mind with the promise of retribution.

She rockets toward him, her legs an inch above the ground, and he darts away, his breath sawing up and down his throat. One glance reveals that Echo and Flora are dragging the now free Chase toward the opening to this catacomb of death. All they have to do is get him past the entrance and the Worker will leave them alone.

The Worker leaps and River throws his body to the side in a desperate attempt to avoid the attack. He loses his center of gravity as he lands, which costs him precious split-seconds as he scrabbles to gain momentum.

Each beat of his out-of-control pulse counts the moment when he'll be captured.

His feet finally gain traction and he shoots forward. A glance over his shoulder reveals the Worker has attached herself to the shelf as her front legs and antennae poke and prod the crumpled skeleton. Her head snaps to look at him, gears and lights flickering behind her glass eyes.

"River!" Echo screams. "Quick!"

Her voice is like a whip around his body, because River launches forward with speed he didn't know he possessed. Echo and Flora drag Chase over the last few feet as he reaches them and he bends down to grip the same arm Flora has. Together, they haul Chase through the archway that separates the crypt from the dark corridor.

The Worker runs for the entrance, but just like last time, she doesn't follow them. She shrieks her fury at their desecration of her nest, making Flora duck instinctively.

"Come on," Echo pants. "We need to get Chase out of here."

She and River return to dragging him, yanking a pained moan out of him. Flora looks from Chase to the Worker and back again, her face pale in the gloom.

"What...what about the programming Oren spoke of?" she gasps.

"All the more reason to get moving," Echo growls.

Flora jolts into action, joining Echo so they can both pull at the same arm. River glances over his shoulder. The light from the main room beckons. The Worker watches them, her antennae twitching and metal jaws working. But she doesn't attack.

They only need a few more minutes.

River's just caught sight of the Alphadome when the glow at the other end of the tunnel shuts off. The crypt is plunged into darkness. River stops, as do Echo and Flora.

"That's a good thing?" Flora asks tremulously. "She's going to sleep?"

Except that didn't happen last time.

The Worker wouldn't sleep.

As if she heard River's thoughts, the rounded entrance bursts to life. The circle on the back of the Worker fills the corridor with blue-tinted light, illuminating her metallic outline.

"River..." Echo says.

She doesn't need to finish the sentence. They both know this isn't good.

That they're now staring at a completely different Worker.

Oren's words seem to fill the air. *Our Worker will be switched over to crave the living instead of the dead.*

Her antennae twitch forward, then backward toward the crypt, then forward again. And stay there. Her eyes flash with brilliant, cold light.

And she shoots toward them.

"Run!" River screams, bending down to grab Chase again, Echo already doing the same.

"We need to get him into the Alphadome," Echo gasps.

"Yes!" River hisses. "The Alphadome."

For once, that glass dome can protect someone from a bee, not trap them inside with one.

Chase groans as they wrench him along, no longer worried about the pain this could be causing him. Behind them, the corridor fills with the whirring and clattering legs of the Worker. The sound grows faster than they can escape it.

Flora darts past them. "I'll open the door!"

River grunts as he and Echo half-run, half-stumble, hauling Chase with them. The head start they had on the Worker rapidly shrinks as her six legs power her down the corridor.

"Hurry!" Flora calls from the open door of the Alphadome.

Except River and Echo are already going as fast as they can. They pull Chase into the main room, the white light illuminating exactly how bruised and bloodied he is. His eyes are puffy and his lip is split in three places. His clothes are charred...as are multiple weeping sores anywhere his skin shows. But he's alive.

For now.

The Worker bursts from the corridor only a second or two after they do and her gleaming black wings snap out. Making her bigger.

Giving her more speed.

Flora appears by Echo's side. "Quick," she sobs, helping them drag Chase.

The Worker leaps, her front legs snapping out to impale Chase's feet. River and Echo pull him up hard and the metal tips smash into the tiled floor, cracking it. The Worker leaps again and Flora screams.

Just as they drag Chase through the door of the Alphadome.

The moment they're inside, Flora slams the door closed before the Worker can spear a leg through. The robotic bee shrieks, becoming a frenzy as she crawls over the hexagonal dome, looking for a way in.

River pants as they pull Chase to the center, a rapidly moving shadow crossing over above them. The crystalline sound of the Worker's legs rapidly tapping on the glass seems to match his heart rate.

Then it spikes when the sound stops.

The Worker hovers above them, lights flickering deep in the machination of her eyes. One antenna reaches down and scrapes over the glass, sending ripples down River's spine. The second antenna joins the first as the Worker explores the surface of the Alphadome.

Takes her measure.

More lights flicker inside the mechanical predator's mind. But what's most terrifying is the whirring sound that follows. It's muffled by the glass, but the meaning is unmistakable.

The Worker is excited.

She has a plan.

Flora throws herself over Chase's body, already sobbing. She knows she has no ability to protect him. That if the Worker gets through, she'll be dead moments before Chase.

The Worker lifts a front leg high above her and spears it down. River and the others duck as it slams into the glass. He waits for shards to rain down on them. For the first flimsy pane to shatter.

But the glass holds firm.

"Oren would've made it strong," Echo gasps. "So the Green Borns couldn't escape."

Relief and horror churn in River's gut. The Alphadome's strength could be their savior. Because it was designed to be someone else's tomb.

The Worker screeches, bringing a second leg down with even greater speed. More force.

But the glass doesn't smash.

She starts to circle, her legs tapping and scratching over the glass. The sound feels like it's doing the same over River's skull.

He and Echo stand up on either side of Chase and Flora, watching the deadly machine as she plans her next steps. Without warning, she strikes the glass in the same place.

Again.

And again.

"She's not going to give up," Flora sobs, pulling Chase closer.

River stills as he realizes something. While they're all in there, the Worker will smash through the glass to get to them. Her prey is trapped in a bubble, the only thing separating them are sheets of hexagonal glass. No matter how tempered or strengthened they are, it's no match for the Worker.

And Flora's right.

The Worker won't give up. It's in her *programming*.

Making a decision, River runs for the door. "I'll distract her."

"No, River!" Echo cries, darting to his side. He turns to her, wanting to tell her it's the only way, but she grabs the handle. "We both will."

She's yanked it open before he can respond.

The Worker's response is instantaneous. She scrambles over the Alphadome, a fresh blast of whirring filling the air as she shoots toward the noise that just alerted her.

Her prey is coming to her.

River and Echo sprint out of the Alphadome as Flora slams the door shut behind them. There's no chance to glance at each other, to have a plan beyond creating as much distance between the Worker and the Alphadome.

With unspoken agreement, they split up. Echo darts left while River darts right.

All he can hope is that the Worker will choose him first.

TWENTY-FIVE

ECHO

Echo waves her hands above her head as she runs, desperately trying to attract the Worker's attention away from River. He'd darted in the opposite direction, leaving him nowhere to go. The Worker is powering after him, closing the gap.

With her eyes on River, Echo crashes into the far wall, wincing as her shoulder takes the force. But her pain is quickly forgotten as a section of the wall withdraws, revealing itself as a door when a handle emerges from one of the tiles.

"Over here!" she shouts to River, hardly daring to believe what she's seeing.

At the sound of Echo's voice, the Worker expertly changes direction, spinning on her six legs and advancing.

"No!" River pauses his steps, then runs around the glass dome, his eyes focussed on Echo.

Echo pulls on the door handle, hoping there's no lock. It doesn't budge, so she pulls harder, sweat pouring down her forehead.

"It slides!" River barrels up beside her and tugs on the

handle. The door rolls to the side and River pushes Echo through and slams it closed behind them.

There's a loud crash as the Worker throws herself at the door and it shudders on its tracks. River keeps hold of the handle on the other side, using his full weight to keep it closed.

But the Worker is too strong and the door inches open.

Echo lunges forward, helping River to close the gap.

"We won't be able to keep her out." River's face contorts from the strain.

Echo yelps as she pushes harder, knowing he's right. The Worker is mechanical with seemingly limitless endurance. Their human strength is already weakening, and they've only been holding the door closed for a few seconds.

Glancing around the room, she takes in their surroundings. They're in a smaller version of the LaB. There are dozens of glass columns stretching from ceiling to floor, and benches are covered in test tubes, bottles and canisters. Reed would love it in here. Perhaps he was the one to set it up? But Echo has no time to think about that now. She needs a plan, and she needs it fast.

"Can you hold the door closed?" she asks on a groan. "Just for a few seconds."

The door shudders more violently as the Worker tries to break her way in.

River repositions himself to put more force behind his grip and nods. "I think so."

Echo darts across the small room and takes a canister of adrenacure as well as a black one that looks like the venom that Daphne shot Trid with. She shoves them in her back pocket, trying not to think about the unnecessary risk they put themselves in when they went to the Sting to retrieve something they could have taken from here if only they'd found this room earlier.

She spins around, seeing the door has opened a couple of inches. The Worker has pushed one of her long metallic legs through the gap and is waving it around wildly as she tries to force it open further.

Echo rushes back and helps River slam the door closed. The Worker screeches as her leg thrashes, then flops as it's crushed by the sudden force of the heavy door.

"Again!" River pulls the door open a crack, then immediately slams it closed.

Echo works with him and together they open and close the door four more times before the leg clatters to the floor. It twitches like it's still alive then goes completely still. Meanwhile, the Worker's screams rattle around the room on the other side of the door like she can feel the pain of the amputation. Hopefully Flora and Chase are still safely locked inside the glass dome.

"Let's do it again!" River cries as his green eyes light up. "We'll take another leg."

Echo nods her agreement. If they can destabilize this beast, they might have a chance of overpowering her.

"Ready?" River asks.

"Ready."

They pull the door back by two inches and wait. It doesn't take long and another long leg pokes through the gap. River and Echo don't hesitate to slam the door closed with as much force as they can muster. The Worker screams as her leg is crushed, and they pull back the door, preparing to go again.

But this time the leg withdraws and the Alphadome falls silent.

"She learned what happened," says Echo, her eyes wide with awe.

"Just wait." River holds his position. "She'll be back."

Echo draws in some deep breaths, keeping her body tense,

but at the same time giving her muscles a brief reprieve. Just how clever is this evil creation of Oren's if she can learn from experience and apply it to her future actions?

"Where is she?" Echo whispers.

"She's there." River keeps his focus on the small gap in the door. "She's trying to take us by surp—"

An almighty shake rocks the door as it's forced back several more inches. Echo pushes forward with everything she has, knowing River's doing the same. But it's not enough. Despite missing a limb and having another damaged one, the Worker has the advantage of strength over them. Bit by bit, the door opens further.

Instead of poking one thin leg through, the Worker edges her entire much more robust body into the gap.

"It's no use!" screams River as the door opens further. "We can't hold her back."

"Lure her over to you." Echo lets go of the door and scoops up the severed mechanical leg.

River's eyes flare, but he nods, trusting her completely as he lets go of the door, placing himself directly in front of the gap. He's the most brave and beautiful sight Echo's ever seen and it's all she can do to hope that her plan is going to work.

The door flings open all the way and the Worker leaps. She wobbles slightly as she finds her balance. Her remaining damaged front leg hangs limply by her side, while her hind and middle legs support her weight. She screeches when she spots River. With antennae twitching and the large light on her back flashing, she advances on her prey.

River backs into a corner with his hands up and Echo moves so she's behind the terrifying beast. Steadying her shaking hands, she raises the severed limb above her head and waits.

The Worker rears up and a high-pitched noise erupts as her middle legs swipe at River.

Echo sees her chance and slams the severed leg down on the Worker's back. The glass circle shatters and light spills out, bathing the stark room in yellows and reds and greens and blues. In the center of the rainbow made from tiny globes is a pink, spongy substance that's pulsing like a heartbeat.

The Worker squeals but doesn't turn. Instead, she grips River by the neck with one of her middle legs and lifts him from the ground. His face twists in pain and Echo catches sight of her locket dangling on his chest.

It wasn't supposed to be like this! She was the one who was putting herself in danger. There's no way she can allow the guy she loves to be taken so mercilessly by an evil creation of his father.

With a scream of her own erupting from her lips, Echo drops the bee's mechanical leg, snatches the adrenacure from her back pocket and injects the Worker directly into her spongy heart.

Two terrifying seconds pass where nothing happens. Then the Worker lifts River higher and his hands clutch at his throat as she tightens her grip on him. The adrenacure has had zero effect.

"Damn it!" Echo screams, reaching for the venom gun and shooting it into the beast's heart. She hopes it's deadly to the Worker. Because if that doesn't work, she's going to have to reach in with her bare hands and remove that pulsing life-source herself.

The Worker immediately freezes with River still dangling in the air. Then she trembles and River's released, sent tumbling to the ground in a heap. He clasps his throat as he heaves for air. The Worker wobbles then crashes to her side, falling against one of the tall glass columns and smashing it to pieces. Her giant body twitches violently, then goes still.

Echo isn't sure where to turn first. She wants to go to River to make sure he's okay, but she needs to know the Worker isn't going to come after him again.

She goes to the Worker and squats down beside her, getting ready to tear out her heart at the first sign of movement. But the pulsing has slowed to a stop, the pink color of the fleshy organ quickly turning gray.

"She's dead," Echo says, letting out a long breath of disbelief. Her plan actually worked. It had felt like such a long shot when she'd thought of it, but she'd literally had no other options.

Picking up the empty venom gun, she reads a label on the side. *Apitoxin.* She's going to have to ask Flora what that means.

A movement to her left has Echo tensing once again and she stands and spins around, seeing a bee flying around the shattered remains of the glass column she was being held captive in. The insect lands on the Worker's lifeless heart and Echo freezes, studying the long abdomen, short wings and shiny hairless back.

There's no doubt whatsoever she's looking at a queen.

A groan rattles from the corner of the room and Echo holds up a hand. "River. Don't move."

She may have managed to kill the Worker, but in the process, she released another equally deadly threat.

"What's wrong?" River whispers.

"There's a queen," she replies, without taking her eyes off the small creature that's very much still alive. "She was released when the column broke."

"Stay back." River's voice increases in volume.

"But isn't that exactly what we came in here for?" she asks.

"We have another queen." She glances at River as he carefully sits up. His neck is purple, but he otherwise appears unharmed. "It's safer to test you out there."

Echo squats back down in front of the queen. It's no safer in the Alphadome. River's just buying time. He's not ready to do what he knows must be done.

And while nor is she, she can't bear to wait another minute. Plus, she needs to remove the threat to River. While this queen is loose, he's in grave danger.

The tiny queen rises from the Worker's body and hovers in the air in front of Echo.

They stare at each other, waiting to see who's going to make the first move.

Echo swipes, her hand darting out and missing the queen by an inch. The creature flies off in River's direction and Echo chases after her. She will *not* let River come to harm.

"Stay still!" she screams. "I've got this!"

River sits like a statue, doing exactly as he's told. But she can see in his eyes that he's terrified—not of the bee itself, but of what might happen to Echo when she catches her.

The bee circles River's head, flying at a rapid speed, before landing right on the top of his tousled mop of dark hair. Echo dives forward, skimming her hand across River's head and trapping the queen in her palm.

She stands and holds out her closed fist, feeling the deadly sovereign buzzing in her tiny, dark prison.

"No, Echo!" River scrambles to his feet and Echo can see the bruises flaring around his throat. She'd come so close to losing him. All so they could test if Echo is the Sovereign. This can't go on any longer or someone really will die.

It's time to end this once and for all.

She shakes her hand, aggravating the bee, and feels a tiny stab on her flesh.

"It's done." She winces as the angry queen stings again.

Balling her fist tighter, she crushes the bee, feeling one last defiant sting on her finger as the deadly insect dies. She opens her hand and lets it fall to the floor.

River dives for the box of adrenacure and gets a canister ready. "How are you feeling? Can you breathe?"

"I can't tell yet." Echo becomes aware of the rapid rise and fall of her chest and the way her heart is racing, but there's no way to know if it's being caused by the sting or the stress of the situation.

Flora chooses that moment to burst into the room. She scans her surroundings and sees the giant, dead Worker and River standing beside Echo, ready to inject her.

"What happened?" Flora asks with wide eyes.

"I've been stung." Echo holds up her palm with the three tiny dots where the queen pierced her skin.

"I don't understand." Flora looks to River, whose eyes are glued to Echo. "What stung you? The Worker?"

"No, we killed the Worker." Echo shakes her head. "With the same thing Daphne used to kill Trid. I thought it was bee venom, but it was labeled Apitoxin."

"That's just a fancy name for bee venom." Flora picks up the empty canister and studies it.

"Echo killed her," says River, dismissing the credit she gave him. "I just sat in the corner and screamed."

"That's not true." Echo puts her hand on her chest, checking to see if her heart is slowing down. "But when she died, she fell on a glass column and a queen flew out. She stung me."

"How do you know it was a queen?" Flora asks, her brow creasing into a sea of furrows.

"See for yourself." Echo points to the ground and Flora dives on the bee to study her.

"Can you breathe?" River asks, still focussed on Echo's health.

Echo turns over her hand and sees the marks have swollen into red lumps. A lightheaded feeling sends her senses spinning.

River grips her by the arms as he steps in closer, preparing to catch her. His eyes fill with tears as he studies her.

"I can breathe." She puts a hand to her stomach, wondering if she's going to throw up. Terror wraps itself around her chest. Something's happening to her. Something... not good. Is it possible that after all this, she's not the Sovereign? She knew there was a possibility of dying from this test, but the reality of it is far worse than she expected.

"It's definitely a queen," says Flora, coming to a stand. She has sweat beading on her forehead and her eyes are wide. "You should be struggling to breathe by now. The venom would be well into your system."

"I don't feel right." Echo moves her hand from her stomach and draws in a deep breath. "My mouth is dry. I'm dizzy. The room is spinning."

Flora takes her hand and presses her shaking fingertips to Echo's wrist and counts.

"Your heart is beating fast," Flora says. "But not as fast as I'd expect. Are you sure that queen was what stung you?"

"She's sure," River answers for her. "You saw the body."

"So, she didn't get those bite marks from anything else?" Flora lets go of Echo's hand and tilts her head, deep in thought.

"We told you." River sounds annoyed now. "She was bitten by a queen."

"And I really don't feel great." Echo leans forward to press her face to River's chest and he grips her tightly.

Flora starts to pace the small room, her hands raking her

hair as she thinks. "River, you need to prepare yourself for the worst."

"She's just having a panic attack," says River, aghast. "If she was having a reaction to the queen's venom, she'd be dead by now. You said as much yourself. Her heart should be beating faster by now."

Echo blinks. The room steadies, just as the swirling in her stomach subsides. With each deep breath she draws in, she begins to feel more normal.

She straightens, strength flowing back into her limbs.

Her hand no longer stings.

She feels...fine.

"Echo?" River pulls back slightly so he can look at her, keeping hold of her in case she loses her balance.

"What?" She looks up into his beloved face and her own eyes fill with tears as the meaning of his words sink in.

"You're the Sovereign." River's voice breaks with emotion. "It's you."

TWENTY-SIX

RIVER

E cho tilts her head up to look at River, her eyes wide. She blinks. Then blinks again. "I'm the Sovereign?" she whispers in wonder.

River cups her face, a grin that feels bigger than any Zone bursting across his face. "You're the Sovereign."

Her own smile takes his breath away. "I'm the Sovereign."

River angles down as she simultaneously moves up and they seal the words with a kiss. It's a kiss of celebration. Of victory.

Of a future that just changed for every soul on the planet.

They pull back, grinning at each other. It's time to produce Immunity.

"I don't understand," Flora says, still pacing the room. "It was definitely a queen, wasn't it?"

River rolls his eyes. His sister has confirmed that more than once. "Yes, it was. And Echo's still alive."

That's how they unequivocally, without a doubt know that Echo's the Sovereign.

Flora turns wide eyes to them. "I don't understand..." she repeats.

"What's there not to understand?" River asks, still grinning. "This is what we came here for."

In those endless seconds, his breath was extinct, his heart didn't beat as he waited to see if Echo would survive the queen bee's stings. It was a moment he'd been dreading since they found out this is what they had to do.

He should never have doubted it, he thinks ruefully. Of course Echo's the Sovereign.

Echo's still smiling as her eyebrows lower quizzically. "You're not happy, Flora?"

His sister spins around. "Of course I am!" Her own smile explodes across her face. "This is wonderful news."

"It really is," River says, squeezing Echo's shoulders.

"Sorry," Flora says, shaking her head. "It's just...a bit of a shock."

Although every atom in River's body is rejoicing, he can understand that his twin is struggling to process this. It's big.

It's massive.

Flora's eyes fly to the door. "I need to check on Chase," she says, quickly exiting the room.

River glances down at the floor. They've been left alone with the dead Worker and the dead queen. He grimaces. "Let's get out of here."

"Agree," Echo says, already leading the way.

They quickly follow Flora, closing the sliding door behind them. Inside the main room, River's surprised to find Chase standing. Admittedly, he's leaning heavily against the side of the Alphadome even as Flora supports him, but he's standing.

He looks at Echo as if he's seeing her with new eyes. "You're the Sovereign," he says, his puffy eyes blinking.

Echo holds up her hand only to look at it more closely. The three welts are gone.

River grins. "She sure is."

Chase looks down at Flora as she props him up a little higher. "What's next?"

Her brow puckers in thought. "We have to harvest some spinal fluid. Then we can produce Immunity for others."

River frowns. "But that means we have to go back to the Sting."

It means Echo has to be harvested by the Worker.

Echo shrugs even though she's a shade paler. "Then that's what we have to do."

Flora chews her lip as she regards Echo. "Maybe we could do it here."

"How?" River asks, jumping on the idea. Going back to the Sting isn't something he wants to contemplate.

Flora's thoughtful gaze goes to Chase, then Echo, before falling on River. "We need Reed. He knows what needs to be done."

River's barely thought of the guy he once called a friend since they left the Green Zone.

"Reed?" Echo asks. "He'd never agree to it."

"Maybe he will," River offers. "Once we tell him the truth."

Echo looks at him skeptically. "Maybe."

"Only one way to find out," Chase grunts, taking a step toward the stairs leading out of the Alphadome.

River leaps forward to help, but Chase holds up a hand. "I've got it," he pants.

"But—"

"I've been dragged around enough, thanks." There's humor in Chase's tone, but also steely determination.

River steps back, acknowledging the leader of the Razers is trying to salvage his pride. Flora throws him a grateful glance before leading Chase to the stairs. River and Echo follow them as Chase limps on, leaning heavily on Flora. Echo nudges River and he looks down, seeing her pointing at the floor of the glass column that houses the queen bees.

A small, dead body is curled up on the tiles.

"Another one?" River mouths. A second queen is dead?

Echo shrugs, clearly wondering at the chances of two dying so close together. Then again, this queen was snatched from her hive in the Betadome, then transported here by Flora. The chances of her surviving that were probably low.

River looks down at Echo, marveling at the brave, strong girl he's holding. If she hadn't grabbed the queen in that room, choosing to get stung before they had a chance to prepare, they may never have found out the truth. Gratitude wells through his heart, filling it, overflowing, and crowding his chest.

He gets to be the guy who protects the Sovereign. Gets to love her. He vows he'll do both with everything he has.

She smiles up at him. "I love you, too," she whispers.

He grins back at her, liking that she can read him so well. Before he can answer, a pained groan comes from Chase, and they both sober. The time to celebrate will be later.

The climb up the stairs is slow and punctuated by Chase's harsh breathing, but they make it to the hatch. River slips past, noting Chase's pasty skin beneath the bruises, and pushes it open.

Outside, the night air is just as dust-tainted and arid as it was when they entered. But everything feels different. River draws in a deep breath, realizing the clogged, dirty feeling in his throat will one day be gone.

Soon, the Dead Zone will cease to exist.

A rustling sound from behind the large rock has River jolting into high alert. Beside him, Chase leaps in front of Flora, swaying dangerously.

Makk runs toward them. "Chase, you're okay." He reels back as he gets close. "Well, you're kinda okay..."

River lets out a relieved breath. "Whoa, Makk! A bit of warning, okay?"

The little boy shrugs. "Sorry?"

River shakes his head, but it's a timely reminder that the threat of Oren is far from gone. In fact, now that they know Echo's the Sovereign, it's even more present. The stakes have just multiplied.

If his father gets his hands on Echo, then Immunity will be gifted to the selected few. To Oren's selected few.

"I'm fine," Chase says through swollen lips. "They only did this because I wouldn't talk."

Makk's chest puffs with pride. "I knew you wouldn't."

River's impressed. He saw a side to Daphne in the Betadome that sends chills down his spine. She looked as if she'd do whatever it took to make Chase talk.

But he didn't.

"I need you to do something—" Chase starts.

"I'm on it," Makk says eagerly.

"Get a message to Tuff. Tell him that Reed needs to come to the Betadome at dawn. Tell him it's urgent."

Makk's gone before River can question whether Reed would even agree to something like that.

"Chase!" Flora gasps.

He crumbles to the ground with a soft groan, taking her with him. River and Echo rush over, but stop when Chase throws them a glare. "I just need a minute."

Echo puts her hands on her hips. "How about you rest right about there?"

"I think that might be a good idea," Chase replies, his lips twisting wryly.

She takes River's hand and tugs him away. "We'll stand watch."

They move to the other side of the rock to give Chase and his pride some privacy, and settle themselves down, their backs against it. River weaves their hands together, staring at their skin in the darkness.

Still the same hands.

Yet everything's changed.

He nudges Echo with his shoulder. "Do I get to call you my queen now?"

She throws him an unimpressed look. "No."

He grins wider. "Your wish is my command, my—"

An elbow lands in his gut, huffing a chuckle out.

"I'm still me," Echo says softly. "A Dead Born."

River presses a kiss to her temple. "You were never just a Dead Born, Echo."

She leans her head against his shoulder. "None of us should ever have been led to believe we can be defined by a label."

Realizing how true that is, River rests his head on hers. As the adrenaline finally fades, as the revelations slowly become their new truth, they sit in silence. River realizes he's exhausted. And hungry. And thirsty. And his neck where the Worker had gripped him hurts like hell.

Yet that's all going to have to wait. These couple of hours of rest are going to have to be enough.

In many ways, their work has just started. Immunity now has to be shared.

And he has no idea what that looks like.

River must doze, because when he opens his eyes from what he assumed was a blink, the sun is casting its first glow on the horizon, gently illuminating the Extinction Zone. The scraggly trees cast wobbly shadows over the barren soil, looking like fragile veins.

Echo sits up and looks around. "We need to get to the Betadome."

To see if Tuff's been able to convince Reed to go there, too.

River climbs to his feet, extending a hand to help Echo up. Together, they circle the rock to go back to Flora and Chase, only to stop. She's curled up beside him, and even though he's bruised and battered, Chase is wrapped protectively around her.

River and Echo glance at each other, wordlessly deciding to let them sleep. Soundlessly, they turn away and trek toward the silvery dome catching the first morning rays. They've just reached it when Makk appears, separating from the pale shadows cast by the trees inside.

"Get down," he hisses. "Reed's coming now."

He grabs River's hand and drags them down the incline, then onto the ground. Lying on their stomachs, they peek over the top. Just as Makk predicted, Reed's passing through the green door.

River's old friend looks just as he remembered with his mop of red curls and freckles that can be seen even at this distance, but what he notices most is the healthy tone to his skin. The way he fills out his suit. River had to notch his trousers tighter this morning because he's already lost weight.

Reed enters the Betadome more fully, looking around. "Hello?" he calls out.

River wonders if Tuff is here, too, but no one else passes through the green door.

Reed plants his hands on his hips. "Ah, hello?" He spins one way, then the other. "It would help if Tuff could actually talk so I'd know why I'm here," he mutters.

He executes another spin, looking more and more irate.

With a huff, he turns back to the green door. "Last time I get yanked out of bed with some cryptic note."

River's about to get up when Makk grabs his arm. "You can't go in the Betadome, remember?"

Because of the cameras.

But how are they going to talk to Reed, then?

Makk answers the question when he shoots to his feet and runs to the black door. Without hesitation, he yanks it open and darts into the Betadome.

Echo gasps. "What's he doing?"

"Something stupid, from the looks of things," River replies, wondering if he should go after the kid.

Makk makes a point of shutting the black door with a thud, making River wince. Noises like that are guaranteed to irritate the bees. Yet Makk acts as if he's running into a play dome. He leaps up and grabs a pear, catching Reed's attention. Makk gives him a jaunty wave, then runs to the next tree and plucks an orange.

"Hey!" Reed shouts, then quickly ducks his head. "You can't take those!"

"Stop me," Makk calls out, this time grabbing a plum, shoving it in his mouth, then snatching two more. He whips around the tree and runs back to the black door.

"That kid has no fear," Echo says in wonder.

Yet, he has Reed racing after him.

"Quick," River says as he pushes to his feet and breaks into a run.

Echo's right beside him as they rush to the black door. They burst through just as Reed's grabbed Makk by the scruff of his neck, a burst of smoke enveloping them. The haze clears and Reed releases the boy the moment he sees who's in front of him.

"River!" he gasps. "Echo!"

Makk slips out of Reed's grasp and darts behind them. "My name's Makk, by the way." He spits out a plum stone and bites into another. "And I was hungry."

Reed ignores him. "What...we were told you were..."

"Well, we're not," River says. "Oren lied."

Reed glances over his shoulder. "Does he know you're here?"

"We don't have time for all the answers," Echo says urgently. "We've found the Sovereign."

Reed's head snaps back toward them. "Impossible!"

"You're looking at her," River says.

Reed's eyebrows shoot up so high that his glasses slip down his nose. He's too stunned to push them back up.

"We need you to come with us," Echo says. "So we can make Immunity for everyone."

Her words snap Reed out of his stupor. "Sure. Come to the Sting and—"

"No," River says sharply. "We're not going back there. We have somewhere we can do this."

Reed takes a step back as his gaze darts to the black door. "Ah, that's not happening."

River recovers the space his friend just created. "You have to. Don't you realize what's riding on this?"

"Of course, I do," Reed says indignantly. "I'm the one who's been slaving away in the LaB trying to find the Sovereign, remember?"

"Well, the Sovereign wasn't in the LaB." River points at the Dead Zone beyond the door. "The answers were always beyond the walls of Oren's precious Sting."

Reed's gaze darts between Echo and River, clearly weighing up his options.

Makk snorts. "He's gonna run."

River acts before he can give himself time to think through

the decision he just made. He whips his arm out wide and connects his fist with Reed's chin. There's a click as his teeth clash. His eyes roll back. And he crumples to the ground.

"Whoa, go River," Makk says, letting out a low whistle.

Echo looks at Reed where he's lying, his glasses askew. "You knocked him out?"

River shakes his hand, wincing. It hurt more than he thought it would. "He thinks he understands, but he doesn't. We need to show him."

Echo grins. "Well, this will make sure he listens."

River bends down and heaves Reed over his shoulder, grunting at the weight. A Dead Born would weigh half as much. Echo opens the door and he walks through, ignoring the strain. "We'll take him to the Alphadome."

"Go take that fruit to your family," Echo says to Makk.

Makk hesitates. "Pears are my mom's favorite."

Echo shoos him on. "Go then. You've helped us more than enough."

"Yes, my queen," Makk says in the deepest voice his little body can make. "Your wish is my command."

River almost chuckles as he notes Echo's sour expression, but he focuses on turning toward the Alphadome. Makk darts away, leaving the two of them to move as quickly as they can before they're seen.

Despite his exhaustion and hunger, River maintains a sharp shuffle, kicking up puffs of dust as he goes. The one time he slows because Reed's weight seems to be multiplying with each step, Reed groans. The sound gives River a burst of speed he didn't know he had. He doesn't want to have to hit Reed again.

Flora and Chase scramble to their feet when they see them approach, Flora's eyes widening when she sees River carrying Reed.

"He needed a little convincing," River says, then grunts when he hefts Reed further up his shoulder.

Chase arches a brow, still covered in bruises and burns, but looking more alert after a rest. "Seems he couldn't say no."

Echo rushes past and enters the code into the hatch and opens it. River carefully makes his way down, glad for the lights as his knees threaten to buckle with each step. Inside, he makes his way straight to the glass dome and unloads Reed with relief. He steps back, breathing hard, then rights his friend's glasses. Reed moans and stirs, and River scuttles back out of the door.

He shuts it, then locks it, not liking what he's doing, but not seeing any other choice.

Echo appears, placing a hand on the middle of his back. "Once he sees this, then he'll understand."

As if he heard her, Reed's eyes flicker open. He startles when he sees he's in a white room, his gaze darting around. He leaps to his feet then scowls when he sees Echo and River watching him. The scowl deepens when he registers he's in a hexagonal glass prison.

"What the hell, River?" he demands, rubbing his jaw.

River lifts his chin even as guilt tugs at his insides. "We needed to show you."

"We're in a secret, underground chamber." Echo opens her arms. "This is where Oren brings the poor souls he hopes are the Sovereign."

"So they can get stung by a queen bee," Flora adds, her voice hard.

Reed looks momentarily surprised to see her, but he quickly recovers. "So? It's the only way to test whether some-one's the Sovereign."

"He doesn't need to anymore," River says. "We've found the Sovereign."

Flora steps forward. "And we need to harvest her cerebrospinal fluid then replicate it so we can make others Immune."

"Which is what we need you for," River finishes.

Reed crosses his arms. "No."

"Look around you, Reed," River says through gritted teeth. "Oren built this place in secret. He's been luring people here with the promise of Immunity, then making them disappear when they die. Do you really want to be part of that?"

Reed clenches his jaw. "Sometimes tough decisions need to be made."

Chase launches forward, slamming his fist on a glass pane. Reed leaps back in fright. "You Green Borns just want to keep it all to yourself, you greedy bastards."

"Said like a true, clueless Dead Born," Reed mutters.

Flora quickly draws Chase back before he launches himself at Reed, probably straight through the glass of the dome.

"Even if I wanted to, there's no point," Reed says, glaring at River. "We don't have the Sovereign Code."

"What Code?" River demands. "What are you talking about?"

"It's a formula. A recipe outlining the ingredients and steps to mass produce Immunity." Reed rolls his eyes. "Have you even considered how you were going to do that?"

River hates the flush that spears up his cheeks. "Then tell us."

Reed glances at Echo. "Without the Code, she'll have to be harvested over and over again."

River's blood turns to ice.

"And it would take years, and I'm talking decades, to produce enough Immunity for everyone."

Echo would have to endure the agony of the Harvest countless times. She'd have to be terrified each time they did it.

"Then where's the Code?" River grinds through gritted teeth. The scenario that was just painted in his mind isn't one he's willing to entertain.

"No one knows. It was stolen several years ago. Any record of it was wiped from our systems."

"Are you saying we can't produce Immunity for all?" Flora demands, then tightens her grip on Chase when a rumble of fury rips through him.

Reed takes a cautious step back. "Yes, that's what I'm saying. It's why Oren knew we'd have to start with a selected few. Then if we cracked the Code again, we'd be able to move onto everyone else."

River takes a quick step to the side, slipping between Chase and Reed's line of sight. He's not sure if he's protecting his friend from Chase or whether he wants to pummel him himself. "People are dying in the Dead Zone," he almost shouts. "We have to do something!"

Reed flinches, but doesn't lose the hard edge to his jaw. "We are."

But for the Green Borns only.

If it were up to Reed, he'd let Oren harvest Echo to save those he deemed worthy.

His own fury rippling through him, River unlocks the door and yanks it open. He reaches in, ignoring his sister's gasp, and grabs Reed by the arm. "Come with me."

Reed's eyes widen with terror even as he lets himself be led out of the glass dome. "What are you doing?" His voice rises with each syllable. "Where are you taking me?"

Echo arches a brow. "Are you going to let him hang out with the Worker?"

The color drains from Reed's face. "There's a Worker here?" he squeaks.

"Sure is," River growls, not bothering to mention she's nothing but a hunk of lifeless metal now.

Reed digs his heels into the tiled floor, looking more and more terrified. "I promise, I won't tell anyone about any of this. About the Alphadome. Or that you're here. If you let me go, I'll pretend none of this happened."

Echo slips in on his other side, clamping her hands around his arm. "We just want your help, Reed."

"Keeping a couple of little secrets is no big deal," Reed rushes on as if she didn't speak. "I would do that for you, River. We grew up together. And Echo, I always liked you. You remind me of my cousin, Prairie. I would never want to see either of you hurt."

River drags Reed past the Alphadome and toward the dark corridor leading to the crypt. Echo quickly realizes his intent, and she helps escort the struggling Reed. When he sees the looming darkness they're stepping into, he struggles even harder.

But River just tightens his hold.

Reed needs to see this.

The moment they reach the crypt, Reed stills. His face grows another shade of pale as he takes in the shelves staggered up the walls of the round room. As he registers the bodies in various states of decay.

River doesn't stop until they've marched him right up to the body of the girl who lost her life because she resembles Echo. Reed's knees give out and River and Echo release him as he crumples to the ground. "Prairie," he moans.

River's gut clenches. The girl was Reed's cousin?

"She was the most recent Green Born to be tested for the Sovereign," Echo says, her voice soft, but firm. "She was so scared when she died."

"A Worker kept them here," River adds, deciding that Reed needs to know it all. "She fed off their dead bodies."

"Don't you see, Reed?" Echo asks. "What other secrets has Oren kept from you?"

River clenches his hands. "When is the price too high?

Reed staggers to his feet, glancing around the room. There's a green tinge to his white complexion. "I...I can't."

River releases a breath. Finally, Reed understands. "That's why—"

Reed shoves him so hard he crashes into Echo. "I can't let their sacrifice be for nothing," he gasps.

River and Echo stagger but can't keep their balance. As they tumble to the floor, Reed spins on his heel and runs out of the crypt.

There's a crash somewhere in the main room, and a shout from Chase.

Then Reed's receding footsteps up the stairs and out of the Alphadome.

CHAPTER
TWENTY-SEVEN
ECHO

Nobody runs after Reed. It's not worth it. He's made it clear which side of the net he stands on. And he's given them some valuable information. Even if it's not what they wanted to hear.

"Who would steal the Code?" River asks, his brows furrowed as he paces.

"Someone who hates Oren even more than we do." Chase slides down the glass wall of the dome and sits on the floor with a groan.

Flora shoots him a concerned glance. It's not like Chase to complain. Daphne really left her mark on him. He's very lucky to still be alive.

"How many days do we have left?" Echo asks, trying to focus on what they need to do next. "When's Harvest Day?"

"Two days," says Flora. "Which isn't enough time. The Code's been missing for years. We'll never find it before then."

Echo lets out a long sigh, not wanting to accept they failed when they've come so far. "But we have to try! It's possible, isn't it?"

Flora nods slowly. "It's possible. Although, it would be easier if we were all Immune."

"You heard what Reed told us." River looks across at Flora, his face full of concern. "We can't produce enough Immunity for everyone without the Code."

"But we could make enough for the three of us," Flora says quietly, pausing as she waits for her words to sink in. "Then we could go safely to the Green Zone to look for the Code."

"How do we do that?" Chase's head snaps up.

"By harvesting Echo's cerebrospinal fluid." Flora winces before River's even had a chance to step forward and protest.

"No way!" he says. "We can't put her through that if it's not going to benefit everyone."

"But maybe it will," Echo says. "If it means we can all search for the Code without fear of being stung, maybe we can find it in time. Maybe it would even fix your allergies."

"I have serpentwood seeds for that." River pats his pocket where he still carries the pouch of seeds Clover had given him.

"Serpentwood is an endangered species," Flora reminds him. "And that's beside the point. It's Immunity we're talking about here."

"So, how do we do this?" Echo pulls back her shoulders, trying to look braver than she's feeling. The last thing she wants is a needle in her spine, but if there's a way to keep River safe, she's prepared to do anything.

Flora tilts her head, deep in thought. "We need somewhere sterile. The glass dome is probably the best place. But I'll have to strap you to the chair."

"I can sit still," says Echo, not liking the idea of being strapped down.

"It will hurt." Flora winces apologetically. "You'll likely move without meaning to. We need to keep you very still. It's safer to use the straps."

"Have you done this before?" River asks.

Flora shakes her head. "Of course, not. But I know what to do. All the equipment I need is in that secret LaB."

"Let's do this then." Echo steps away from River, hoping he doesn't notice the way she's begun to shake. She can at least act like she's brave, even if her feet are wanting to follow Reed's path up those stairs and away from this dungeon of death.

"Chase, can you help me, please?" Flora puts out a hand to help Chase up from the floor. "I need to get a few things prepared."

"Yep." Chase grimaces as Flora drags him to his feet. He wraps his arm around her and walks slowly to the LaB. They close the door behind them, which feels a little unnecessary but Echo is glad to be alone with River. Perhaps Flora and Chase need the same.

The Alphadome instantly feels bigger now that it's just the two of them and Echo frowns, not liking the way River's neck has bruised up after the Worker's attack. It's just one more reason why she needs to go through with this, no matter how painful it is. If they can find the Code before Harvest Day, she can save Nola from being harvested, along with all the other poor souls trapped inside the Hive. And they can bring Immunity to all. There's nothing in the world more important. She can't back out now.

"Are you sure you want to do this?" River goes to Echo and puts his hands on her shoulders. "You're shaking!"

"I'm just a little cold," she tries. Then when she sees he hasn't bought that excuse, she shrugs. "And a little scared."

"Maybe being a little scared is a good thing if Flora's taking your spinal fluid?" River drops a kiss on her forehead. "Like in the Hive."

"Hmm. Maybe." Echo hadn't thought of that. She slides her

hands around his waist and enjoys the comfort of having him so close. Her shaking subsides as her heart picks up his steady beat. She's always better when she has River by her side.

"Can you strap me into the chair?" Echo asks. "It won't feel as awful if you do it."

"Of course." River lifts a hand to stroke her cheek. "I won't leave you. I'll be right on the other side of the glass the whole time."

A sadness fills Echo as she thinks of the time Chase promised to wait for her on the other side of the net during Confirmation. And he had. But it hadn't helped one bit as she'd been declared Immune and her whole life had been turned upside down. She'd been so angry with him for not giving her the pollen she'd asked for, but she knows now that it hadn't made a scrap of difference. She's the Sovereign. She could have been stung by a thousand bees and she'd have lived. And the person she'd really needed to wait for her was already there, blinking those green eyes at her in anger as he'd tried to process the loss of his twin.

Flora and Chase emerge from the LaB and Echo and River pull apart. Flora is holding a tray of sharp implements that Echo doesn't want to look too closely at.

"Come on." River opens the door to the glass dome and waits for Echo to enter.

"You need to wait outside, River." Flora rushes forward. "I need space to work. I can't have you in there."

"I will." He closes the door behind them before she can follow. "Once I have Echo secured in the chair."

Echo sits down and lifts the back of her top so that her spine is exposed. She folds the worn fabric so that it stays up, while River straps her ankles to the legs of the chair. Next, he straps her wrists, then loops more of the wide straps across her waist and chest.

"Is that too tight?" he asks, his handsome face filled with despair.

"It needs to be tight!" calls Flora from outside the dome. "Make it as tight as you possibly can, so she can't move."

"I'm okay," Echo reassures him. "It can be a little tighter."

River works his way around the straps, pulling on them in turn. With each tug, Echo's heart beats faster. She keeps her eyes on River, reminding herself why she's doing this. It's for him. And Flora and Chase. And every last human left on this dying planet. They have to overcome the devastation caused when humans saved the bees in the worst possible way—by turning them into tiny assassins.

River takes her by surprise when he presses his lips to Echo's. She consents to the kiss in the only way she can. By kissing him back. Her lips part and he increases the pressure, filling each of his small actions with love.

"Ah, you do know we can see you in there," says Flora.

River pulls back, not seeming amused by his sister's comment. He's too concerned about what's about to happen. Not that Echo will die this time, but at the pain she's about to experience.

"I love you," she whispers. "I'm okay."

"I love you, too." He gives her another kiss and steps away. "I'll be right outside that door. All you need to do is say my name and I'll be back in here."

She nods, her head the only part of her that she can move.

River leaves the glass dome and Flora enters with her silver tray, setting it down behind Echo's chair and dabbing something cold on the base of Echo's spine. She thinks of all the people who've been strapped to this chair before her as they waited for the queen bee to sting them. Their fear hangs in the air like it's part of the fabric of this strange dungeon itself.

"This will make sure you don't get an infection," Flora tells her as she continues to dab at her spine.

"Okay. Thanks." Echo listens to the clinking of implements on Flora's tray. She doesn't want to see the needle that's about to invade her spine, grateful that Flora is keeping it hidden.

"I'm ready," says Flora. "Keep your eyes on River."

Echo looks up at River whose face is almost pressed against the glass, along with both his palms. Chase is beside him, shuffling his feet nervously. She really does love both these guys, just in very different ways.

"You're okay," says River, biting down on his bottom lip. "It will be all over soon. You're in safe hands."

Chase makes a sudden movement that has Echo's head swimming with confusion as she tries to piece together what she's witnessing. He has his arm wrapped around River's already bruised throat and there's the unmistakable glint of a sharp blade.

Echo's pulse shoots for the next stratosphere as River struggles and a thin line of blood seeps down his neck.

"No!" she screams. "Chase! Let him go!"

"Green Born scum!" Chase shouts. "It's time to die. And your traitor of a girlfriend can do nothing to save you this time."

River kicks back at Chase but even in his injured state, Chase has the advantage over him. This is a hold he knows well. And his blade is pressing closer with each of River's desperate movements. How could Echo have gotten Chase so wrong? She trusted him. Before River came along, he was the best friend she ever had.

"No! Chase! Don't!" Echo screams, pulling at the straps binding her to the chair as tears of pure terror pour down her face. River was supposed to be the one watching her in danger, not the other way around. "Stop him, Flora!"

River groans and there's a sudden sharp pain in Echo's

spine that pulls another scream from her lungs.

It's agony.

The only thing she's felt that came close was being harvested in the Hive. But despite the pain, her eyes remain on the struggle on the other side of the glass as her first love tries to take the life of her true love.

The pain in her back intensifies then evaporates as a cold pressure is applied.

"Enough, Chase!" shouts Flora. "I have what I need."

Chase lets go of River and stumbles back, clutching his own injuries as his knife clatters to the floor.

River lurches toward Chase then seems to figure something out and stops. His hands go to his throat, and he heaves for breath.

"River!" Echo calls, sobbing with relief to see he's survived.

"I'm so sorry." Flora rubs Echo's back in the same way she remembers her father doing whenever she'd been unwell as a child. "We needed you to be scared. It was the only way we could think of."

Echo blinks as her head spins once more. River had never been in danger. Chase wasn't going to hurt him. But he needed Echo to think his attack had been real. Which means he also needed River to believe it.

River opens the door to the glass dome and rushes toward Echo. She breathes in, hardly able to wait for the moment he embraces her so she can feel his lifeforce pumping through his very much living veins. She'd been so certain she was going to lose him.

But it's not Echo he runs to.

It's Flora.

He grips his twin by the collar of her shirt and forces her to drop what she's holding and take two steps back until she's pressed against the glass wall.

"No, River!" Echo cries, hating what Flora did but understanding it. She needed Echo to be scared when she harvested her spinal fluid. And having her believe River was about to be murdered in front of her is easily the most frightening thing Echo could imagine. Her life would be impossible without him.

"I'm sorry," Flora sobs. "I did it for you. For all of us. It was the only way."

River drops his hold on Flora and pulls her to him, half hugging her and half seeming to want to strangle her.

"I'm sorry," she says again, and his hug becomes more gentle. Then, seeming to remember that Echo is still strapped to a chair and in pain, he lets go of Flora and squats down in front of her.

She pulls on her straps, wanting them undone as soon as possible so she can wrap her arms around this gorgeous guy she thought she almost lost.

He works quickly on the straps. As each one loosens, she feels relief sliding down her spine and easing the agony of the harvest that just took place. The last strap falls to the floor and she stands. River hugs her cautiously, not wanting to cause her more pain.

"I'm okay." She presses her face to his, reveling in the soft warmth of his skin. "As long as you're okay, I'm okay."

"Did you get what you need, Flora?" Chase asks from the corner of the room as he drags in a ragged breath. Echo lets go of River to look at her old friend. He's clearly in mental as well as physical anguish. Attacking River couldn't have been easy for him in the state he's in. Not to mention scaring Echo like that.

"Yes," says Flora, her eyes burning with excitement as she holds up a large syringe. "I got exactly what I need. It's time to make all of us Immune. It's time to find the Code."

CHAPTER

TWENTY-EIGHT

RIVER

Flora's words hang in the air, seeming to dominate the room.

It's time to make all of us Immune.

It's time to find the Code.

River blinks. Then blinks again. Then one more time, just for good measure. They're so close now.

"We're halfway there," Echo whispers.

His dazed gaze drops to where she's tucked into his side, and he's stunned all over again. Echo's smile is dazzling. It amplifies the sweetness of this moment. The joy. The knowledge that although three of them are bruised and battered, it was worth it.

They have the Sovereign.

In fact, he's holding her.

River leans down to kiss Echo, then winces when the cut on his neck stings. The crusted blood cracks, releasing a fresh trickle.

Echo frowns. "We need to wash it with clean water while we have it."

Flora moves toward the LaB on the other side of the Alphadome. "There's a care kit in here," she says, ducking in.

"A care kit?" Echo asks.

River tightens his arm around her as he leads her to the glass door. "Yeah, we had them in most areas of the Sting. They have basic medical supplies in case anyone has a minor injury."

Chase snorts as he shakes his head. "That's...nice."

The furrows on Echo's forehead deepen. "No one dies of an infection in the Green Zone, do they?"

River doesn't answer, knowing the question is a rhetorical one. Flora returns with the white hexagonal case that River always took for granted growing up. Tucked anywhere a red bee symbol could be found, he'd had quite a few cuts and scrapes tended to with their always-full contents.

River squeezes Echo's shoulder a second before releasing her so she can step through the door first. He notes the way she's holding herself extra upright. At least they'll have an opportunity to rest while Flora does whatever she needs so that one syringe of pale-yellow fluid can make them all Immune.

The moment they're out of the glass dome, he tucks her back into his side. "This is why we went through all that." The knife at his throat. Their joint terror as they believed Chase had been lying all along. Echo's agonizing harvest. "Everyone will have access to it all."

Not just Immunity.

But food for all.

And access to all the things Green Borns take for granted. Medical care. Clean water. Shelter that stays upright.

Echo nods, her face hardening with determination. "Everyone," she vows.

Flora was opening the six-sided case she's holding, but she pauses. "These even have adrenacure in them."

Chase snorts again, possibly realizing that a cure for bee venom had been tucked in the Dead Zone all along. "I need a break from this place," he mutters as he half-strides, half-staggers to the staircase leading out of this bunker.

For once, Flora doesn't rush after him. She sighs. "He just needs a minute." Instead, she points to a nearby chair. "Sit, River. I'll clean you up."

He does as he's told, conscious Flora was the one who took over tending to any scrapes and grazes after their mother died. It was the one time she cared for him, rather than him caring for her. For some reason, it feels nostalgic and bittersweet. Those days are as dead as their mother.

Flora pulls out some squares of soft, white cloth, along with a bottle of antiseptic. Echo watches in fascination. She leans over the case, taking in the contents. "There's a lot of stuff in here."

"Everything a person needs to tend to bleeding, bee stings, or even broken bones until the medics can arrive," Flora says, wetting one of the cloths.

A curse echoes from the top of the stairs. Chase's disgruntled voice reaches them. "Damned hatch."

Flora looks down at the cloth now saturated in antiseptic, seeming torn.

"You finish that, seeing as you know what you're doing," Echo says, already walking to the stairs. "I'll help Chase."

Flora accepts with a grateful smile and Echo disappears up the stairs. Focusing back on her task, Flora gently wipes the cut on River's neck. Even though he was expecting the sting, he winces. Turns out a cut to the throat is more sensitive than he anticipated.

"It's not big," she says, grimacing in apology. She throws

the bloodied cloth onto a nearby bench and grabs another one, wetting it with antiseptic.

River's about to say it's fine, but he hesitates. "You could've told me," he says softly.

Flora shakes her head. "And risk Echo not believing it? And having to do the spinal tap all over again?"

He falls silent as his twin once more cleans his wound. River barely notices the burning flash this time. Maybe it's because this cloth comes away cleaner.

Or maybe he's struggling to accept Flora's words.

"There had to be another way," he says, knowing he's being stubborn, yet unable to shake the thought.

Flora frowns as she takes a dry square of cloth this time and dabs at the moisture on his skin. "Like what? Wait until a better idea came along? Hope Oren doesn't visit the Alphadome in the meantime and discover something's up?"

River clamps his mouth shut, wishing he had the answer, but knowing he doesn't.

"I just..." He sighs, not liking the words forming in his mind. When Flora tries to dab at his clean, dry cut again, he gently pushes her hand away.

"You just?" Flora prompts, watching him closely.

"I just don't want to turn out like him," River says, the words part confession, part promise. "Where anything is justified if it's in the name of the greater good."

Flora's eyes flash with green fire. "Everything I'm doing is so I don't turn out like *him*."

She spits out the last word as if it's dirty. Bitter. As poisonous as bee venom.

Her ferocity startles him a little. But then again, Flora's had longer to process exactly who and what their father is. And Oren barely acknowledged his daughter's existence. She has far more to be resentful about.

To River's surprise, his sister smiles brightly. "Not that it matters. We have the Sovereign." She tucks the unused supplies back into the care kit. "We've practically won."

"Well, not quite," says Echo, entering the room. "But we've definitely cleared the first hurdle."

River finds himself smiling. He's looking at the prize for that victory.

The Sovereign.

Echo scrunches her nose at him as if she knows exactly what he's thinking. "I think we should head back to the colony. We don't want to be in the Alphadome at night."

Because that's when Oren visits. Although it's not likely to be soon, when he does he'll discover the Worker is dead, which isn't something they want to be around to witness.

Flora takes the care kit to return to the small LaB while River makes his way to Echo. "Is Chase okay?"

"Better once he was out of here." Echo smiles. "And Makk was up there, waiting for us."

River chuckles. "That kid has an uncanny knack of being around just when he's needed."

Flora returns and they make their way up the stairs and out of the hatch. They find Chase leaning against the large rock, Makk nowhere to be seen. Chase straightens, looking just as bruised and battered, but as Echo said, also looking as if the afternoon sun has invigorated him.

"Let's get back. I'm starving."

River's surprised at his choice of words, and he notices Echo is too. Flora just giggles as she rushes to his side. In pairs, they make their way back to the village, giving the Betadome a wide berth.

"You'll be able to go in there soon, just like I can," Echo says as they pass it.

"Thanks to you," River says, pressing a kiss to the crown of her head.

"Thanks to all of us," she corrects.

Grinning, River can't help himself. "Yes, my Quee—"

The gentle but firm elbow to his gut cuts him off. "Watch it. That beautiful face of yours will only get you so far."

He grins wider. "It got me the Sovereign."

"No, that was your courage and selflessness and your ability to make me smile, no matter what." Echo presses a hand to his chest. "It was your heart."

Suddenly looking forward to a night alone in their hut, River squeezes her close. Sharing a moment of heated anticipation, they focus on returning to the village. They might even have a few rations waiting for them.

As the Betadome slips behind them, River squints, his eyes roaming the Sting spearing into the sky on the other side. That's where they have to go back to search for the Code. It's a daunting thought that sobers him. A little part of him can't help but feel betrayed by Reed. He'd thought once he saw the truth of Oren's deception, he'd understand. That maybe they could have an ally on the other side of the net.

"River."

Although Echo says his name softly, it vibrates with alarm. He yanks his gaze back, seeing that she's looking toward the village.

A mass of people have congregated. Waiting for them.

River is instantly tense. He steps in front of Echo, conscious she's only just gone through a harvest. She'll be more than willing to fight, but she's also drained. There's no way she'll last long against that many people.

"Relax, hero boy," Chase says, rolling his eyes. "They're here to welcome us."

"Welcome us?" Echo asks, confused.

It's the crowd who answer. A murmur of excitement ripples through them as they sight her and the others. And then they begin to chant.

"Sovereign." Feet stomp. "Sovereign." Voices raise. "Sovereign."

"You told them?" River gasps.

Chase shrugs, a grin splitting his face. "I told Makk. Who then must've passed on the good news."

Who clearly passed it onto every person in the Dead Zone.

They rush forward, the chant dissolving into excited chatter. Echo looks like a horde of queen bees are coming at her.

"Do not leave my side," she hisses under her breath.

River moves closer. "Never."

The crowd of grinning people contract as they come closer, becoming a battering ram that has its target.

Echo.

"My queen," a woman calls out, falling to her knees as she tries to kiss Echo's feet.

"No, please," she says, trying to help her up. "There's no need for that."

The woman tears up, her hands clutching at Echo. "She touched me! She touched me!"

The rest of the crowd closes in, and River pushes back the grasping hands and desperate bodies.

"Our queen!" someone shouts.

"The Sovereign," another calls out, adoration lighting up his face.

"Let me touch her! Get out of the way!"

Many of the elated smiles reveal toothless gaps or nothing more than bleeding gums.

Echo shrinks back, clearly uncomfortable with the attention and adulation. Hands brush over her as if her Immunity is contagious as more people crowd in, trying to shove those who have been blessed with a touch out of the way.

River tries to keep up, but there are too many. He has no idea what to do. The people's joy is understandable.

Yet Echo never asked for this. She doesn't want to be worshipped.

River's just about to demand the people step back and give her some room when Chase shoves his way forward. "My people," he calls out, raising his arms. "It is a time of celebration."

The crowd stops as a cheer breaks out. "Yes! Celebration!"

Chase takes a few steps forward, forcing the people back, then opens his arms, creating a bubble of space around Echo and River. "We have the Sovereign!"

The roar is a wave of joy that rises from the crowd, the voice of every woman, man, and child lifting their spirits collectively. It's a stark contrast to the silent clapping favored by the people in the Green Zone. River allows himself a sigh of relief. Chase's speech has given them some room to move.

Chase turns one way then the other, beaming at the Dead Borns. "And it's only a matter of time before we find the Code and every one of us will be Immune!"

Another explosion of excitement carries into the air.

Chase forms a fist and holds it up high. "Then the Razers will make sure no one is forgotten. That everyone is Immune. Who's with me?"

Hands punch into the air, mirroring him. This time, the cries are harder. Thrown out with more force. They puncture the air in an unapologetic onslaught.

"Pick me, Chase!"

"Take me, I can fight them Green Borns!"

"I would give my life for the Razers!"

River realizes that's what this pep talk was really about—recruiting people to Chase's army.

So they can storm the Green Zone when they finally have the Code.

Chase is beaming as he surveys his people. "Everyone, man, or woman, is welcome to join us." He takes a step forward, parting a few of the people. "But for tonight, we celebrate!"

The cheering returns and the crowd separates as Chase walks toward the village. River grabs Echo's hand and quickly follows, wanting to make the most of the narrow path being forged.

Yet the people don't stop their desperate grasping. A few throw handfuls of shredded material that was probably once colorful, but is now frayed and gray. It rains down over Echo and River like ash, catching in their hair and settling on their shoulders. When an old man shoves a piece of stale, flat bread into River's hand, he startles.

"Take it," the old man wheezes. "You need your strength."

River quickly passes it back. "Thank you, but I can't." Although his stomach rumbles painfully, this man needs it far more than he does.

The man opens his mouth to object, but a woman shoves past him, pushing him back with her elbows. "He don't want no bread," she snaps. She pushes something into River's hand and wraps his fingers around his. "Here, I've been saving this for a special occasion."

River looks down at the half-cob of dried, dirty corn. "Thank you, but—"

The woman shakes her head, her lanky hair whipping her cheeks. "Take it!" she hisses. "It's an insult to everything we've been through if you don't."

She blends back into the crowd, her gaze on Echo as if she's more than a Queen. As if she's a divine being. It's beautiful, yet disturbing all at once.

A child with pale hair wearing nothing more than a tattered sack slips through the legs of the adults. "My queen!" she cries. "My queen!"

Echo turns, smiling when she sees the little girl. River registers her hands are also full of the meagre scraps of food the Dead Borns have been able to gift. His chest tight, he extends his half-cob to the girl. Her eyes widen at the prize and she snatches it before he has a chance to blink. He smiles as she darts away, no doubt thinking that meeting the Sovereign was her luckiest day yet.

"Good idea," Echo whispers, then passes a handful of withered beans to an old woman on her right.

The old woman bursts into tears as she crumples to her knees. River wishes they could comfort her, tell her it was never their food to begin with, but the momentum of the crowd keeps them moving.

Up ahead, he sees that people are spreading out through the village, singing and dancing and crying with happiness. River realizes that the Dead Zone is coming alive now that the Sovereign has given them something they've never had.

Hope.

It has him smiling, even relaxing a little. Tonight will be about celebrating their victory, rather than worrying about the next battle. Tonight will be about Echo.

Tomorrow they can worry about the Code.

He's about to lean down and jokingly tell Echo that it seems he has some serious competition for her attention when he pauses. Many of the Dead Borns are congregating to their left, most of them male, and he registers Chase is at their center.

"The Razers will protect you," he calls out, then shoves

something white and withered in his mouth. River realizes Chase knew this would be waiting for them. That's why he made the joke about being starving. "They will fight for you."

"The Razers will fight for Immunity!" the crowd calls back, already familiar with the chant.

Their fervent, impassioned faces show they're not only prepared to fight for that ultimate promise, but to die for it.

As Echo and River continue through the village, the dirty stream coming into view where people are already congregating, his smile fades.

These hours of joy and celebration are going to be short-lived.

In fact, that's probably why the Dead Borns are so determined to make the most of it.

For the first time, River realizes what finding the Code will mean.

War.

CHAPTER
TWENTY-NINE
ECHO

Echo is back in the Alphadome much sooner than she expected. It became quickly obvious they couldn't stay in Nola's hut. The Vulnerables are worshipping her like she's their savior, when she can't save a single one of them.

Not without finding the Code.

The desperate people of the Dead Zone had crowded around Nola's door, marveling that their Sovereign was inside. The walls had started to wobble from the pressure of the crowd touching its fragile frame. Echo couldn't let it continue or the whole hut would've fallen down. Nola needs somewhere familiar to return when they get her out of the Hive. Literally the only thing she asked of Echo was for her to look after her chair. And she can't do that if Nola's hut has no walls.

So, they'd returned to the one place they felt safe. Which is ironic given it's a place that's filled with fear. There's no concern about Oren finding them in the Alphadome. With Chase's burgeoning army of Razers pacing the dirt outside, Oren won't attempt to enter his dungeon of death.

River is sleeping beside Echo on the floor. She'd also dozed off for a while during the night, enjoying the quiet after the ordeal they'd put themselves through, and knowing there's still far more to come. She snuggles in closer and he makes a small noise to let her know he's awake even though his eyes are closed.

"How's Flora?" he whispers. "Any progress?"

"Not yet." Echo looks toward the small LaB where Flora and Chase are locked inside, turning Echo's spinal fluid into Immunity. Flora has said there should be enough for three shots, although Echo's secretly hoping there's enough for four. Makk's made it clear he's not against breaking the rules. He'd almost given Echo heart failure when he'd run into the Beta-dome to lure Reed out. If anyone needs immediate Immunity, it's him.

The door to the LaB flies open and Flora fills the space. She's holding a canister and there's a wide smile stretched across her face.

"I've done it," she announces proudly. "I made the Immunity."

Echo's heart pounds. She can hardly dare to believe this is actually happening. Not only is she an Immune but River is about to become one, too. And it's all because of the incredible connection they made. None of this would have happened if they hadn't been thrown together in Confirmation.

River sits up. "Flora, I can't believe you did it. You're amazing."

She waves away the compliment. "It only took me all night. Come on. Let's make you Immune."

"You go first," he says, pulling himself to a stand.

Flora blushes. "Oh, I already did my shot. And Chase's. I had enough fluid to make four canisters."

"We can give the extra one to Makk," says River, smiling.

Echo's heart fills with love to know he's on exactly the same page.

"Good idea." Flora steps into the main chamber.

Chase appears in the doorway behind her, yawning. "I'll go find Makk. Knowing him, he's probably in the Betadome getting stung by a bee right now."

"He'd better not be," Echo calls after him as he heads up the stairs.

"Sit down, River." Flora goes to her twin and waits for him to get comfortable. She crouches down beside him, positioning the canister on his thigh on the outside of his clothing.

Echo leans in closer and holds her breath. This is the moment she's been waiting for. And a big part of the reason she agreed to endure that painful harvest. After this, the bees won't be able to harm River. Maybe he'll even be able to breathe like a regular person.

River looks up at Echo and holds her gaze. He understands the gravity of this moment, and she knows the only reason he'd agreed to use a canister on himself is so that he can do whatever it takes to save everyone else.

"One. Two," Flora counts. Her hand jolts and there's a click as Immunity is released into River's bloodstream.

"You didn't count to three," River complains, rubbing at his thigh.

"I never said I was going to," she counters.

Biting down on her lip, Echo fights back a tear.

"You okay?" River asks, noticing how emotional she's become.

She nods. "I'm better than okay. I'm happy."

River grins then shifts his gaze to Flora. "How long does it take to become effective?"

"Just a minute or two." Flora stands. "Congratulations, River. You're officially an Immune. A real one this time."

These words are like the sweetest song Echo's ever heard and this time she fails to contain her tears, letting one slide down her cheek.

"Did it hurt?" she asks, kneeling beside him as Flora takes the empty canister back to the LaB.

River shakes his head. "No more than an adrenacure shot. And a whole lot less than what you went through earlier."

"The harvest wasn't that bad." She tentatively touches his thigh, imagining the Immunity racing through his veins. "The worst part was thinking I was going to lose you."

"I really hate that you had to go through that." River lifts his hand and wipes away Echo's stubborn tear.

"I'm okay," she whispers.

"Thank you," he says, trailing his fingertips down her cheek. "I've just received the greatest gift because of you."

"We're a team, River." She looks into his green eyes and kisses him gently. His neck still looks so sore. And now his leg.

"I won't break," he murmurs, sensing her hesitation as he pulls her in closer to deepen the kiss.

"But my eyes might," says Flora, coming back out from the LaB with another canister. "Is Chase back with Makk yet?"

Echo and River pull apart and the hatch opens right on cue. Heavy footsteps clomp down the stairs.

River snaps to attention as he quickly gets to his feet. "That's not Makk with him."

Echo listens more closely and realizes he's right. There are three sets of footsteps, and none of them are light enough to be Makk. Positioning herself beside River, she readies herself to face whatever, or whoever, comes down those stairs.

"That better not be Oren," River mutters, angling himself slightly in front of Echo.

Chase is the first to appear, followed by Ruff. For a moment, he looks so much like his brother that Echo does a double take. But he's thinner than Tuff, and his skin sunken and sallow. And he's missing the deep wrinkles caused by years of the anguish of inflicting so much pain. It's definitely the richest man in the Dead Zone, not Oren's right-hand man. And he has his daughter with him. Both of them are wide-eyed as they take in the stark white cavern that's been right under their feet their whole lives.

Echo tries to remember Ruff's daughter's name, certain it was a color.

"Hello again, Ruff," says River. "And...Emerald?"

"Navy," Ruff corrects, shaking his head. "You forgotten me daughter already? And here I was thinking you two had a special connection. She's still got all her teeth, you know."

"What are you doing here?" Flora asks, holding the canister behind her back to keep it out of sight. "We were expecting someone else."

"He overheard me talking to Makk." Chase shoots them an apologetic glance. "And then Makk ran off saying I should do whatever Ruff says."

"I've done a lot for the cause and that boy knows it," says Ruff. "Passing messages back and forth like an overworked raven. Hiding the girl when she first came into the Dead Zone." He points at Flora.

"And being rewarded nicely for it," Echo reminds him, remembering the generous rations of food that were on his table, even if they were meagre by Green Born standards.

"You owe it to my brother to help me," Ruff sneers. "He saved your lives. More than once. It's time for you to take care of his family now. So, what's this I heard about you having some Immunity?"

Echo's shoulders sag, cursing Makk for running off.

"We only have one shot," River says quickly. "And we all agreed it should be for Makk. We can't possibly give it to you."

"I'm hardly asking for it for myself, am I?" Ruff laughs. "My time's just about up. It's Navy who needs it. She's only a few years older than Makk. Did I tell you she's still got all her teeth?"

"You may have mentioned it." Echo shakes her head at his brazenness. But she can't help being a little touched by the way this man stops at nothing to ensure his daughter has a better life. And at least this time he's not trying to sell her to River.

"She's worth Immunity," Ruff says. "Just as worthy as any of you."

"That's true," says Echo, cautiously. "Everyone is worthy. But this shot is for Makk. I'm sorry, but it's not available."

Ruff crosses his arms. "Are you saying that boy's life is worth more than my daughter's? Because that's what I'm hearing here. Maybe you've been hanging out with the likes of Green Borns too much with an attitude like that."

"I'm..." Echo runs out of words, knowing she can't possibly argue for one life being valued more than another. Especially given that's the exact cause they're fighting so hard for right now.

"She didn't say that," says River. "All she said was that the shot's already been allocated."

"Then it looks like your communication link to the Green Zone is about to be cut off," growls Ruff. "If my Navy isn't Immune, I'm not going to feel much like talking to my brother for you, am I?"

"That's why I agreed to it," says Chase, frowning. "We can't afford for Makk to be our only link to Tuff."

Especially if he won't have the chance to be Immune.

Seeing that he's backed them into a corner, Ruff pushes his daughter forward. Her hair falls over her eyes as she looks at the floor, seeming embarrassed by her father's behavior. There's a fine sheen of sweat coating her forehead.

"Hey, Navy." Flora goes to the girl and puts her free hand on her shoulder. "It's okay. Don't be scared. If it can't be Makk, I'm glad it's you."

Flora leads Navy to a quiet corner and instructs her to sit down. She immediately does as she's told in the compliant way of someone who's used to following orders. Flora squats down beside her and after a few murmurs, there's the familiar clicking sound and Navy's face pulls into a wince.

"It's done." Flora looks up at Ruff. "In a minute or two, she'll be Immune. Unlike Makk..."

Ruff grins broadly, proving two things. First, he couldn't care less about Makk. Second, he certainly doesn't still have all his teeth.

"Thank you." Navy blinks up at Flora.

"Don't thank me." She stands and tucks the empty canister into her back pocket. "Thank Echo. She's the Sovereign."

"Thank you, Sovereign," Navy obediently chimes.

Echo nods, feeling just as uncomfortable as when River had called her his queen. She doesn't think she'll ever get used to this.

"Well, that's part of the debt paid off." Ruff nods.

"Are you joking?" River's hands fly out. "Your daughter just got given the most sought-after gift in both the Green and Dead Zones. Immunity. There are plenty of people out there who would kill for that. And one in particular who won't be getting it now."

Ruff has the decency to look at least a little chastised. He nods, returning his gaze to his daughter.

"We'll find another way to look after Makk," says Echo quietly.

"The Razers have a lot of work ahead of us," Chase tells

Ruff. "We expect your continued help with whatever is necessary."

"Yeah, yeah." Ruff waves away Chase's request as if it's a given.

"And don't tell anybody Navy's Immune," says River, a frown crossing his features. "It'll cause mayhem. And that was the last shot of Immunity. We can't make more."

"Fine." Ruff nods, although Echo doesn't believe him for a moment.

She looks at River, biting her tongue to stop herself from correcting what he just said. They *can* make more Immunity. But it would require scaring her again, and she's not sure she's ready for that just yet. In time, if they can't find the Sovereign Code, she may have no choice. However, that's not something she wants to think about right now. Being terrified and harvested over and over for years on end would be a living nightmare. She'd be sure to lose her mind. Even so, she knows she'd do it if it was the only way to save everyone. Which makes her even more determined to find that missing Code.

"I'll walk you out," says Chase, stepping toward Ruff.

Navy rushes to her father and Chase ushers them up the stairs.

Flora heads back toward the LaB. "I'll be in here if you need me. I have some tests to run."

"What are you testing for?" River asks.

"I kept a small part of Echo's spinal fluid." Flora's eyes light up. "I'm running some tests to see if there's a way to produce Immunity using less genetic content."

Echo's brows shoot up. "Is that even possible without the Code?"

"Doubt it." Flora shrugs. "But when have we ever let odds get in our way?"

Echo smiles. "Fair poin—"

There's a shout from the hatch and Flora immediately drops the empty canister and runs up the stairs. River and Echo are right behind her.

They burst out into the open air and Echo blinks as her eyes adjust to the change in light. Hopefully she doesn't get mobbed the moment the people see her.

But there's no chance of that. The Razers, along with dozens of other Vulnerables, are rushing toward the Betadome in the early morning light. More are pressed up against the net, watching something taking place inside. Chase is amongst them, shouting something Echo can't make out.

"What's going on?" River secures the hatch in a hurry.

"I don't know." Echo slips her hand into River's and they run toward the chaos.

It doesn't take long to see what's causing the commotion. Navy is inside the Betadome, picking fruit and stuffing it into a large sack.

"Get out of there!" Chase shouts. "It's not safe."

"The bees can't hurt her," Ruff growls as he stands by the black door, rubbing his hands with anticipation.

Echo groans as they reach the net and come to a stop. That's why Navy had been so nervous just now. It wasn't the thought of being injected with Immunity. It was the knowledge of what her father would make her do once she had it.

"It's not the bees!" Chase shouts back. "There are cameras in there. Oren won't stand for this. She'll be killed."

"My girl is fast," Ruff sneers. "And clever. And Immune."

The crowd gasps to hear this as their eyes open wide.

"Make me Immune, Sovereign!" one woman says, tugging on Echo's shirt.

River puts a protective arm around Echo and pulls her in close.

"Help my son!" another says, dropping to her knees. "Give him Immunity."

"And my daughter!" cries someone else.

"I can't make anyone Immune right now," Echo says truthfully. "But we're working hard to make all of you Immune. All your sons. And your daughters. You have to be patient."

"Look!" someone cries, taking the attention away from Echo as everyone turns back to the Betadome.

Navy is continuing to take whatever fruit she can find, her sack now bulging with lumps. But that's not what the people are pointing at.

Echo looks up higher. And then she sees it.

Or, rather, she sees *them*.

There's a swarm of bees rising from a nearby tree like a shimmering black and gold cloud. This shouldn't be happening. Just like Confirmation, if someone is Immune, the bees won't pay them much attention. One or two more curious insects might decide to investigate their intruder, but not a swarm like this.

"Navy!" Echo calls. "Get out of there!"

Somehow, Echo's voice cuts through the noise of the crowd and Navy locks eyes with her.

Echo lifts a hand to point at what Navy hasn't yet seen. In what feels like slow motion, she looks up. And drops the bulging sack of fruit.

Apples, pears and plums roll across the soft grass and Navy's hands fly to her mouth.

"What are you doing?" Ruff shouts. "You're safe! Pick up the food and bring it here."

"I have to help her." Echo tries to run for the black door, but River pulls her back.

"We can't," he says, his face full of anguish. "It's too late."

Echo looks across at Navy and gasps.

The bees have wrapped her in their blanket of death, sending her falling to her knees. She collapses to the ground and lets out a scream that rattles inside Echo's brain.

Navy isn't Immune.

Which can only mean one thing.

Echo is not the Sovereign.

CHAPTER
THIRTY

RIVER

River is as unmoving as Navy. His stunned mind can't process her swollen body, the angry red welts on every inch of her skin.

The way the bees swarmed her, wrapping her in a cloak of furious buzzing.

They saw Navy as a threat.

As one that needed to be extinguished.

And now she's dead.

River places his hand on the netting of the Betadome, his fingernails catching in the tiny holes that act as a screen between him and her.

If Navy isn't Immune, he isn't either.

None of them are.

And Echo isn't the Sovereign.

A low moan escapes Echo as if she just heard his thoughts and he reaches out instinctively when her knees give out. He hauls her to his side, registering that he only half-feels it. Glancing down, he notes her pale face and shaking hands. Yet he can't think of what to do. In part because he's numb.

In part because he doesn't know what he *can* do.

Echo.

Was never.

The Sovereign.

A gasp has River's head snapping up. His gaze shoots straight to Navy, hoping to find her breathing. Maybe sitting up, rubbing at the fading welts covering her face. Relief is already poised to flood through him, bringing with it a reality he's willing to face.

The Sovereign can still get stung. She just survives it.

Except Navy is even more bloated than she was a few seconds ago. Her skin is stretched tight, now a mottled blue and purple. Her eyes are bulging in their sockets as if there isn't room for them as the inflammation explodes exponentially.

It's the green door that triggered the gasp, that snapped the Dead Borns out of the same shock River can't seem to shake. They're now murmuring and shifting uneasily.

The door is opening.

Four Green Borns enter the Betadome, encased in white suits. Their faces are obscured by dark mesh masks. They stride straight toward Navy, ignoring the crowd that just watched her die.

Two bend down and grab an arm. The other two grip a leg each. Unceremoniously, they lift her distended body.

One of the Green Borns holding an arm glances at her face, physically blanches, then looks away. He shakes his head and River knows it's not in sadness. It's in disgust.

"I'm glad they're all here," he snarls loud enough to be heard as they half-carry, half-drag Navy away. "They need to see what happens when they get greedy."

"They just don't seem to learn," another scoffs.

An angry mutter ripples behind River, but apart from that,

no one says anything. Instead, the Dead Borns watch Navy being hauled away. There will be no burial. No body to mourn.

River's almost relieved when she's taken through the green door. Navy just became a gruesome reminder that Immunity is still out of reach.

The hum of the Betadome quickly becomes the only sound filling the air. River draws in a deep breath, the delicate scent of honey catching at the back of his throat. It makes him faintly nauseous. For some reason, losing the Sovereign makes it feel all the more dangerous.

Once more, they have no way to protect themselves from the superbees.

"I don't understand," Ruff moans, his fingers tugging at his hair. "She was supposed to be—"

Chase grips him by the shoulders. "We'll figure it out, Ruff. Her loss won't be for nothing."

Anger snaps in Ruff's eyes, burning away the grief. It quickly blazes into fury. "She was supposed to be Immune!"

"I know," Chase says reassuringly. "But—"

"You lied!" Ruff cries. He jerks himself free and steps around Chase, his bright gaze surveying the crowd. "They said she was now Immune!"

The first real emotion since Navy's death crawls through River.

Alarm.

Ruff stalks toward the Dead Borns. He points an accusing finger at Echo. "Navy was injected with Immunity from her!"

Dozens of eyes widen. Dart to Echo. Then widen some more.

"And she won't give any to us!" cries the woman who'd begged Echo for Immunity earlier.

"That's because she's not the Sovereign," Ruff shouts, his voice cracking. "They killed Navy!"

River tucks Echo behind him, noting she's still pale, still looks frail as a leaf. "We didn't know—"

"Did you hear me?" Ruff says, his voice rising. "That girl is not the Sovereign. There is no Immunity!"

Feet shift in the dusty soil. People glance between each other. Frowns pull down brows and the edges of mouths.

Chase steps forward, lifting his hands in a conciliatory gesture. "Listen to me. There's been a mistake."

"Is she the Sovereign?" someone at the back demands.

Chase's shoulders tense. "Everything suggested she was. And we're going to keep searching—"

"Echo's not the Sovereign," a woman shouts, her voice powered by shock and betrayal.

It triggers a tidal wave of more shock. More betrayal. Then anger and pain.

"You lied to us!"

"We gave you our food!"

"How many of us were you going to let die in your search for the Sovereign?"

The last one hits River the hardest. It was never supposed to be like that. They even broke into the Sting so no one would have to die as they were tested.

Yet they failed.

"Please, listen," Chase tries again, desperation creeping into his voice. "We—"

"No! We listened to you and look what happened to my daughter!" Ruff shouts with enough force that his face turns red.

Chase recoils as if he was just punched. River suspects this is the first time the Dead Borns have not only failed to listen, but openly defied him.

Echo slips around River. "Let me try and talk to them."

273

Except the moment she becomes visible, the crowd surges. "It's her! She thought she was better than us!"

Crimson blotches of anger flare beneath streaks of dirt. Gapped rows of teeth are exposed by sneer after sneer. River suspects that having so much further to fall after last night's celebrations, after finally tasting hope, has the Dead Borns' emotions running high.

He grabs Echo's arm. "Quick. We need to get to the Alphadome."

She looks like she's about to object, but Ruff is storming toward them, features twisted with fury. "Navy is dead because of her!"

River wraps an arm around Echo, escorting her away. He almost throws an angry glare back at Ruff. He was the one who insisted Navy be administered Immunity. He's the one who told Navy to collect fruit from the Betadome.

Yet ultimately, it doesn't matter.

He's a grieving father looking for someone to blame.

And there's a hard seed of truth in his words.

They don't have the Sovereign.

River glances over his shoulder, seeing that Chase hasn't moved. He's looking around the Dead Borns, his people, the ones who were zealously signing up to become Razers only hours ago, seeming unsure of what to do next.

"Chase!" River shouts sharply. "Now!"

His words snap Chase out of his stupor. He grabs Flora's hand where she's standing beside him, waiting to see what to do, and hurries to catch up to River and Echo. They stride away, River listening keenly behind them.

"Cowards!" someone cries.

"Of course you'd pretend this is nothing!" shouts Ruff.

Flora gasps. "Run!"

River breaks into a jog as he glances over his shoulder. A few Dead Borns have broken from the mass and are chasing after them. Ruff is at the front.

Grabbing Echo's hand, and making sure Chase is smart enough to know when to make himself scarce, River pumps more speed into his legs.

He finds himself gasping at the dust almost instantly. Flora coughs, but Echo and Chase seem used to it. River swallows, hoping his dry mouth can clear it away. They can't have come this far, only to be mobbed by those they were trying to save.

But a quick glance back reveals the Dead Borns have already given up. Ruff is bending over his knees, breathing hard. The odd insult still pierces the dirty air. The Dead Borns chose not to pursue them, although River's not sure why. Maybe they don't have energy to waste.

Hopefully they realize Echo isn't to blame here. Neither is Chase. Or any of them.

Like Chase said, everything suggested Echo was the Sovereign. They were ready to go into the Betadome themselves, assuming they were Immune.

Any of them could've ended up like Navy.

Yet when they reach the hatch, River still closes it firmly behind them, even tugging on it for good measure. They don't know what the Dead Borns are going to do when the initial shock has worn off. They'll either accept that Chase and Echo aren't at fault.

Or be like Ruff, and look for someone to blame.

Downstairs, Chase immediately begins to pace, half-circling the glass dome before returning. His fingers compulsively spear into his hair. "How could we get it so wrong?"

Flora wrings her hands, watching him. "I don't know what happened. None of this makes sense."

"Well it has to," Chase snaps, his voice rising. "I need answers!"

She winces and River takes a step toward her. Flora's eyes dart to him as she imperceptibly shakes her head. She doesn't want her brother protecting her. River stops where he is, willing to humor her for now. But if Chase loses it anymore...

Echo appears by River's side. "I'm so sorry, Chase," she says, her voice hoarse.

"You have nothing to be sorry for," River says, frowning. Echo's the one who went through the agonizing harvest because they all believed she was the Sovereign. "This isn't your fault. It's nobody's fault."

Chase doesn't seem to have heard either of them. He stops his frenzied pacing. "I can't believe we got it so wrong." He raises agonized eyes to Flora. "The Razers are never going to trust me again."

Flora moves toward him, her hands outstretched to cup his face. "Of course, they will. This is just a setback."

River has to suppress his eyebrow raise. This is more than a setback.

They don't have the Sovereign.

Let alone the Code.

Chase seems to think the same because he slowly sinks to his knees. "What will this mean for the rebellion?" he whispers.

Flora lowers herself beside him, unsure of what to do as her hands hover midair. River can't blame her. Everything about Chase—his stooped shoulders, his bent head, the way he looks at his hands as if he's not sure what to do with them now—all adds up to one word. A word River never thought he'd use to describe the determined leader of the Razers, no matter their disagreements.

Lost.

A broken shudder slips through Echo as the hopelessness and helplessness multiplies, becoming stifling. River draws her into his arms, knowing nothing can make things better, but hoping to at least share the pain. She wraps her arms tightly around him as she buries her face in his chest.

River looks over the top of her head at his sister, seeing the tears Echo's clearly holding in tracking down Flora's face. Seeing Chase's desolation is breaking her.

She shuffles forward and cups his face. "We can get through this. I know we can."

"Maybe," Chase says, not sounding like he believes it. "But it will be without me as the leader of the Razers. I don't deserve it."

"You most certainly do," Flora replies, her voice hard with conviction.

Chase opens his mouth as if he's going to object, but River stills as he watches his twin. There's a certainty about Flora. One that's founded on more than just faith.

It's as if she knows something.

Flora holds Chase's gaze. "Because I know where the Code is."

Chase draws in a sharp breath. "What?"

Yet it's River that she turns to as she says the next words. "The Sovereign Code is with our mother."

River draws back, bewildered as he wonders what she means. They're going to have to exhume their mother's dead body?

Yet Flora's unwavering gaze, the slight pinch to her brows, tells him the answer is far more complicated.

That another truth is about to be painfully revealed.

"She's still alive, River. Our mother is why I came to the

Dead Zone. To find her." His sister's face melts into a tremulous smile. "And when we do, we'll have the Sovereign Code."

THE END

Ready for the next book in The Sovereign Code?
Check out Queen Hunt now!
http://mybook.to/QueenHunt

BOOK THREE - QUEEN HUNT
THE SOVEREIGN CODE

Protecting the Sovereign has never been more deadly

Time is running out. The Sovereign needs to be protected before the Green Zone can claim her for themselves. At the cost of everyone else.

As the seeds of rebellion brew, impatience threads its way through the Dead Zone. Vulnerables are questioning the fairness of the life they've been born into. Soon, Echo and River find themselves in danger on both sides of the giant net that's supposed to keep them safe.

Where do you run when you have no place to call home? Who do you trust when nobody is who you thought they were? And is it really possible to save everyone?

Lovers of the Hunger Games and Maze Runner, prepare to be blown away. The authors of the best-selling series, The Thaw Chronicles, have crafted another unique dystopian adventure full of romance, twists, and page-turning excitement.

Grab your copy now!
http://mybook.to/QueenHunt

THE THAW CHRONICLES

Tamar Sloan and Heidi Catherine are the authors of the bestselling series, The Thaw Chronicles.

Get your free prequel now!
http://mybook.to/BurningThaw

WANT TO STAY IN TOUCH?

If you'd like to be the first for to hear all the news from Tamar and Heidi, be sure to sign up to our newsletter. Subscribers receive bonus content, early cover reveals and sneaky snippets of upcoming books. We'd love you to join us!

SIGN UP HERE:

https://sendfox.com/tamarandheidi

ABOUT THE AUTHORS

Tamar Sloan hasn't decided whether she's a psychologist who loves writing, or a writer with a lifelong fascination with psychology. She must have been someone pretty awesome in a previous life (past life regression indicated a Care Bear), because she gets to do both. When not reading, writing or working with teens, Tamar can be found with her husband and two children enjoying country life in their small slice of the Australian bush.

Heidi Catherine loves the way her books give her the opportunity to escape into worlds vastly different to her own life in the burbs. While she quite enjoys killing her characters (especially the awful ones), she promises she's far better behaved in real life. Other than writing and reading, Heidi's current obsessions include watching far too much reality TV with the excuse that it's research for her books.

MORE SERIES TO FALL IN LOVE WITH...

ALSO BY TAMAR SLOAN AND HEIDI CATHERINE

The Thaw Chronicles

ALSO BY TAMAR SLOAN

Keepers of the Grail

Keepers of the Light

Keepers of the Chalice

Keepers of the Excalibur

Zodiac Guardians

Descendants of the Gods

Prime Prophecy

ALSO BY HEIDI CATHERINE

The Kingdoms of Evernow

The Soulweaver

The Woman Who Didn't (written as HC Michaels)

The Girl Who Never (written as HC Michaels)

Printed in Great Britain
by Amazon